HAD A GREAT FALL

HAD A GREAT FALL

A Roxanne Calloway Mystery

RAYE ANDERSON

Doug Whiteway, Editor

Signature
EDITIONS

© 2025, Raye Anderson

All rights reserved. No part of this book may be reproduced, for any reason, by any means, without the permission of the publisher.

Cover design by Doowah Design.
Photo of author by Michael Long.

This book was printed on Ancient Forest Friendly paper.
Printed and bound in Canada by Hignell Book Printing Inc.

We acknowledge the support of the Canada Council for the Arts, the Manitoba Arts Council, and the Manitoba Government for our publishing program.

Library and Archives Canada Cataloguing in Publication

Title: Had a great fall / Raye Anderson.
Names: Anderson, Raye, 1943- author. | Whiteway, Doug, 1951- editor.
Description: Series statement: A Roxanne Calloway mystery ; 5 | "Doug Whiteway, editor".
Identifiers: Canadiana (print) 20250243849 |
Canadiana (ebook) 20250245787 |
ISBN 9781773241531 (softcover) | ISBN 9781773241548 (EPUB)
Subjects: LCGFT: Detective and mystery fiction. | LCGFT: Novels.
Classification: LCC PS8601.N44725 H33 2025 | DDC C813/.6—dc23

Signature Editions
P.O. Box 206, RPO Corydon, Winnipeg, Manitoba, R3M 3S7
www.signature-editions.com

1

VASSILY KOVALENKO KNEW how to drive a car. He'd borrowed one occasionally since he arrived in Canada three months earlier, but soon his Ukrainian licence would no longer be valid in this country. He needed to pass a Manitoba driver's test and his good friend Mike McBain had offered to help.

They worked together, Vassily and Mike, on a building site in Fiskar Bay, a small town on the edge of a big lake, an hour north of the city of Winnipeg. Vassily and his wife, Zlata, had never imagined they'd end up living in Manitoba but there had been a welcome here for people like themselves, recently displaced by war. The farmland in the area where they now lived had been settled by Ukrainians more than a hundred years ago and their descendants had offered support to refugees like the Kovalenkos. They'd found Vassily's small family an apartment in town, provided them with basic furnishings, helped them find work. Vassily and Zlata counted themselves among the lucky ones.

Vassily had been an engineer back home in Kyiv. He'd never expected to find himself employed as a labourer, but this job would do for now. A tall building was going up near the harbour, to house old people who needed care. Working there would provide him with an income right through to next summer. Vassily knew about buildings and he wasn't afraid of hard work. Neither was Zlata. She was a trained physiotherapist, but she'd found a job at a local bakery now that their son, Andriy, was attending the local school.

Other Ukrainians worked on the building site with Vassily. They liked to talk together in their own language but he wanted to improve his English, so he sought out the company of the Canadians on the crew. Sometimes he went for a beer to the local hotel after work with Mike McBain and his friends.

And now here they were, driving around town in Mike's big red truck, Vassily at the wheel, learning the Canadian rules of the road. Four-way stops. School zones. Right-hand turns at red lights. It didn't take long to understand all there was to know about traffic in this little town. Six, seven roads ran in each direction, straight up and down. That was it.

"Let's go out on the highway," said Mike. There were two choices, a long, straight road that went all the way to the city of Winnipeg, an hour south, or another, that hugged the shore of the lake. Mike thought they should drive the lakeside route first, then come back to town on the faster one. They'd have time for a beer, after. Zlata didn't like it when Vassily spent extra time with Mike in the bar but favours needed to be paid for.

It was September, fall already, leaves turning red and gold, the lake a shining expanse of water on their left, but this was evening. The sun was falling into the west and golden light flashed like a strobe between the shadows of the trees that lined the roadside. Vassily screwed up his eyes.

"Won't be like that when you do your test," Mike assured him. "And it won't be snowing yet, either. See, the ospreys are still here."

A big nest sat on top of a telephone pole, a white-headed bird perched on the edge. This was September. Geese were gathering on the water, ready for their big migration south. Soon, they and the ospreys would be gone. Summer vacationers were disappearing fast, too. The ones who owned cottages out in this area were only around on the weekends now. By October, their summer beach homes would be closed and shuttered. On a weekday like this, the roads were quiet.

Vassily drove through Cullen Village, twelve kilometres south of Fiskar Bay. Houses were scattered along the shoreline of the lake. There was a gas bar. A shack that sold burgers and fries at the side of the road was only open for a few hours on Saturdays and Sundays now. Soon it would be closed up for the winter too and the inevitable snowflakes would fall, but Mike said you could buy good Chinese food at the Cullen Hotel, all year round. Maybe Vassily could bring Zlata and Andriy here when they had saved enough to buy a little car. Mike had said he'd keep an eye open for one going cheap.

Past the village, the road straightened out. Fields stretched over flat land to the west. The prairie went all the way from here to the foothills of the Rockies, in Alberta, Vassily had been told. A combine was harvesting a crop; big trucks were waiting to collect the grain. A CLOSED sign sat at the end of a driveway.

Vassily guessed what it said. Reading English was hard. Most of the other words on the sign defeated him.

"Yeah," Mike agreed. "They sell vegetables on Saturdays. Just keep your eyes on the road, eh?"

Sunlight glowed across the fields. Farmyards were shrouded by willows and spruce trees. An occasional oak stood alone, casting long, inky blue shadows alongside the telephone and hydro poles that lined the highway.

They reached a field that was thick with sunflowers. A dense carpet of green leaves stretched as far as Vassily dared to look. The big, yellow-petalled heads had turned away from the sun and they drooped, like they were about to go to sleep. He slowed down, suddenly homesick.

"We grow these," he said. "In my country."

"That's why the farmers here have planted so many this year," Mike glanced at them. "There's going to be a shortage of sunflower oil if that war of yours keeps going." His brother Pete was a farmer and had said so.

If the conflict in Ukraine ended, Vassily and Zlata would be able to go home, but Vassily had little hope of that. They might be in Canada for a long time. He drove onto the gravel shoulder at the edge of the road and stopped the truck.

"I take a photo to show Zlata?" he asked. "And send it home to Ukraine?"

"Sure. Let's get closer. I'll get a shot of you next to a big one." Mike was an easygoing kind of guy and they had the time. The night was young.

They clambered down one side of a grassy ditch and up the other. The edge of the field was thick with tall grasses, spiky yellow flowers that came up past their knees, white daisies and others that were as golden as the sunflowers, with dark brown centres just like them. The big sunflowers that stood, row on row, were almost as tall as they were, bowed heads above leafy skirts. Vassily stood in front of them.

"It's too dark here," said Mike. "Let's go round to the side where it's still sunny," and off he went. He was right. The north edge of the field caught the evening sun. "Stand between these two and hold up one of their heads so we can see it." He took Vassily's phone and snapped a couple of shots. Vassily looked at them.

"They will remind Zlata of home," he said. "After the disaster happened at Chernobyl, and the ground was made bad, we planted sunflowers, to help to heal the land."

"That right? You should pick a bunch. Take them back to her."

"That is not stealing?" Vassily hesitated.

"Two or three little ones? They'll never notice." Mike eyed the regimented rows, looking for likely candidates. Then he noticed a gap, further along the field, running between the thick green stalks. "See, someone's been here already. There's a track. Looks like they've driven right in." He strode off along the edge of the sunflower field to go look.

Vassily followed. Sure enough, the stems there were broken. Twin tire tracks cut a path between them. An ATV had been through, smashing down plants as it went.

"I can take these ones, they will do." Vassily hesitated to walk into the field. It must belong to someone. You didn't go onto other people's land without permission, not where he came from. But he didn't want to fall out with his new friend, either. He picked up a head that had broken off, but it was old, the petals withering.

"Nah," said Mike. "We'll find something better than that," and he walked off again into the grove of sunflowers, following the tracks.

"Should we do this?" Vassily asked, still wary.

"No problem. They'll never know. And it's someone else did this damage. They must've driven through here fast to smash everything down like this." Mike was up ahead now, carefully picking his way over the broken stumps of stems.

"Wonder where they were going?" Vassily hurried to catch up. It was gloomy in here among the big flowers, and quiet, but shafts of sunlight penetrated between the flower heads, enough so they could see.

"Nooky. Or a place to smoke up," Mike replied knowingly. "Look, there's a space they've cleared up ahead." He pointed to an open patch. "Looks like something's lying there. Let's go see."

He picked his way along the track, avoiding more broken stubble and fallen stems, then he stopped and stood still. Vassily reached his side.

A man lay on the ground on his back, his arms stretched out on either side of his body. His hair was grey, he was tall, solidly built, in his late fifties, sixty, perhaps. The front of his chest was a gaping wound. Blood had soaked through an unbuttoned plaid shirt and a T-shirt that had once been white. His eyes stared straight up at the patch of sky above them and his mouth hung open.

"Someone's used a shotgun," said Mike. "He's not someone local. I've never seen him before. Maybe we should get out of here." He backed up a couple of feet.

Vassily stared at the body, dismayed. He had seen enough bloodied corpses back in Ukraine to recognize trouble when it was staring him in the face. The last thing he needed was to get entangled with Canadian law enforcement, especially when he only had refugee status. Still, Vassily was a cautious man. He knew that sometimes, you had no choice but to obey the authorities.

"We should call the police, Mike," he said.

"You think so? How're they going to know we were here?"

Mike kicked at a fallen sunflower head, then he looked back at the dead man, lying on the ground. Mike had had a few run-ins with the cops in his time. Nothing serious but enough to make him leery.

"They have ways of finding out," said the nervous Vassily.

He was right, of course. Mike's red truck was parked out there on the highway for any passerby to see and country folk took notice of such things. It had big black thunderbolts painted along its side. Nobody else around here drove a truck like that and Mike had grown up in this area. Played hockey. Lots of people knew who Mike McBain was.

The ground was soft between the rows of sunflowers. He and Vassily had both left footprints on the tracks that they had followed in here. They had just added to them, scuffing the ground as they walked.

It would just be his luck to get found out, Mike thought. Not that he'd done anything wrong. Just gone for a walk, hadn't he? Taken a couple of photos?

"My sister Izzy works for the RCMP. She's a sergeant, works in the Major Crimes Unit. If this guy's been murdered, chances are she'll be put in charge. Izzy will know what to do," he said, trying to reassure himself as much as his immigrant friend. Mike might get into the odd fix but he knew he was Izzy's favourite brother. She would look out for him and his new Ukrainian buddy, Vassily. He found her number and made the call.

2

SERGEANT IZZY MCBAIN of the RCMP's Major Crimes Unit was not available to help her brother, as Mike had hoped. And she would probably not be assigned to a case of suspicious death in the Interlake. She was in Churchill, Manitoba, way up north on the shores of Hudson's Bay, where there had been too many fentanyl-related deaths lately.

"Call 911, right now," she told her brother. "You haven't been drinking, have you?"

"Not a drop, Iz," he assured her. For once, it was true.

"Well then, just stick to the facts. Tell them exactly what you told me and you'll be fine."

Izzy called her boss, Inspector Schultz, at HQ in Winnipeg, soon as she hung up. She might as well tip him off so he could get things rolling. As a result, Sergeant Rob Marsden arrived on the scene a little over an hour later, just as a constable from the local RCMP detachment was about to take down statements from Mike McBain and Vassily Kovalenko.

Marsden looked exactly as a Mountie should, tall, straight-backed and even-featured with a strong jawline, his brown hair neatly trimmed. He'd once posed for a press photographer in his dress uniform, looking good in his red serge jacket and knee-high polished boots, the traditional brimmed beige RCMP hat set squarely on his head. Strong and assured, a responsible figure that you could depend on to do what was right. But Rob Marsden was not pleased to be out on the highway in the Interlake on a Sunday evening. He preferred to work out of HQ, in Winnipeg, where he was close to the centre of things and knew what was going on in the Major Crimes Unit. He'd just closed a case south of the city limits and had hoped for a similar assignment. Not this.

He glanced around him. A red truck was parked at the side of the highway, in front of a couple of police cars with their lights flashing.

Marsden approached the woman cop and the two men beside her. "What were you doing out in the middle of a farmer's field, in the dark?" he demanded of Mike McBain and his anxious Ukrainian friend.

"Taking a photo, so Vassily here could send it home to his family." Mike was not about to be intimidated by Marsden's rank or manner. He'd met tough cops before and knew how to stand up for himself when he came across one of them. "You know they grow sunflowers over there? Like us? Vassily wanted to show his folks back home how we have them here too. What's the law against that? And it wasn't dark when we got here. There was enough light to see by. We've been stuck here for hours already, waiting. Not done nothing wrong, ask Constable Vermette here. She's got it all written down, ain't that right, Aimee?"

The fact that he used the woman constable's first name did not escape Marsden's notice. Nor did the fact that this guy was a McBain. Inspector Schultz had said that Izzy McBain had called in this case, and hadn't he been told that she came from the Interlake? She was a sergeant, like him, in the MCU. Always sucking up to the boss so she got the best cases. Word was she was fast tracking for inspector. Up in Churchill right now, assisting the drug squad. Making good contacts. Women were always getting promoted these days, ahead of hard-working guys like himself, who got phoned on a Sunday night and sent off out to the boonies.

The uniformed woman that Mike McBain had called Vermette was still waiting to finish taking down statements from the two men. Another constable was making sure traffic kept moving. The cars driving by were few and far between but many of them were slowing down, trying to photograph as much as they could of the scene. Word would be out already on the internet about police activity just south of Cullen Village.

The skinny guy hovering behind Izzy McBain's brother looked scared. Marsden shifted his attention to him.

"You!" he barked. "Why were you really here, out where no one could see you?"

"Nothing." It came out as a quiet whisper, then Vassily found his voice. His English stumbled when he was pressured like this and his accent became stronger. "I followed Mike. Someone had driven in already. We went look. Good we did? There is dead man there. Blood. Someone has shot him with gun."

"Yeah!" Mike noticed Vassily's difficulty and came to the rescue. "You should be thanking us, Sarge, not wasting time bossing us around. Eh, pal?" He wrapped a protective arm around his friend's shoulder. They were about the same height, but Mike was visibly stronger. "If we hadn't happened by when we did, the coyotes would have got at that guy in here. You know how long it takes before they harvest a sunflower field? Not until they're all frosted over. He would have just been bones if you'd had to wait that long."

Mike had a point, and he was probably telling the truth. Marsden decided not to waste time on the two of them any longer.

"Get their statements and send them home," he instructed Constable Vermette. "Leave your contact information," he told the two men. "I'll want to talk to you again." He wasn't going to let them think he was completely done with them. He donned plastic gloves and foot coverings and marched off. A path was now trodden up and down the side of the ditch. He clambered down in the light from the cars, ducked under a strip of police tape and disappeared from view.

"He's talkin' bullshit." Mike watched him go.

"Into the car, Mike." Aimee Vermette had a notepad and pen ready. They watched Sergeant Marsden's flashlight shine its way along the edge of the sunflowers. "This will only take a few minutes, then the two of you can be off."

As Rob Marsden turned the corner onto the north side of the sunflower field, he wished that Ident, the RCMP's Forensic Identification Unit, was already here. They'd be able to rig proper lighting. It was dark out, not a sign of a moon, only an orange glow in the sky from the street lights in Cullen Village, six kilometres further north, an occasional big star and a blinking, moving satellite up above. The local detachment had managed to install a single light at the entrance to the track that led into the rows of plants. Another light, positioned halfway down the path, was the only other source of illumination. The rest was shadowy, the towering sunflowers leaning in like old women, listening.

Wooden planks had been laid down so the police could walk without damaging too much evidence. At least the locals had had enough sense to do that, but it made for precarious walking, especially with plastic bootees on. He picked his way along them. Up ahead another light illuminated the spot where the body lay, guarded by a uniformed constable who looked young enough to be straight out of the Depot, the RCMP's training facility in Regina. A man in a corporal's uniform was bending over the body. He wore a turban. That must be Corporal Anand, temporarily in charge of the Fiskar Bay detachment while their regular sergeant was off on maternity leave. East Indian, by the look of him. Another diversity hire, getting shunted up the ranks, Marsden suspected.

"Stand back, Corporal," he ordered. "I'll take charge of this now. Ident will be here shortly and they'll arrange for the body to be picked up. Get your crew to prepare a path for their vehicles, this side of the ditch."

"Done already. There's room for a van. And there's a driveway into the field by the next intersection." Ravi Anand stood up and stretched, showing no sign of leaving. The young constable stood watching, his hands behind his back. "This man hasn't been here more than a day," the corporal reported.

Rob Marsden squatted down beside the body, making his own inspection. He might as well hear what the guy had to say while he waited for forensics to arrive, so he let him talk.

"We haven't found any ID on the body. No wallet, no phone. This isn't anyone we recognize. It looks like he was shot here. A shotgun blast would do that much damage and death would have been instant. We haven't found a gun, so it doesn't look like this is a self-inflicted wound."

"Not suicide, but maybe a hunting accident?" Marsden eyeballed the body. "How would he have got in here?"

"There's no other vehicle parked nearby." Ravi Anand pointed along the canyon of sunflowers, ghostly in the shadowy light. "The tire tracks look like they've been made by a large-size quad, but there are also footprints. More than one set. Mike McBain and his friend also walked in. Maybe this man came in on the quad, or else he was on foot. As you said, sir, we'll have to wait until Ident tells us more."

"Hey, Ravi!" A voice rang out. A woman had appeared at the far end of the track wearing the same protective boots and gloves as they were. She was waving. The light caught a flash of red hair as she moved forward.

"Hey, Sarge! How come you're here?" Ravi Anand called back in greeting.

"Izzy McBain texted me. Said her brother, Mike, and someone he works with found a body over here. The baby's asleep and Matt's home so I came by in case you needed a hand."

Rob Marsden watched the dark silhouette approach. This had to be Roxanne Calloway, the sergeant in charge of the Fiskar Bay detachment when she wasn't taking time off to have babies. She'd been a member of the Major Crimes Unit back in the day, he'd been told, but wasn't she on maternity leave? Not a working member of the force, right now?

"You don't need to be here, Sergeant," he called to her. "We've got this all under control." But Roxanne kept walking toward them.

"Mike's gone home already?" she asked as she got closer. "Are you Sergeant Marsden?"

Who had told her who he was? Izzy McBain, maybe. Or more likely the woman constable out on the roadside. That must be who had given her the gloves and foot covering.

Calloway moved into the light, in the clearing where the body lay, then she stopped. She stared at the body, her head tilting, first to one side, then the other, like she couldn't believe what she was seeing.

"I know who that is," she said. "He's Cooper Jenkins. What's he doing here, dead?"

"Who?" asked Ravi Anand.

"He used to be a DS, with the city police. I worked with him on a case, about five years ago. This guy saved my life."

Ravi Anand knew that story. Roxanne had been accosted by a killer, years before, in the days when she worked for the Major Crimes Unit. It had happened in a snowstorm, in Winnipeg. Her throat had been cut. She still bore a faint scar under her chin and up to her ear and half her earlobe was missing. A city cop had arrived in time to knock out her attacker with a baseball bat and call for help. This must be that same guy. He watched Roxanne drop on one knee beside the head of her old colleague, take off her glove and reach out to close his eyes.

"You can't touch that body," Rob Marsden objected.

"Don't worry," Roxanne straightened up again and faced him. "I'll tell Dave Kovak that I did it when he gets here. Abdur Farouk, too, if you like. They'll understand."

Kovak ran the Ident Unit for this area and Dr. Farouk was the provincial medical examiner. Marsden got the message. She was making it clear that she knew both of them and he was supposed to be impressed. Like she had equal status here, with him? She didn't, not if she was off on mat leave. She was still talking: "Coop must be retired now. I've lost touch with him. We swapped Christmas cards for a couple of years and that was it. He was going to quit the police around then. Was talking about joining up with some old buddies who'd set themselves up in business as private investigators after they'd quit the police. If he was out here, investigating a case, that could explain why he's lying here, dead."

3

ROB MARSDEN WASTED very little time sending Roxanne Calloway off home where she belonged. She had no business being on the site. Sure, she'd identified the body, but it turned out that Dave Kovak, who headed up the Ident team, recognized the guy too, and he knew more about what Cooper Jenkins had been doing in recent years than Calloway did. Jenkins had retired from the City of Winnipeg Police Service as a patrol sergeant three, four years ago, but he had served as a detective before that. At least she'd got that right.

He'd joined a PI company run by old cops like himself. They were doing well out of it. Did surveillance mainly. That meant spending a lot of time sitting in a car with a camera waiting to see who visited a house when they shouldn't. Insurance fraud, that kind of stuff. Boring jobs, but they paid the bills. Not the kind of casework that would get you shot in the middle of a sunflower field in the Interlake, but it did seem possible that an investigation might have brought Jenkins out to Cullen Village and it had gone wrong. Why else would he be out here, dead? Calloway might have been correct about that, too.

Kovak had given Marsden the name of the PI company. That gave him a good reason to get back to Winnipeg tonight. He'd go check it out first thing in the morning. Once he discovered what Jenkins was working on, he would get this case solved in no time. With a bit of luck, he'd be able to cover most of this in Winnipeg and not have to spend too much out here in the Interlake after all.

He'd been told the whole story about Cooper Jenkins and Roxanne Calloway while Ident got themselves set up and the medics had come to cart the body away, back to the city morgue. Calloway had almost died, several years ago, bled out on a city street in the middle of a blizzard, but Jenkins had been watching out for her. She had survived. She'd quit the Major Crimes Unit shortly after and had taken the job running the Fiskar Bay detachment instead. Dave Kovak said it was because she had a kid and wanted to make sure she lived to see him grow up. That was the problem with women in the force. They had other priorities that got in the way of work. Had babies. Took time off, like she was doing right now. What had made her show up last night at the crime scene when she was off the job?

MATT STAVROS WAS Roxanne's partner. He knew perfectly well why she had gone out that night to find out what was happening at the sunflower field, not far from their home. She had already discovered that something was going on along the highway just south of the house. There had been posts online about a police presence. Then she got a text from her old friend, Izzy McBain, saying that Izzy's brother Mike, the one who was always getting himself into trouble, had found a body out there, shot dead.

"Izzy says the MCU is sending a guy named Marsden to investigate, and he's got a rep for throwing his weight around. Mike doesn't do well with those types. He starts mouthing off when he's under pressure. I'll just go make sure he's all right and I'll be right back," she had said. But Matt understood why Roxanne was so eager to head out into the dark on a September night. She wanted to find out what was really going on.

Roxanne had once been a member of the Major Crimes Unit. She'd moved out to the Interlake so she would have a less dangerous job, but she'd still managed to help solve the occasional murder out here during the past few years. Now there was a body not far from home. She was off on leave, Matt reminded himself.

Maybe this wasn't even murder. Hunting season was just getting started. This could be an accident. Or a suicide. Roxanne wasn't due back on the job until December. Maybe she wouldn't need to get herself involved.

He knew for sure that wasn't going to happen when he came downstairs in the morning and found Roxanne spooning oatmeal into their daughter Dee's hungry mouth with one hand while the other tapped at her keyboard.

"It's Cooper Jenkins that's lying out there, dead." She looked up at him, hollow-eyed from lack of sleep.

"Who?"

"You remember! He's the guy that saved me that time when I got my throat cut. City DS. We were working on the same case." The baby yelled for more food. Roxanne loaded up a spoon again and fed it into Dee's open, red mouth.

Matt knew exactly how that had happened. That incident had convinced Roxanne to leave the Major Crimes Unit and return to uniform. It was what had led her to take the job running the Fiskar Bay detachment.

"What was he doing out here?" Matt reached down and lifted his daughter out of her high chair. Dee squealed with glee, oatmeal dribbling down her chin. She looked like him, olive skinned, but there the resemblance ended. Matt was quiet, Dee was not. He took the spoon from Roxanne, propped the baby on his knee and took over the job of feeding her. Matt Stavros liked being a dad. His baby loved him right back.

Roxanne sat back in her chair.

"It seems like he was working as a private investigator these days." She had found some information online. "He joined a PI company after he retired but it didn't work out, so he went into business for himself a couple of years ago. I think he was working from home."

"You can't get yourself mixed up in this, Roxanne." Matt wiped mush from the baby's chin. "You're on leave, remember?"

"I know. But it's Coop." She bit her lip as she closed the lid on her laptop. "If he was on a job out here, why didn't he call the detachment and ask to speak to me?"

The last time they had been in touch, Roxanne had quit the MCU and was living with her son, Finn, in Fiskar Bay. That was long before she and Matt had moved in together, and before she and Finn came to live here in the house Matt had built just west of Cullen Village.

"He might only have come out here for the day," Matt reasoned. "Maybe he only needed to come this far. He wouldn't have known you lived here, now."

"So where's his vehicle?" Coop had liked big trucks. He'd driven a green Silverado when she had known him. He'd lent it to Roxanne once. "I should have stayed in touch with him," she said. "I found his daughter's name online. Hailey. Maybe I'll talk to her. Tell her I'm sorry this has happened."

Matt raised an eyebrow. He knew where this was leading. Roxanne intended to ask some questions. "Do that if you must. But otherwise, shouldn't you leave this alone?" he reminded her. "The Major Crimes Unit will have to figure this one out."

"I suppose you're right." Roxanne stood up. She stretched and yawned. "Come on, Dee. Your dad needs to get ready for work."

Matt's law office was in Fiskar Bay. He dropped Finn off at school on the way most mornings. Finn was still asleep upstairs and it was time that Roxanne woke him. She took the baby back from Matt and carried her upstairs.

Spending the summer on leave had been okay. Finn had been home; Matt had taken time off and they had spent hours at the beach. Dee loved the water. They had watched Finn play baseball. Had barbecues. But now Finn was back at school, Matt was busy at work again, it was fall and Roxanne wasn't due back in the office until December.

Matt and her son soon drove away, leaving Roxanne at home with a baby and two dogs for company. Once a week she picked up a supply of vegetables from her neighbour, Vera Klassen. The Klassens ran a market garden and sold shares in their crop. Their vegetables were not registered as organic but were grown as if they were. Their small farm lay right on the highway, one road north of the sunflower field where Coop Jenkins's body had been found. She phoned Vera.

Mornings were busy on the farm. Vera and her husband, Armin, would be harvesting fall vegetables like beets and squash today. They dried garlic bulbs and Vera needed to help package those, too, but she was more than ready to stop for a minute and talk about what had been going on last night, just down the highway from where they lived.

"The police were there past midnight," she informed Roxanne. The farmland that included the sunflower field was owned by a couple called the Carlsons. "The ones that built the straw house," she added. "They moved in just last year."

Roxanne knew exactly where that was, only a road over from the Klassens' place. She and Matt had driven by as that house went up, thick walls made of piled-up bales with an overlay of concrete. It looked quite ordinary but it had geothermal heat, they had been told, and there were solar panels.

"They've got beehives out the back, and a big shed they call their honey house," Vera continued. "The old farmhouse has been turned into an Airbnb for now. Andrea Carlson was telling me it's doing quite well for them. Summer's over but now hunting season's starting, so they're still getting bookings and they'll get ice fishers during the winter. They only use about ten acres of their land themselves. All the rest of it's rented out to Pete McBain. He uses it as pasture for his cattle, mainly, but those are his sunflowers that were getting trampled down last night. His truck drove past, just before you called. He'll be there right now, I suppose, inspecting the damage."

"Really?" said Roxanne, eager to get going. "I won't keep you any longer."

"Stop by for tea on Thursday." That was vegetable pickup day. Vera hung up, most likely eager to get outside to the vegetable plots where her husband would already be hard at work.

Roxanne bundled up her baby and went out to the car.

"You two stay home," she told their dogs, Maisie the Lab and Joshua the terrier, and shut them inside the house. Matt had installed a dog flap in the mud room so they had access to a fenced yard. They came and went all day as they pleased.

Soon she reached the highway. Four roads south of her road end, the sunflowers stood in rows, their faces raised to soak in the September sunlight, and a large truck with the words "McBain Farms" lettered on the driver's door stood in the spot where the police cars had been parked last night.

A skein of geese honked overhead as she strapped Dee into a carrying harness and clambered across the ditch to the other side. She came face-to-face with Pete as she turned onto the north side of the field.

"Roxanne Calloway!" Pete was an old acquaintance, a member of the Fiskar Bay town council, one of the most prosperous farmers in the area. Pete and Roxanne had served on several committees together over the years. He shared the same blond Icelandic look as his sister Izzy. They took after their mother. Their brother Mike was darker and stockier, more like their dad. "You've come here to have a look?"

"Been already, last night," she said. "Izzy let me know that Mike had found a body."

"Yeah. She might have let me know. I didn't find out that it was in my sunflower patch until this morning." Dee kicked and babbled her version of a hello. Pete grinned at her and waved a hand. "This one's growing, isn't she?" he said, but he was more interested in finding out what was going on with Roxanne and the RCMP. Pete liked to keep up to date. "When do you get back to work?"

"Middle of December," she told him.

"Be good to have you there. So Izzy made sure that you knew about this situation?"

"Well." Roxanne shifted Dee in the harness so she was more comfortable. Dee was a heavy baby and wide awake, trying to bounce up and down. "She said she wanted me to look out for Mike. Make sure he didn't open his mouth and stick his foot in it."

Pete nodded his head.

"Hey, thanks for looking out for him. But have you seen the mess in there? Come look." They ducked under some police tape and walked back along the line of flowers. The yellow heads were bright, their green leaves stretched wide in welcome. It was a different scene from last night. The body was gone. Roxanne picked her way over the uneven ground, keeping her balance with the baby in front of her. The boards for walking were gone and the pathway in between the flowerheads was well trampled.

"I'm going to lose some of my crop," Pete complained. Roxanne wasn't fooled. Only a small part of the sunflower field had been affected. Row on row of heads, laden with seed, remained. Pete would still have a decent harvest.

Roxanne reached round to hold Dee's hand and get her to settle. The baby raised her small face to the patch of blue sky above them, her mouth open as she stared. The occasional yellow-petalled head peeked over the leaves. It was not as spooky in here as it had been last night. Instead it was quiet and peaceful, shady.

"I hear the guy the MCU's sent out's a bit of an asshole." Pete prided himself on being well-informed. "Ravi Anand's a good guy but he's a bit of a pushover. Too bad you're not back in charge, Roxanne."

"It can't be helped. Ravi's doing fine for now. Don't worry. He keeps things under control."

"Yeah, but he's never had to deal with anything like this on his own before."

"MCU will take care of it. Maybe it will get sorted out soon. How long have you rented this field?" She changed the subject.

"A year past May." They had reached the clearing where the body had lain. "It belongs to that couple that built the straw house. The Carlsons. You've met them?"

"Not yet," she replied.

"Can't think why they wanted to buy a whole farm. They only use ten acres. I've offered to buy the rest of the land but they're not selling, yet. This is where they found the guy?"

"Right here." Roxanne looked down at the empty spot where Coop had lain. There was a bloodstain but it wasn't as much as she had expected. Maybe Coop hadn't been shot here after all. His body might have been brought here so it would be out of sight.

"When would you have discovered him?" she asked. "If Mike hadn't come in here last night?"

Sunflowers were the last crop to be harvested. That could be late November, December even—two, three months away—so the body would have been found, eventually. What was left of it. There would be considerable less of Coop Jenkins by then. Plenty of wildlife inhabited this area.

"You think he came in on a quad? Or was he on foot?" Pete looked around the clearing. "And someone followed him?"

"I don't know." There was no visible gap between the plants, aside from the path carved in by the quad, but there was enough space for someone to walk or run between the stalks. "Coop could have come in on foot, perhaps to hide from someone. Or he might have already been dead, and they brought the body in on the quad."

"There's plenty of folks around here own one of those." He pointed north, toward the Klassen farm. "Vera and Armin have one. The Carlsons, too. An old one that came with the farm. They keep it in the barn over at the old farmhouse. You know they rent the house out?"

"I've been told," she said.

"You gonna be checking things out a bit more?" Pete asked as they walked back along the canyon of sunflower stalks. "Does the RCMP let you do that, if you're not really working right now?"

"I'm just taking an interest, Pete," she replied.

"You do that, Roxanne," he said and laughed. "Keep me up to speed, will you? I gotta go."

They emerged into bright sunlight. More geese were flying over, heading inland, looking for freshly harvested fields where they could gorge on fallen seed, fatten up before the long flight south. Dee chortled and waved at the sight of them.

Once she had fastened the baby back into the car seat, Roxanne turned around and drove back up the highway past the Klassen house. She turned onto the next road west. It led to the property that the Carlsons had bought. A driveway led past a stand of willows to a farmyard. There was a farmhouse, outbuildings and an old, hip-roofed barn that rose behind them. Roxanne slowed down, then stopped her car.

A green Silverado truck, exactly like the one that Coop Jenkins had driven when she'd known him five years ago, was parked in front of the house. She drove into the yard, then called the office she usually occupied at Fiskar Bay RCMP.

"Hi, Aimee," she said. "It's me, Roxanne. I need to talk to Ravi right away."

4

"ARE YOU SURE it's his truck?" Ravi asked. "There's lots of Silverados around."

"I'm going to go look." Dee had dozed off, strapped into her car seat, lulled by the short drive over and Roxanne had parked in the shade of a big ash tree. She opened a window so the baby would have fresh air and got out of the car.

The Silverado was an older model, rust beginning to show at the bottom of the doors and the tailgate. It was about the right vintage to be Cooper's, she told Ravi, still on the phone.

"Don't touch a thing. Todd Brewster's out on highway patrol. I'll send him your way."

Roxanne was already close to the big green truck. She didn't carry latex gloves with her but having a baby meant her car came well supplied with plastic bags. She took a couple of those and stuck a hand in one of them before she reached for the truck door. It was locked, but on the front seat she could see a couple of well-worn ball caps, one beige, one grey. Coop Jenkins had often worn ones like those. She walked around the truck, peering in the windows, her other hand still clasping her phone.

"I'm sure it's his, Ravi," she told him. "There's a baseball bat lying on the floor, behind the driver's seat. Coop always had one of those handy." She was probably looking at the exact weapon he had used to clobber the man who had attacked her on that snowy night five years ago.

"Okay. I'm calling the MCU and I'll be there, soon as," said Ravi.

"I'll wait." Roxanne looked at the farmhouse. Coop must have rented it. The single-storey bungalow was older but freshly painted, dark grey with a lighter trim. Two steps led up to a front door, now fuchsia pink, signalling the house's new role as a short-term holiday rental. Wrought iron planters full of pink and purple petunias stood either side of the steps. Roxanne walked over, reached out her plastic-covered hand and turned the handle. The door swung open, revealing a darkened hallway. New laminated flooring stretched inside. Empty coat hooks hung on the walls. A siren howled, a white police sedan roared into the driveway and screeched to a halt behind her, red lights flashing, and Constable Todd Brewster jumped out.

"Don't go in there!" he hollered. "I'll take care of that."

Todd Brewster was large and muscular, not turned thirty yet. He'd been assigned to the Fiskar Bay detachment shortly after Roxanne had taken her leave. She'd only met him casually, two or three times, usually with Dee on her hip, never as his boss, but she'd be back in that role in less than three months.

"You need to tape off this site first, Brewster. That truck likely belongs to the man that was shot yesterday," she advised him. She saw him hesitate. Roxanne wasn't a working member of the RCMP right now. Was he questioning whether this woman, in jeans and a sweat jacket, could tell him what to do? The ruckus he had made driving in, the red lights flashing in the car window, had wakened Dee. She began to wail.

"Look, Constable." Roxanne hurried to her car. "I may be off duty right now but I've worked many cases like this and I know what needs to be done. Turn off those flashers. We don't need to let the whole neighbourhood know that we're here." Not that that damage wasn't already done. The Klassens would know that the police were here. So would the Carlsons, if they were home. Her screaming, red-faced child was making a racket, too. She lifted her out of the car.

"Okay. Sure." Constable Brewster reluctantly went to the police car and turned off the flashing lights. Then he walked over to look at the Silverado, peering in the windows, just as she had already done. He hadn't gone to tape up the site as she had asked, not yet. Next, she saw him look at the open front door of the bungalow.

"Was that locked when you got here?" he asked, asserting his right to be in charge.

"No, obviously. I told Ravi Anand I'd stay until he got here." She took a breath. She should back off. There would be plenty of time to make sure Constable Brewster knew who was boss once she was back in uniform.

"Wait outside while I go look," Brewster ordered.

He hopped up the front steps and disappeared inside. Roxanne was glad to see him go. She didn't want to challenge him right now, not while she was officially on leave. She bounced Dee up and down, got her settled once more and walked to a big front window.

Well-established shrubs grew in front of it. Dogwood, she thought. She stood between a couple of bushes and peered inside. A black leather bomber jacket was suspended across the back of a chair. Cooper had worn one just like it when she had known him. There were papers scattered on the table in front of it. She couldn't see Todd Brewster. His large bulk had disappeared in the direction of the kitchen. She wiped Dee's snotty nose.

A tall, lean man in light brown cotton pants, a golf shirt and clean, newish sneakers rounded the corner of the house at the other side of Coop Jenkins's truck.

"Just what is going on here?" he asked.

"Roxanne Calloway. RCMP, when I'm not off duty." Roxanne pocketed a damp tissue. "You must be Alan Carlson, who owns this house?"

He looked past her. Brewster had reappeared, stepped onto the doorstep of the house.

"Why are you searching these premises?" Carlson asked. He spoke directly to Todd and ignored her question. Having a baby attached to her hip seemed to make Roxanne invisible. She sighed, then noticed another police car approaching. Ravi Anand had arrived.

Alan Carlson introduced himself to Corporal Anand. He was dismayed to learn that the man renting their house had been found dead in a sunflower field on land he and his wife owned, just a short distance down the highway. He hadn't heard a thing about it. The Carlsons had spent Sunday afternoon and evening in Winnipeg, returning home just before ten. They hadn't spoken to anyone since.

He didn't know who their weekend renter was, but his wife, Andrea, would have met him. She handled all their Airbnb bookings and liked to stop by to say hello and make sure guests had everything they needed. Perhaps the police should go over to their house and speak with her? It was just on the other side of the trees. He pointed toward a patch of bush on the west side of the farmyard. Roxanne noticed a path running through it—the way Carlson must have come.

Ravi Anand turned to his constable. "Tape this house off, and the truck," he told him, just as Roxanne had already done, "and tell Sergeant Marsden that he'll find me next door when he gets here."

This time Todd Brewster went straight to his patrol car to get tape and do as he was told. Ravi turned to Roxanne. "Everything's under control, Roxanne," he said. "The MCU's on its way. And Ident. Thanks for finding the truck so quickly. We were looking for it."

"You're welcome," she said. "But you should know that there's a leather bomber jacket inside that house that looks exactly like one Coop Jenkins used to wear. Those outbuildings will need be taped off too. I've been told there's a quad inside that old barn."

Then she took Ravi's advice, buckled her child back into the car seat and drove away, feeling somewhat mollified at having done her small bit.

She went back the way she had come. The road to the highway was quiet, not another car in sight. She slowed down and looked across a green field dotted with black cattle. The sun was high in the sky now. She could see the sunflower heads fringing the horizon to the south. The Klassen farm was visible to the east. She stopped so she could have a good look.

It wasn't far from the farmhouse where Coop had been staying to where he was found dead, especially if you cut across the fields. Had he left the door unlocked? Had he taken his phone with him? Had it been on the body? She didn't know.

As a working PI, he might have been armed. If so, where was the gun? In the house, or had his killer taken both his phone and his gun from his body?

Had he run across the pasture, pursued by someone on the Carlsons' quad? Tried to escape by hiding among the sunflowers? Or had he been a passenger—willing or taken under duress? Was he already dead by then, killed in the house behind her? A large quad could carry a lifeless body. Had he been dumped in the sunflower field in the hope that his remains wouldn't be found until Pete McBain harvested the crop? That wouldn't happen until two, maybe three months from now.

There was another possibility. The quad could have taken a different route, gone along the road she was on right now. They were usually driven off-road, on the other side of the ditch. It could have turned at the highway just up ahead and headed along past the Klassen farm to the sunflower field.

If Coop had been alive and taken against his will, he might have tried to escape and hide among the tall plants. Had the quad's driver pursued him in and found him? Cut him off and shot him right there, on the spot? Was the track the quad had made as it smashed through the sunflower stalks the only one? Would Ident have thought to check for footprints leading from the road to where Coop's body was found?

So many questions and she had no answers. Usually she would find out. As the sergeant in charge of the local detachment she would be kept informed, but right now she was not in a position to ask. She bit her lip in frustration. It was her old buddy Coop who had been killed here. How was she supposed to stand aside and wait? Do nothing?

She reassured herself that she'd already made a useful contribution by identifying the body, locating Coop's truck, and discovering where he'd been staying. That might have to be enough for now. If the case dragged on until she returned to work in December, she'd have the right to know how it was progressing. But investigations like this were best solved while the evidence was still fresh.

Should she cut her leave short and go back to work now? Sooner than she had intended? That was going to be difficult. She had no childcare set up for Dee and all the daycares were full. She would be lucky to have a place when it was actually time for her to go back into her office.

She glanced in her rearview mirror. Cars were approaching from the other highway. Marsden from the MCU? The Ident team must be coming to resume the search, but she, Roxanne, wasn't in a position to know what they might discover.

This case was happening right in her neighbourhood, and she had past knowledge of the victim. There was no reason why she shouldn't take a neighbourly interest, she told herself. Local gossip was often useful. She could pass on what people were saying to Ravi Anand. Make herself useful as best she could. Just as she had been doing since the body had been discovered.

Her old friend Roberta Axelsson lived further north on the highway, closer to Cullen Village. Roberta kept chickens. Lots of people stopped by her house to pick up eggs and Roberta talked to all of them. Roberta was inquisitive, interested in what went on around her. She knew most of what went on around Cullen Village. There was no reason why Roxanne couldn't go and find out what, if anything, Roberta knew about their new neighbours. She drove to the highway and headed in that direction.

"Roxanne! And Dee! Come on in!" Roberta stood in her open doorway. A brown tabby cat took the opportunity to stalk inside, brushing against her legs as it did so. Fat hens strutted around in a wire enclosure behind the house. Roberta looked quite like one of the white ones, her round, smiling face surrounded by a mop of silvery curly hair, a large, fluffy, home-knitted sweater draped around her ample body, her feet in bright red slippers, also of her own making.

She reached out and took Dee from Roxanne without asking. "I've just made some soup. Why don't you stay and have some? What was going on down the highway last night? Is it true that someone's been found dead in that big sunflower field? Do you know who it was? Come and tell me all about it!"

5

A COUPLE OF hours after Roxanne Calloway had gone off home with her baby and some eggs, Roberta Axelsson played her usual Monday afternoon Scrabble game with her friends Margo Wishart and Sasha Rosenberg. They were seated around a table in Margo's lakeshore house at Cullen Village.

"That baby looks more and more like Panda," Roberta said.

Panda had been their friend. She had lived and died in a house nearby. It had burned down and the land had been left to her favourite nephew, Matt Stavros. Dee wasn't just like her in looks and manner, she was named for her.

Panda's ashes, and those of Annie, her partner, were buried under a pair of mountain ash trees not far from the house where Matt and Roxanne now lived, and Matt had wanted his baby daughter to have her name. Panda's Greek immigrant parents had baptised her Delphia. Panda had hated it and had never used it unless she had to.

"Roxanne didn't want that name either, but her mother was called Rose Anne, so she and Matt settled on Roseanne Delphia. Rosie for short. But then she had a big baby with a head of thick, black hair. No Rosebud is she! Matt called her Dee instead and that stuck." Roberta laid down her letters, first ones on the board. "BROKEN," she announced. "Double points for the B and a double word. I get thirty for that."

"Very good, Roberta." Margo noted the score. "Does Roxanne know anything about that body they've just found down the highway?"

"She went there and saw it! She recognized who it was! It's that detective that saved her from getting killed years ago in Winnipeg, just before she moved here."

"Cooper Jenkins?" Margo knew exactly who he was. She had helped with the same case Roxanne and Detective Sergeant Jenkins had worked on years ago, but only with Roxanne herself. She had never met the DS in person.

"That's right. And Roxanne is stuck at home on mat leave so she can't work on the case. Not officially, anyway." Roberta watched as Margo added 'Z' and 'O' to her letters, the 'Z' on a triple point square.

"ZOO. Thirty-two points," said Margo.

"No fair," Roberta complained, then she shrugged. Margo usually won at Scrabble but it was fun to play and a good excuse to spend an afternoon together. "Jenkins was staying in that old farmhouse that the Carlsons rent out. The one next to their new straw house."

Margo didn't know the Carlsons, but Sasha did. She had made some wrought iron plant holders for them. Usually she twisted metal into sculptural shapes but she also made serviceable metalwork to help pay the bills. The Carlsons had offered her a good price for the set of holders. She lifted some letters from her rack.

"WELT. That's the best I can do. I get seven." Sasha watched Margo write down the number. "The Carlson guy's quiet. Doesn't say much but she seems okay. Kinda fun, actually."

"Andrea is great! I like her. You should see the kitchen in that new house—granite countertops, glass doors, stainless steel everywhere, copper pans. It must have cost a fortune."

Roberta had also met Andrea Carlson and had been shown inside the straw house. She reported that it looked quite ordinary. The thick straw bales inside the walls were there for insulation.

"Don't they attract mice?" asked Sasha.

"Not a problem, they say. Everything's covered in with concrete." Roberta also knew that Alan Carlson planned to go into serious beekeeping. "He only kept a few hives this year, but he's planted a big patch of clover so he can make clover honey. He's been talking to the Klassens. Their son, Nick, is helping him set up a vegetable garden. Vera told me."

"I think Andrea Carlson's in my new yoga class," Margo commented. "I haven't talked to her yet."

"I don't have any vowels," Roberta complained. "I'm going to have to dump my letters and get new ones." She reached for the bag that contained the tiles. "Roxanne must want to get back to work. She was asking about babysitting."

"How long is it until her leave is up?" asked Margo.

"Not until December, but all the daycares are full. She's not sure what to do about that."

"So now Cooper Jenkins is dead, right here, near where we all live, and she wants you to take care of her baby?" asked Margo, putting all the facts together. "Does she want to go back to work so she can help find out who killed him?"

"You'll be stuck taking care of the kid full-time if you do it," Sasha muttered. "Would you be okay with that?"

Sasha had never had children. She preferred dogs. Her old hound had died a few months ago. Her new pup, part basset, the rest of his parentage unknown, was outside in the yard with Margo's dog, Bob. She called him Albert. Albie for short.

"Not really," Roberta admitted. She took new tiles from the bag and ranged them on the rack in front of her. "Dee's a good baby and I could use the extra cash, but I don't want to get myself tied down. I told her I could do a couple of days a week. Three, sometimes. That's all."

ROXANNE HAD MADE up her mind while she talked with Roberta. Being sidelined on this case wasn't enough for her.

"I'll have to find another part-time babysitter if I want to get back to work. Roberta's been a good mom. She knows all about babies and Dee loves her already, but she can only do three days at best and I've no idea who else to ask. I've called the daycares again to find out if they can push me up the wait list but I'll be lucky to get a spot by December as it is," Roxanne said to Matt as they loaded the dishwasher after dinner that night. She'd need to talk to Ravi, too, if she cut her leave short. Make sure she wasn't ousting him from the job before he was ready.

"Maybe you should give the MCU time to do the job." Matt didn't share her enthusiasm. "It's just this murder that's making you want to get back. Because it's Coop Jenkins."

He wasn't completely right about that. Roxanne had been sergeant at the Fiskar Bay detachment for over four years. Running it, day by day, was no longer much of a challenge, but it was the job she had settled for and sometimes an interesting case came her way. It was being at home alone with a baby for another ten weeks that didn't thrill her. She had been off long enough.

"Aren't you a bit too close to this one?" Matt continued to object. "I know you feel like you owe it to Coop to find out who killed him, but you're emotionally involved, aren't you?"

"That just makes me more determined to do it. Are you saying I'm too tied to this case to think it through clearly enough?" Roxanne leaned back against the kitchen sink and folded her arms. She had expected Matt to be more supportive. "Don't you think I'm more professional than that?"

"I didn't say that. But you do have a personal connection to the victim, right?"

"Someone blasted Cooper with a shotgun, in our neighbourhood. It wouldn't matter who it was, I'd want to know who did that. It's Coop and I owe him big time. I am involved, whether I like it or not," she replied.

"Okay," he said. "I get it. Do what you need to do. Just don't put yourself into any danger, will you? We kind of need you here, don't we, Dee?"

The baby sat in her high chair, waving her arms and yelling at her daddy to pick her up, but he needed to leave. Finn stood by the door, eager to go. Tonight there were hockey tryouts for his age group at the arena in Fiskar Bay. Afterward, he planned to go to his best friend Noah's house to play video games. Matt was staying in town to catch up on some office work and would pick him up later. They wouldn't be home until after nine. Soon they were gone.

Roxanne parked Dee in a playpen with a stack of toys and went online.

A search for Winnipeg-based private investigation services yielded *Jenkins Investigations*. She checked out their website. A headshot of Coop showed him looking just as she remembered, cropped grey hair, the corner of his mouth lifted in a half-smile. His bio described his many years of service with the city's police services, how as a detective he had specialized in solving difficult crimes.

His daughter, Hailey, was co-owner of the business. Her photo appeared below his. Her hair was darker, parted down the middle, and she wore lots of eye makeup. She had Coop's long face without the quirky smile. She stared, straight faced, at the camera. Hailey, it seemed, had a background in telecommunications. She specialized in online surveillance.

A list of recommendations followed. They helped find missing evidence, worked on divorce cases and fraud. They were reliable, discreet and reasonably priced. Delivered results in good time, the comments said.

Contact information gave a telephone number. Roxanne listened to a recorded voice, a woman's, that of Hailey, she presumed, as it delivered the usual message.

"Hi, Hailey," she said, after the beep. "You don't know me but I worked on a murder case with your father several years ago. I am so sorry that this has happened to him. I'm with the RCMP, off on maternity leave right now, but I live close to the place where Coop died, near Cullen Village, and I'd like to know more. Maybe I can help. Please call me back. My name's Roxanne Calloway." And she left her number.

Less than five minutes later, her phone rang and Hailey Jenkins's name came up on the screen.

"Are you the same RCMP woman that almost got herself killed on the job? The one that my dad saved?"

"That's me," Roxanne admitted. "We were working on the same case. Two bodies, one found outside Winnipeg, the other inside the city limits, so the RCMP and the Winnipeg police needed to collaborate."

"That was years ago, right?"

"Yes, it was. I'm sorry I didn't keep in touch with Coop," she said. "I moved out to the Interlake shortly after."

"That's right. I remember because Dad got a commendation for it. He said you chickened out after. Took a cushy number out at the lake."

"Coop quit being a detective himself," Roxanne reminded her.

"He didn't have much choice. The city only lets cops like him work out of uniform for four years at a time. He went back on patrol, but he got fed up with that. Took an early pension and went into business for himself."

Hailey didn't mention that he'd tried working with some other old colleagues first. Maybe that hadn't worked out. Cooper Jenkins had never been much of a team player.

"You went into business with him?"

Hailey had lost her job during the pandemic. "Yeah, sure. I got let go. Tried working with a friend. That tanked, but I know my way around a computer, and crime didn't stop just because of the lockdown, so Dad and I joined up. I do all the bookings and the accounts too. Dad was shit at that."

"Was he investigating something out here?"

"Kind of. The police are saying they found his body in the middle of a field and he'd been shot."

"That's all that they've told you?" Roxanne asked.

"'Course. You cops can be real jerks sometimes," Hailey retorted. "You tell people nothing. Ident's been in Dad's office all day and I'll bet they'll have taken his work computer away, and his files. It's just as well I work from home myself most of the time. I've got enough here to keep going." There was a hint of Coop's old toughness in the way Hailey spoke.

"You work out of separate offices?"

"Yeah, I've got a kid to look after and Dad and I both liked our own spaces."

"I went out to the field where Coop was found last night."

"You're kidding. How come?"

"It's minutes away from where I live. Someone I know in the Major Crimes Unit told me there was a body and I went to go look. It was me that identified your dad."

"You saw him?"

"I did. You know that he was found lying in the middle of a sunflower field?"

"No. They just said it was out in the country and he was shot."

"He was hit in the chest. A shotgun wound. It would have been instant. He wouldn't have suffered at all." Roxanne tried to soften that information but Coop Jenkins's daughter wasn't buying it.

"Yeah, but wouldn't he have seen the shooter?" she countered. "He'd have known that this was it, wouldn't he? That he was going to die?"

Hailey was probably right. Coop must have been facing his killer when he was shot.

"Aren't you supposed to be off duty? On leave?" she asked warily.

"I am," Roxanne replied. "But it's your dad that died. I wouldn't be here if it wasn't for him. If I can help find whoever killed him, I'd like to. If I come into Winnipeg tomorrow, can we get together and talk? I'll tell you what I know so far."

"Well, maybe. Can you make it in the morning? My boy, Liam, will be in kindergarten. I'll be home then." There was still a hint of caution in Hailey Jenkins's voice, but she had agreed to that much. Roxanne got directions.

"Great," she said. "I'll be there."

Hopefully, Roberta could take Dee off her hands for the day. She made that call, next.

"Sure," said Roberta. She could keep the baby all day. Roxanne hung up and stretched. She felt quite like her old working self. Not quite, but almost.

6

HAILEY JENKINS LIVED in a townhouse in a relatively new development at the south end of Winnipeg. The row of attached homes sat slightly back from a busy highway, leaving room for a parking lot and a green, grassy area with play structures out front. A group of mothers stood nearby, watching their kids climb, swing, and dig in the sandpit. Soon, snow would blanket the entire area, bringing outdoor playtime to an end.

Roxanne asked for directions. A mom holding a coffee mug pointed the way. As she walked toward Hailey Jenkins's place, the group watched her go, heads together, speculating about who she was. They probably all knew that Hailey's father had just died. Maybe they thought Roxanne was a relative. She passed a row of identical townhouses: two windows upstairs, one down, a patch of scrubby grass in front, a path leading to each door, no fences. She found the number she was looking for and knocked.

The door slowly and a cautious face peeked out. From what Roxanne could see, Hailey was tall and rangy, just as Coop would have been when he was younger, but everything about her was darker. Straight black hair hung either side of her face. She wore black jeans, a dark grey tunic over a black, long-sleeved T. Her face was covered in pale makeup, the eyes sooty black, as were the lips. One hand, silver rings on the fingers, nails painted black as well, held the door open. The sleeve was rolled back, revealing a tattooed arm.

"You're Roxanne?"

Roxanne said she was and the door opened wider.

Two bikes were parked in the hallway—one adult-sized, the other small, silver and blue—along with a buggy, the kind used for hauling a child or groceries. Three doors branched off the hallway, one leading to a combined living room and kitchen. Hailey led them up a wooden staircase. The house had two bedrooms; one had been converted into a home office. She must share the other with her child.

Hailey didn't offer coffee. She pointed to an empty upright seat and lowered her leggy self into a large black desk chair. Three computer monitors were ranged behind her. One was turned on. It showed the doorway to a house and part of a street.

"You're monitoring someone?" Roxanne asked.

"Yep. Restraining order but the guy keeps showing up." Hailey clicked the keyboard and the screen went blank. "I'll check it later," she said. The camera would continue to record.

"So you do online surveillance and Cooper did the legwork? Is that how you worked?"

"Something like that." Hailey Jenkins leaned back in her chair. "You're here to tell me about how my dad died," she reminded Roxanne. "How come you found him if you're not working right now?"

She crossed her arms and tucked her hands under her armpits, out of sight. Roxanne had seldom seen Coop without a twinkle in his eyes, a sardonic lift to his mouth. He'd used humour as a weapon and a defence. Without it, his daughter looked sullen, but she had a right to be sad, resentful even, considering how her father had died.

"Didn't you quit being a detective way back when you knew my dad?" Hailey demanded.

"I'm RCMP. We don't call ourselves that," Roxanne reminded her. "But we do investigate, especially when someone dies in the area where we work. And there's been a couple of suspicious deaths since I moved to the Interlake. I've kept my hand in."

"That right?"

"You and he were both PIs? Was that what he was doing out where I live? Investigating a case?"

"Sure. The police know all about why he was there. They're dealing with this." Hailey Jenkins wasn't about to give up any information.

"I told you. Your dad had my back when I needed him. You know he saved my life once, in a knife attack. Now he's died, on my turf. Of course I'm taking an interest. I know my neighbourhood, and the people in it, so I can ask around. And I didn't just identify his body. I found his truck."

"You did? The cops have got it?"

"It was parked outside an Airbnb where he was staying."

"I rented that place for him," Hailey remarked. "Just for the weekend. Do you know if they've towed the truck away?"

"I don't, but I can check. I'll let you know."

"How come they didn't tell me that they've found it? The cops aren't saying much." Hailey's demeanour thawed. The information about Coop's truck had worked. "Dad's in the morgue. I don't know when they'll let me have his body. They wanted his keys and his passwords. I haven't been able to get over to his place yet. I had Liam last night and I couldn't drag him over there. I would have taken the bus this morning, once I got him off to school but I couldn't because you were coming. You have a car. Can you give me a ride?", she asked.

"I thought you only had the morning free?" Roxanne replied.

"Hey, I asked one of the neighbours to pick Liam up and keep an eye on him until I get back. If you don't drive me I can still take the bus."

"Sure, I can. Let's go." Roxanne rose to her feet and found her car key. This was better than she had hoped. She'd be able to get a close look at Coop's apartment.

It was a twenty-minute drive away, enough time for Roxanne to learn that Hailey was a single mom, that Liam's dad was long gone. She'd worked in the IT department of a large store that specialized in electronics. "They liked to have a girl out on the floor to sell to women," she said. "That's why they hired me. But I got to work in the back room too, fixing computers. I learned a lot from those guys. When the pandemic hit and we went into lockdown, three of us set up in business for ourselves."

That hadn't lasted, but by then Coop had discovered that working with a bunch of old cops as a private investigator wasn't for him, either.

"He said they gave him all the boring jobs. And Dad always was a bit of a loner, y'know?"

Roxanne suspected that his daughter was, too.

By now, they were crossing the river, just minutes from the building where Coop had lived. Roxanne turned onto a main thoroughfare—the road that led out of town and westward, out onto the wide prairie.

"So you got your PI licence?" Roxanne asked, checking. She pulled up at a red light, beside a large semi.

"Sure, I did. And we divvied up the work. He did all the legwork. I did the office stuff. I told you already."

Hailey gazed out the window at the blank side of the semi, her expression inscrutable. Roxanne could read the signs. Hailey was pretending everything had been going well, but it was clear things were tight in that small household—financially strained by a lost job, a failed venture with friends, and the demands of raising a child. She hadn't just lost her father; she'd lost her business partner—the one who set up trail cams so she could monitor them from home and who travelled to places like the Interlake to gather information. Their work still required someone to be on the ground now and then. How was Hailey Jenkins supposed to manage that as a single mother, with a child still in part-time kindergarten?

They pulled into Coop Jenkins's parking spot, the same one Roxanne remembered from years ago. The building was a wall of windows and balconies. Some had flowerpots on them, flowers still blooming. Not Cooper's, five floors up. Hailey had a set of keys. She let them in through the front door. An elderly woman with a small dog on a leash walked towards them.

"Hailey!" the woman said. "I just heard the news. It's your father? I'm so sorry." Hailey froze, but the old lady continued, undeterred. "Will you be having a service for him?" Roxanne held the front door open for her and her dog. "You know the police were here last night?" the woman added, pausing, clearly hoping for more details. But the elevator doors had already opened, and Hailey was walking toward it.

"I'll let you know," she muttered, barely loud enough to be heard. "Gossipy old bat. She's lived on the same floor as Dad for years," she said as the door slid to a close. "Always needs to know everybody else's business."

The building's hallway was carpeted and bare-walled, but the moment they entered Coop's apartment, his presence seemed to fill the space. Hailey gasped audibly, and Roxanne watched her struggle to fight back tears. An ashtray, half full, sat beside a folded newspaper on the coffee table. A nearly empty coffee cup had been left behind. A well-worn brown leather chair faced a large-screen TV. On the wall hung a framed photo of Hailey with her son as a baby, and another of Coop in uniform, receiving an award from the city's police chief. Everything looked just as it must have on the day Coop left for the Interlake, fully expecting to return.

There were two bedrooms. In one, a comforter had been hastily thrown over the bed, with a heap of clothes piled on a chair. The second bedroom had been converted into an office, now in a shambles. The police had opened desk drawers and left them emptied. The top drawer of a filing cabinet hung gaped; its files scattered across the floor.

"They've taken his safe." Hailey had wiped her eyes and now surveyed the mess. "And his computer."

"He didn't take it to the Interlake with him?"

"Don't expect so. Dad liked to write things down by hand. He was old-fashioned that way." Roxanne remembered that Coop had carried a small notebook and a pen with him, always.

"Have they found his wallet or his phone?"

Hailey was rooting through a top drawer. "They're gone, along with all his notes," she said. "Whoever left him there must have thought it would be months before he was found and didn't want him identified. Or they just stole them?"

"Did he have a gun?" asked Roxanne.

"Sure, he did. I don't know if he took it with him, though. It would have been in the safe if it was here." Now she rifled through a half-empty filing cabinet.

"His baseball bat was in his truck." Roxanne stayed by the doorway and watched.

"Well, he always took that." Hailey's head swung up. For an instant the wary look on her face reminded Roxanne of her father. "You saw it?"

"It was in the truck, behind the driver's seat, where he usually kept it," said Roxanne. "What exactly was he looking for?"

"A missing person, name of Meagan Stephens." Hailey leaned against her father's desk and folded her arms. "She worked the beach patrol at Cullen Village all summer. The job wrapped up, the Monday of Labour Day weekend, just a couple of weeks ago. Meagan should have gotten home by the next morning. She'd told her parents she was getting a ride. University started the next day but she didn't show up. They waited a week before they talked to us. They thought she'd maybe gone off with a boyfriend, nothing serious enough to report to the police. Maybe they didn't want to set off alarm bells, something like that? The girl had led a pretty quiet life up until then. It was her first job away from home. Maybe she wasn't ready to go back. She'd had her first taste of freedom, you know. They wanted to know where she'd gone. That she was okay, that's all."

"Did they talk to her friends?"

"I don't know. That's all Dad told me. We've done cases like this before. The kid usually shows up when the money runs out. Dad went out your way to find out about a boyfriend. To talk to the woman she had stayed with. Anyone else she had hung out with. Otherwise I don't know much."

"Do you know the boyfriend's name?"

Hailey shook her head. Coop hadn't said.

"Did Meagan have a car?"

"Nah. She packed up her suitcase and left while the woman she was staying with was out, so someone must have picked her up. That was it."

"So that's all the police know, too?"

"Unless they found something on Dad's phone. Or in his notes. I gave them the Stephens's address. That's pretty well it."

"When did Coop go out to Cullen Village?" Roxanne asked.

"Friday. He was going to stay the weekend. I booked the Airbnb for him until Monday morning. I didn't hear anything from him but that's how Dad's always operated. He does his end of the job and I do mine. He comes by my place now and then for something to eat and to catch up. To see Liam."

"So you haven't talked to the Stephens parents yourself?"

"No. They always talked to Dad. I just emailed them the work contract and they paid by e-transfer. I'm not sure how I'm going to manage without him," Hailey admitted, her eyes fixed on the floor in front of her. "I can't get out and about like he did. I don't know much about how that side of the business works. I just left it to him. And I'm like you. I want to know what's happened and the police aren't going to tell me. You've got a better chance of finding that out." Her dark hair had fallen over her face. She pushed it back and looked at Roxanne.

"I can find out what he uncovered in my neighbourhood and get back to you, if that would help," Roxanne offered. "Maybe we could share what we know? I want to find out what happened to your dad too.

"I need to head home by midafternoon," she added, "but there's still time to see if anyone's home at Meagan Stephens's place."

"Nah." Hailey stood up and looked around her. "I need to stay here and clean up this mess. Find out what's been left of Dad's and what's been taken. I can get a bus home. You go. I'll give you the address." She took out her phone and found the contact. "You'll tell me, though? If you find out anything?"

"Sure, I will," said Roxanne.

7

THE STEPHENS FAMILY lived in a neighbourhood that was almost new, a development in the southwest corner of the city named Spring Woods, in spite of the fact that it had been built on reclaimed farmland, once tall grass prairie, barely a tree in sight. The roads curved around bays that all looked alike.

The houses Roxanne passed varied in size and design, but all were constructed from the same materials, with similar roofing, windows, and doors. Young trees had been planted in small plots beside wide driveways. Hanging flower baskets were popular, though most were past their best this late in the year. Nearly every house featured a double garage, and the Stephens's home was no exception. It was one of the larger models, two storeys, built to accommodate a big family.

Carrie Stephens, mother of Meagan, was home. She received Roxanne coolly but welcomed her inside once she had explained that she was an off-duty RCMP sergeant and a friend of the Jenkins family, trying to clarify what had recently occurred.

"We were so shocked to hear what has happened to the detective we hired." Mrs. Stephens took Roxanne's jacket and hung it in a closet. "Who would imagine that anyone would come to such harm in Cullen Village, of all places? Such a quiet spot. We are praying for his soul, and for the safe return of our daughter."

She was a small woman, with prominent cheekbones and a straight nose. Her hair was scraped back into a bun at the back of her head. Some curly wisps escaped, softening the effect. A long skirt almost reached her ankles.

This was a Christian household. There was a picture of Jesus at the end of the hallway and Carrie Stephens wore a small gold crucifix on a chain around her neck. A grand piano dominated the room into which she showed her unexpected guest.

"I teach music," she told Roxanne. "I have a student coming for a piano lesson at one. But I can spare you a few minutes."

A photograph of her children hung on the wall—all five of them, grouped together. Meagan was the oldest, bigger than her mother, but she had inherited those good cheekbones and she had a broad smile. She was pretty, as her mother must once have been. Her hair was darker and cropped short.

"She swims every day, so it makes sense to keep it cut like that," said Mrs. Stephens.

Roxanne sat on a straight-backed chair, the kind placed for a waiting parent, while Carrie Stephens taught a child their scales. She took the piano stool, her back straight, long fingers knotted in her lap.

Meagan was studying biology at the local university, intending to become a marine biologist. She had her lifeguard certification and taught swimming lessons at a nearby pool when she was home. Her parents had been surprised when she'd applied to join the summer beach patrol program out at the lake.

"We think that her swimming instructor put the idea into her head. At first we said no, but she was offered a place at Cullen Village and a friend of mine who lives there agreed to let her stay at her house while she was there. We thought she'd be perfectly safe, but now we are so concerned."

The friend who lived at Cullen Village was named Susan Rice.

"I know who that is," said Roxanne. "She teaches yoga. I've been to her house."

"I've known Susan since we were children. We went to school together. She's given some workshops for the women's group at our church. She let Meagan board with her in exchange for some child care. Susan's a single mother, you know, and Meagan's always been good with little ones."

Susan Rice's children were growing. Both of them were in junior high, old enough to be left alone for an hour or two, Roxanne thought, but Susan was a careful parent. Working the beach patrol was a full-time job. If Meagan was expected to keep an eye on the Rice kids while Susan taught evening classes at her studio, she wouldn't have had much time for herself. Perhaps Carrie Stephens had figured that out before she let her daughter go.

"Why didn't you tell the police that she's missing?" she asked.

"We hoped she was just staying with some new friend, but now we've learned that Meagan was seldom at Susan's. She spent a lot of time with the other three lifeguards. They were sharing a cottage. Sometimes Meagan didn't sleep in her own bed." Carrie Stephens frowned. "We are so disappointed in Susan. We thought she'd take better care of our girl. And in Meagan, too. We didn't raise her to behave like that. There was a boyfriend, it seems. Mr. Jenkins thought she might have gone off with him. The boy drives trucks for a living."

"Did he give you a name?"

Carrie Stephens shook her head. "Now Mr. Jenkins has been killed, and the police are involved. We are so worried." A fat teardrop appeared in the corner of a pale blue eye. She thumbed it away and composed herself once more. "An officer from the RCMP visited my husband at work yesterday. He was quite abrupt, John said."

It had to have been Rob Marsden, Roxanne thought. That was just his style.

John Stephens was the principal of Spring Woods Christian Academy, located in a building near their church, not far from their home. All their children attended the academy for elementary school, then moved on to a collegiate run by the Mennonite community where they would continue to be taught according to Christian values.

"Does Meagan have friends? From school? At university?" Roxanne asked.

"She knows lots of people her own age. Swims every morning. Sings in the church choir and teaches one of our younger classes at Sunday school. Meagan gets along with everyone." That didn't add up to friendship, Roxanne thought. "And of course she has her university classes. She works hard. She needs to get good grades if she wants to get into grad school."

"She has a computer? A phone?"

"She took them all to the beach with her. We thought she had maybe gone astray this summer, and didn't want to come home. I so hoped Mr. Jenkins would find her, then we could bring her home without too much fuss and talk some sense into her. I pray, morning and night, that she is somewhere safe. I do hope that what's happened now doesn't mean something absolutely awful has happened to her. But maybe it has." Another teardrop appeared. This time she reached for a box of tissues.

"The police know that she is missing now, and the two cases must be linked," Roxanne said. "They'll be putting all their resources into finding Meagan."

"Yes, but that won't be their main priority, will it? John says the sergeant who interrogated him made it quite clear that he thought Meagan was just some silly girl who had wandered off. He insinuated that we'd been too protective of her. Said she was twenty years old, an adult. Entitled to a life of her own."

Roxanne found herself inclined to agree with Rob Marsden about that. But Meagan had disappeared out at Cullen Village and Coop had also died near there.

"Are you working on this in an official capacity?" Carrie Stephens asked suddenly, as if the thought had just occurred to her.

"I knew Cooper Jenkins in the past, when he was with the city police. We investigated a case together," said Roxanne. "Currently I'm on maternity leave but in December I'll be back at work. I am usually in charge of the Fiskar Bay RCMP detachment." She watched Carrie Stephens absorb that information.

"So you are involved too?" Carrie persisted.

"Any murder or missing person case that happens this close to home concerns me." Roxanne sidestepped the question once more. "I know the people in the neighbourhood very well. Someone must know where Meagan has gone. I'll ask around and see if I can find out anything. She couldn't have left Cullen Village by herself."

"We'd be grateful for any help that you can give us. God bless you," said Carrie Stephens.

It was almost one o'clock—time for the next music student to arrive. Soon after, Roxanne backed out of the driveway. Another car had pulled up outside, waiting to take her spot. Carrie Stephens stood in the open doorway, ready to welcome an elderly woman with white hair. Many retirees were returning to the music lessons they had abandoned in their youth.

Roxanne had plenty of time to reflect on what she had learned as she drove home. It might end up being a city matter. Meagan was from Winnipeg, and it seemed she had left Cullen Village after work on Labour Day weekend. The boyfriend could have been another beach patroller, or a holidaymaker, or someone who, like Meagan, had only worked the summer and was now long gone from the Interlake. The person who drove into the sunflower field on a quad might have been a visitor as well. There might not be much Roxanne could do.

Still, she could talk to Susan Rice—find out who had worked beach patrol that summer and whether any of them had a cottage at Cullen Village. She was especially eager to learn the boyfriend's name.

ROB MARSDEN WAS avoiding spending too much time at the RCMP detachment at Fiskar Bay, but he was still in the Interlake. He was eating lunch alone, in the Tim Hortons parking lot, trying to stay under the radar. Not that that would work for long in a small town like this, where people watched out for strangers, especially when the summer visitors had gone home. He'd kept a room at the hotel for another night. It wasn't bad. Overlooked the beach. He'd gone for a jog this morning along the boardwalk and watched a work crew rake the sand. There must still be a few tourists around, although he hadn't seen any. Fishermen had been unloading their catch at the harbour. Maybe, if he ended up stuck out here through the weekend, he could bring Fran and the kids. Treat them to a couple of days at the lake. They'd like it here.

The RCMP building in Fiskar Bay was typical, built of red brick, two storeys, with a front desk and offices branching off from it. There were interview rooms, holding cells, and a fenced-off area out back for prisoners, though it was empty at the moment. Everything was quiet. Not much was happening.

The Sikh man running the place didn't have an accent, so he must have grown up here in Canada. He was trying to explain to Rob that he couldn't spare anyone; they were already one person short. He himself was filling in for that Calloway woman who'd shown up at the crime scene on Sunday night. Technically, another sergeant should have been assigned to replace her, but the force was stretched thin. The bosses had decided that Anand, who was Calloway's second-in-command, could cope. He seemed pleased with himself for managing through a busy summer. But now, he really couldn't spare anyone to serve as Marsden's local backup. That was annoying.

Not that there was anyone at the detachment that Rob would want on his team. One little French chick. A guy that grinned all over his face and looked like he had some Mexican blood in him. A rookie, not long finished the six months job training that followed graduation from the Depot. Another guy called Brewster that Rob hadn't met yet. There was a civvie doing desk work. That was it. For now, he'd have to stick around and ask questions himself.

He'd already done some of the legwork. Ident had tried to find tire tracks to identify the make and model of the quad that entered the sunflower field, but without much luck. Foot traffic in and out had messed up the ground, and the boards the idiots had laid down had flattened everything. They'd had no better luck beyond the field: the quad had travelled over grass. But they'd found marks that made them think they might have been made by a brand of tire often used on a Polaris vehicle, so Marsden had gone looking.

He'd knocked on most of the doors between the sunflower field and Cullen Village. Three households had that type of ATV. A young guy at a market garden, only a block from where the body had been found, explained that the dealership in Fiskar Bay sold and serviced Polaris vehicles, so they were popular. His dad had one, but it was in the shop right now for repairs.

The Carlsons, who owned the field, had a quad, too, but they hadn't been home. Marsden left a message but hadn't heard back. It had been a frustrating morning.

He'd glanced through the notes Cooper Jenkins had left on the table in that rental house near Cullen Village before Ident took everything to the lab in Winnipeg. From them he knew Jenkins had been working a PI case, searching for a missing girl. Jenkins hadn't seemed too worried. The girl had packed up and left a thank-you note for the woman she'd been staying with. She'd walked out on her own two feet, suitcase in hand, after finishing her summer job as a beach lifeguard at Cullen Village. She'd just been paid, so she had cash of her own. It sounded like her parents were churchgoers who kept a close watch on her and expected her to come home. Chances were she'd taken off—wanted to cut loose, that was all. Nothing to get excited about.

So why would anyone want to shoot Cooper Jenkins? If there was nothing to hide out here, it didn't make sense. Was something else going on? Jenkins was an old city cop and there was always someone nursing a grudge against a guy like him, someone he'd put away years ago and who wanted revenge. Could he have run into one of those out here, in the quiet little Interlake? Someone who hated him enough to chase him down and kill him? Maybe they shot him somewhere else and dragged the body out to the middle of those sunflowers, dumping him where he wouldn't be found until the snow came. Whoever did this had wanted the body hidden, at least for now.

Jenkins hadn't been killed in that house where he'd been staying. There was no sign of blood there. Whoever had done it had taken his ID. Whoever had done this hadn't wanted his body identified for now.

Ident had checked out the files that they'd found in Jenkins's apartment in Winnipeg. He had a couple of other cases going, but those were just Mickey Mouse stuff: a woman who thought her ex was hanging around, watching her; a small business that was pretty sure someone who worked for them was fiddling the books. Nothing worth killing for, and no reason for anyone to be out here at the lake.

Which brought it back to the missing girl. She had stayed with a woman at Cullen Village who had let the kid go party with the other lifeguards and didn't worry too much if she stayed out late.

"Meagan's not stupid," Susan Rice had told him when he'd stopped by her house last night. "She just has some catching up to do. Her whole life at home's all taken up with the church and her family. And swimming. My guess is that Meagan has chosen to go away. She didn't want to go back to her old life. I think she's moved on."

Was there a guy in her life? Susan had said she wouldn't be surprised. Meagan was a pretty girl, attractive. But she didn't know exactly who it might be. Meagan hadn't shared that kind of information with her.

There was, however, a name in the notes Cooper Jenkins had left on the table in the rental where he'd been staying. It looked like Jenkins had tracked down the lifeguards Meagan had worked with and spoken to a couple of them in Winnipeg just before coming out here to find out who Meagan was seeing. The name CORY ANDREYCHUK was printed and underlined twice. Rob figured he'd better go talk to the guy. Get him crossed off the list.

8

FINDING THE ANDREYCHUK place wasn't easy. It was tucked up a back road behind the Cullen Village dump and looked like an extension of it, though the actual dump was much better organized. Scrap metal littered the property. Cars, trucks, and assorted vehicle debris were scattered across a couple of acres that must once have been a working farm. The remains of a yellow school bus and a derelict motorhome had been ransacked for parts. Wheels were missing, doors hung open, hoods ripped off. Someone had once tried to park the wrecks in neat rows, but that effort had long since been abandoned.

A bungalow stood beside a front yard, flanked by a workshop that might still be functional and an old garage. Three vehicles were parked outside: a semi, a haulage van, and a truck. The semi bore faded stickers on the back. FREEDOM NOW! one of them proclaimed, in big capitals, alongside a large red maple leaf. They were remnants of a movement that had protested government pandemic measures a few years back.

As Rob Marsden pulled in, the front door opened. Two blue heelers barged out, barking and snarling, with a Jack Russell terrier right behind them. A large woman in denims stepped onto the porch, arms folded. She made no move to call off the dogs.

Rob opened the driver's window.

"Call in your animals, ma'am," he hollered, and held up his ID so she could see it. "RCMP!"

"That right?" The woman looked unimpressed. She stepped off her porch and walked toward his car. She looked to be in her fifties and carried some extra weight. Her iron-grey hair hung to her shoulders, lank and in need of a wash.

"Okay, you guys, shut it," she yelled at the dogs. They stopped barking but hung around, watching, as she reached the passenger side and banged on the window for him to open it.

"Whaddaya want?" She propped her forearms on the window frame and peered in. Fat cheeks, downturned mouth, eyes scrunched up, suspicious.

"Sergeant Marsden. Major Crimes Unit. You got a guy called Cory Andreychuk living here?"

Rob would rather have got out the car but the heelers had moved round to his side and hunkered down, watching his every move. Rob was careful around dogs. He'd been bitten by a Rottweiler early in his career. He couldn't see the Jack Russell. It must be sniffing around, close by.

"Cory? What's goin' on? Cory's a good guy, done nothing wrong."

"You're related to him?"

"I'm his aunt, Mister. Judith Andreychuk." She offered her name grudgingly. "You're with Major Crimes? How come you're asking?"

"We're investigating a murder," Marsden informed her. "A man was found dead, not far from here, Sunday night."

"I heard something. Nothing to do with us. Or Cory. He wasn't here."

She stood and slapped the side of the car, as if to tell him he could leave. All Marsden could see was her wide waistline. A leather belt with an ornate metal buckle faced him, carved with a woman's head, mouth open in a scream, snakes sprouting from her skull.

"Look, ma'am," Marsden called out, raising his voice just enough to carry. The pointed ears of both heelers twitched. "You can invite me in so we can talk, or you can meet me at the detachment in Fiskar Bay."

"That right?" Her large face reappeared in the empty window frame. "On the other hand, you could just open this door and let me sit down, couldn't ya?"

Rob unlocked the door. She slid her large bulk into the passenger seat. He got a faint whiff of body odour. She left the door open. The Jack Russell jumped up into her lap.

"You don't mind if Charlie joins us? He likes to take care of his mom," she said and nuzzled the top of the dog's head. "Don't you, boy?" The dog licked her nose. Rob did mind but he chose to put up with it, for now. He turned on the fan in the car. At least it cleared the air a little.

"We've got nothing to do with that dead guy you found. Us or Cory," she said. "He's in Brandon. Went to deliver a load of furniture couple of weeks ago and he's staying there for now. Got an old pal to visit, then he's bringing another load back this way, be here by the weekend."

"So he does haulage for you?"

"Sure does. Good kid, Cory, ain't he, Charlie?" She rubbed the dog's ears. The heelers outside the car had inched closer.

"Did someone come looking for him? Last weekend?"

"Nope." She stared out the windscreen. A pair of crows settled on a tree branch opposite.

"You sure about that? Tall guy? Grey hair, maybe wearing a black leather bomber jacket?"

"Never seen him." But one hand curled around the dog's collar, and her mouth tightened. Rob was sure she was lying. She knew that he meant the dead man found in the sunflower field, but she wasn't about to admit it.

"Cory had a girlfriend?" he asked instead.

"Sure. Lots of girls liked Cory. Which one?" She smirked at him and stroked her dog.

"A girl called Meagan?"

"Never heard of her." The answer came a little too quickly.

"When did he head out to Brandon?"

"Well, let's see. He stuck around Labour Day. We had a barbecue out back. Took off first thing the next morning."

"And he didn't bring a girl called Meagan with him to the barbecue?"

"Told you. There was no Meagan." She snapped her head toward him, beetle-browed, chin jutting defiantly.

"You know how we can contact Cory?"

"Whatya need to do that for? I told you. He's in Brandon."

"Just give me the number, lady."

She pushed the dog off her lap and reached into the pocket of her jeans jacket for a phone. Found a number and gave it to him. There was no address.

"That's it? I can go now?" She didn't wait for an answer. She hauled her heavy body out of the car and slammed the door shut behind her. Then her face reappeared in the open window.

"Charlie just peed on your back wheel." She grinned. "See ya."

She turned and walked away. The Jack Russell trotted after her toward the house, but the two heelers stayed put. Marsden closed the window and backed up. The heelers crept closer.

Judith Andreychuk disappeared inside without a backward glance, but the terrier soon rejoined his two buddies.

Rob revved the engine and pulled out of the yard. All three dogs barked furiously at his wheels. He wouldn't have minded hitting one of them, but he didn't. They chased him halfway to the road before finally giving up and turning back.

ON WEEKDAYS, SUSAN Rice taught yoga classes mornings and evenings, so afternoons were the best time to catch her. Roxanne made it back to Cullen Village from her Winnipeg visit just in time. She texted Matt. Could he pick up Dee at Roberta Axelsson's house on the way home? And pizza for dinner?

The school bus arrived just as Susan welcomed her in. There was still an hour before supper, so they had time to talk; that was no problem, she assured Roxanne. The teenage girl headed upstairs, and Susan's son disappeared into another room. A few minutes later, the sound of a video game drifted through the house. It felt out of place in Susan's peaceful living room, with its statues of Buddha and Ganesh, the scent of incense curling from a burner, rooibos steeping in a teapot and small porcelain bowls set out for tea.

Roxanne had been here before. She knew the squishy armchairs sank almost to the floor, so she found an upright chair against the wall and pulled it forward.

"Are you sure you're comfortable?" asked Susan, sinking easily into a cross-legged position on the floor, prepared to chat. She and Roxanne had been acquainted for years. Roxanne was a neighbour, their local police officer, off duty right now, just asking questions out of interest. She saw no reason why she shouldn't say what she knew about Meagan and her family.

"It's too bad Carrie met up with John Stephens and got caught up with the evangelists," Susan said. "Although she was always…" She searched for the right words: "Spiritually inclined."

Carrie had met John Stephens while they were students. She got married, soon as she graduated. John was already teaching and involved with the church.

"Carrie took to that place right away. She was studying music. The church had this big organ that she could play. She loved it. It wasn't long before she became their choir director. She fit right in. Have you seen the building?" Susan asked, sipping her tea. "It's huge. Loads of money. They have tithing, of course. Ten percent of everything their congregation earns. That church is loaded." That explained how the Stephens family could afford the big new house in Spring Woods.

In spite of their differences, Susan and Carrie had stayed in touch.

"She's had five children. Home, family and Jesus, that's been her whole life these past twenty years." Meagan was supposed to do the same. Carrie had a couple of young men in mind as suitable husbands for her, both from good, church-going families.

"But she was studying to be a marine biologist," said Roxanne.

"Meagan was good at school. She won a scholarship, so they agreed to let her go to university, but they still kept her on a tight rein. She was a good swimmer. I think that's how she got interested in marine biology. She'd seen it on TV.

"I like Meagan," Susan continued thoughtfully, her feet tucked into an effortless lotus position. "She helped out one day when I taught a workshop for the mothers' group at the church for Carrie. Meagan fetched things and tidied up for me."

She set down her cup, a new thought forming. "I've been thinking about starting a class here, Roxanne—mother-and-child yoga. Would you be interested?"

"I'll be back at work in a couple of months," Roxanne reminded her. "Sorry."

"All the more reason. Self-care, you know." Susan smiled, emulating the picture of Kuan Yin, the female buddha of compassion, pictured on the wall behind her. "And so good for the little one.

"Anyway, I was happy to hear Meagan would be coming out here for the summer. Carrie said she could babysit for me, but I don't need much of that kind of help any longer. My two are old enough to stay home by themselves in the evening. But I did think it would be good for Meagan to have some time away from home.

"She was so happy here, you know. Lovely girl, good natured, friendly. I think she thoroughly enjoyed her summer. She liked talking to the families at the beach. Borrowed my old bike so she could get around and hung out with the rest of the lifeguards and their friends. They were all staying at a cottage, not far from the beach, that belongs to the family of one of them. Willa is her name, I think. Sometimes Meagan stayed over. I didn't mind. She needed to have a bit of a life. You should see what she was expected to wear." Susan rose in one smooth movement. "Come upstairs, I'll show you."

She led the way to a small bedroom. There was a single bed, neatly made. In the wardrobe hung three dresses with long skirts and sleeves. Susan opened the drawer in a dresser to reveal underwear of the sort Roxanne's mother liked to wear.

"She got new clothes. I took her shopping as soon as she got paid. She took them all with her and left these behind. I'm quite sure she left of her own accord, Roxanne. She didn't want to go back to that house again, to being her mother's helper. I could see her getting worried about it as we got closer to September."

"Did she have a boyfriend?" Roxanne ran the fabric of one of the dresses through her fingers, a cotton and polyester mix with small flowery sprigs printed on it. It looked homemade.

"Oh, more than one! She was pretty, you know. So was Carrie until the church made her go all frumpy. Meagan and one of the lifeguards liked one another for a while, I've been told, but at the end, she was more interested in a local boy called Cory. Last name's Andreychuk. You know about them?"

Roxanne certainly did. Brad Andreychuk was the son of a local farming family. She'd first encountered him while investigating a murder in the area, when a body had turned up in the Cullen Village dump, and Brad had been a suspect. He hadn't been the killer, but he'd always been trouble. Right now, he was in jail. He'd been caught during a break-and-enter and had nearly killed the couple who confronted him. Roxanne had played a key role in making sure he'd be locked up for a long time. He still had a couple of years left to serve.

"I don't think Cory's like the rest of his family at all. He dropped by once to pick up Meagan. Nice looking. Good manners. I wouldn't be surprised if he knows where she is. You just need to go and ask him."

GOING TO THE Andreychuk farm right now was not an option. The afternoon was late and Roxanne had to get home. Matt was already there, food on the table, Dee in her high chair, gnawing on a pizza crust. She was teething. Both dogs were parked below her, hoping for fallout.

"How'd it go?" Matt asked.

"Hailey Jenkins is a computer nerd," she told him. "Dresses like a Goth. I don't know how she'll manage without her dad to do all the in-person work involved in being an investigator."

"So you've decided to help her out?" Matt knew Roxanne well. He had bought Hawaiian pizza. Ham and pineapple was not her favourite topping but he and Finn loved it. They had devoured half already. "You sure that's a good idea? I hear there's a sergeant called Marsden from Major Crimes staying at the hotel."

"Yes," she said. "But I'm just taking an interest. And you know what I've found out already?" She told him about the Andreychuk connection.

"Okay. Why don't you go tell Marsden what you've found out and leave it at that. Offer to pass on any local gossip, if you must. And if they tell you they don't need you, leave it be. You'll be back on the job soon enough," her sensible, lawyerly partner advised.

"Yes, but Hailey Jenkins isn't able to get out here." She picked the pineapple off a slice of pizza and nibbled.

"Not your problem, Roxanne. Asking some questions around the neighbourhood is one thing, but you're getting deeper into this. Going to Winnipeg and interviewing people is active investigation. How would you take it if someone poked their nose into a case you were running?"

"Depends," she replied, chewing while she thought about it: "If they were going to be useful I might want to use them as a resource."

"Well then, go see if Marsden can use you, but if he says he needs you to back off, you should. You don't want to compromise your job, do you?"

"It won't come to that," she assured him. "I'll be back in my office in December. But yes, you're right. I'll do as you say."

She'd have liked to go ask questions at the Andreychuk farm tomorrow, but Marsden might already be following up on that lead. Instead, she'd go to the detachment first thing and do as

Matt suggested: offer what she knew and maybe find out how things were progressing on their end. Then she'd decide for herself if, going forward, she had a useful role to play.

9

AS SOON AS Matt had left for work next morning with Finn, Roxanne bundled up her daughter and drove to Fiskar Bay. The sky had turned grey and a slight drizzle fuzzed the windshield. Dee chortled along to the swish of the wipers and music on the car radio. Country-and-western wasn't Roxanne's favourite but it kept her baby happy.

Todd Brewster was manning the front desk at the RCMP detachment when she arrived with Dee on one arm, a box of jammy doughnuts in the other. Bringing doughnuts was a tradition, at least when Roxanne had been in charge. Sergeant Marsden wasn't in. Brewster said he'd check if Corporal Anand was available, but before he could, Ravi was already at his door.

"I thought I heard your voice. Come on in." He beckoned her into his office.

Constable Brewster didn't smile. Maybe he couldn't wrap his head around the idea of a skinny, red-headed mom as his boss. He'd have to, soon enough, Roxanne reminded herself. She'd be in uniform then—and without the baby. That would make a difference.

Jan Bjornson, the civilian office manager, took charge of Dee and the doughnuts. She carried both toward the lunchroom. Jan knew Roxanne would soon be her boss and, unlike Brewster, she intended to make a good impression.

"Where's Rob Marsden?" Roxanne settled into the visitor's chair. The furnishings were still the same in her old office but any sign that it had once been hers was gone. A picture of Ravi's wife and three kids was displayed on top of a cabinet, where she had once placed one of Matt and Finn.

"We haven't seen much of him." Ravi took a seat opposite. "He put in an appearance yesterday morning. Had a look at the room upstairs but didn't stick around. He wanted someone to go door-to-door down at Cullen, asking about ATVs, and he wasn't pleased that I couldn't release one of my team to him. He met Brewster when we visited that Airbnb yesterday. He'd like to have him but that's not going to happen."

"You sure about that? I'll bet Brewster would like it."

"Certain." Some people thought Ravi was soft because he was quiet spoken, but Roxanne knew that when he dug in his heels there was no moving him.

"How did it go with the Carlsons?" If Marsden wasn't available, she could at least find out what Ravi knew while she was here. The last time she'd seen him, he was heading toward the straw house two days ago with Rob Marsden and the owner, Alan Carlson.

"They couldn't tell us much." Ravi sat back in his desk chair and swivelled it back and forth as he talked, just as Roxanne had once done. "Airbnb handled the rental. Andrea Carlson gave Cooper Jenkins the keys on Friday and showed him around the place. That was all she saw of him. She said the truck was gone most of Saturday but it was parked outside both nights."

"You know that he was trying to track down a girl called Meagan Stephens?"

"I heard." Marsden had told Ravi that much.

"Did he tell you that she was seeing someone called Cory Andreychuk?"

"One of the Andreychuks? Well, then!" That name caught Ravi's attention.

Police business had taken both of them out to the Andreychuk farm more than once, though not since Bradley Andreychuk had gone to jail. He'd been on their radar for the past few years. His father, who had worked the land, had died of a heart attack in the barn some years ago. Afterward, Brad's formidable mother, Maggie, moved to Winnipeg to be closer to her other son.

Jeremy Andreychuk had considerably more sense than his brother. He worked for a bank and had no interest in running the family farm, so Brad was left to manage it on his own. He had sold off his father's herd of cattle and leased the pastureland. The Black Angus herd now owned by Pete McBain had likely once belonged to the Andreychuks. The land brought in a steady income, allowing Brad to focus on other, more profitable ventures, until his arrest. That income would continue to accumulate while he served time in the local penitentiary. The last time Roxanne had seen the farm, old cars had been piling up beside it. Brad was selling spare parts. Years before, John Andreychuk had taken pride in maintaining the place. Under Brad, it had become an eyesore.

"It looks even worse now," Ravi commented. "His cousin, Ed, moved in last year. He's a trucker. Has a semi and a few other vehicles besides. A big box van. He's set up a moving business, mainly household goods, picks up junk for people, too, and takes it to the dump. Cory's his nephew."

"Have you had any trouble from him?"

"Clean as a whistle, so far."

There was a knock at the door. Todd Brewster stuck his head inside.

"There's a man on the line," he told Ravi. "You should take this call." He closed the door without looking in Roxanne's direction.

Ravi reached for his phone. Roxanne caught mention of a body. Cullen Village. He stood abruptly. "We'll be right there," he said, then turned to Roxanne: "Got to go. Tell you about it later." As he spoke, he was already pulling on his jacket and cap, clearly in a hurry to leave.

"Get hold of Aimee Vermette and Sam Mendes. Tell them to meet me at the wood, south end of Cullen Beach," she heard him say to Brewster as he headed out the door.

Roxanne went to the lunch room. Dee was covered in jam, Jan Bjornson doing her best to clean her up.

"She loves doughnuts," Jan said, almost apologetic, but she was glad to see Roxanne. She needed to get back to her desk. Roxanne thanked her and followed Ravi outside, wiping her sticky daughter's face as she went. By the time Dee was strapped into her car seat, the police car was long gone, siren wailing and lights flashing.

She wanted to follow, to go and find out who was dead, but she should offload the baby before she did that. Dropping Dee off at Matt's office was not an option. He had said something about visiting a rural client this morning. She called Roberta Axelsson and got voicemail. She was stuck with an eight-month-old child on her hands. The best she could do was go and look.

She drove to Cullen Village, the rain falling harder now. The houses curved around a long bay, known to visitors for its sandy beach. But on this rainy September morning, there were no visitors in sight. At the centre of the village, a cluster of shops including a restaurant and a hotel, both shuttered for the winter, faced the bay and a parking lot, where a couple of police cars were parked at the far end.

A white police cruiser had drawn up alongside a Chevy Tahoe SUV. Aimee Vermette, dressed in rain gear, was taping it off. Dee had finally dozed. Roxanne pulled up and wound down her window.

"Hey, Aimee. What's going on?" she asked.

"Sergeant Marsden. Can you believe it? He's dead, lying in the wood over there." Aimee pointed south. A stretch of bush bordered the beach just south of them. Ravi's car was parked at that end of the lot. "This is his SUV. A dog walker found him. Looks like someone hit him on the head. He was wearing runners and a sweatshirt, so he must've gone jogging last night."

On a sunny September evening, the area would have been quiet. Marsden could have run along the boardwalk that stretched most of the beach, then followed the grassy path skirting the woods. Now, the rain was pouring. The body had to be getting soaked. Roxanne hoped Ravi had a tent handy to cover it.

"What's in his car?" asked Roxanne.

"A jacket on the back seat. A bag for garbage. That's all I can see. No one's looked inside yet. Ravi'll leave that job for Ident."

Aimee knew that Marsden's keys, wallet, and ID were still in his pocket. His killer hadn't taken anything. There had been no attempt to conceal Marsden's identity. That was unlike what had happened in Cooper Jenkins's case.

"Did he have his gun with him?"

"If he did, it's been taken. But it's maybe locked inside there." Aimee shrugged a wet shoulder in the direction of the Tahoe. Her hands were stuffed inside deep pockets and raindrops streamed off the visor of her hood. If the killer had taken Marsden's gun, that was bad news. "He wasn't holstered," Aimee said. "He mustn't have taken it with him when he went running. He must have been off work when this happened."

The rain was coming down even harder. Aimee scurried off to take shelter inside her cruiser. Dee stirred and woke up.

Roxanne drove towards home. Obviously, Rob Marsden had been killed because he was searching for Cooper Jenkins's killer. Was this connected to the disappearance of Meagan Stephens? She had no way of finding out.

She had barely reached the house when her phone rang.

"Calloway! What's with all this shit that's happening in your neck of the woods?" Inspector Schultz asked.

"You've heard?" she asked. "About Rob Marsden?"

"Sure, I have. Just got off the blower with Anand. How come you know about that already?"

"I was at the detachment talking to Ravi when the news came in. I stopped by the crime scene. I've just come from there."

"And?" he asked. She could picture him, sitting toadlike behind his desk, fishing for information.

"I don't know much—just that he died last night. It looks like he went out jogging. He was unarmed, so he must have thought he was safe. He was hit on the head, which is a different method than what was used on Cooper Jenkins. You heard about him? The man found lying in that sunflower field near here last week?"

"Sure, I did."

"And you know Cooper was the city sergeant that I worked with five years ago?"

"Yes, I do. And you've been snooping around ever since that body showed up," he said. "Marsden told me."

"I've been useful," she protested, but she laughed as she said it. Roxanne knew how to get along with Schultz. "I was able to identify Jenkins and it was me who found his truck. I've been in touch with his daughter. I know about the missing girl. Do you know that her boyfriend was related to Brad Andreychuk?"

"Yeah, yeah, yeah," he said. "So you're kinda up to speed already?" The reason why he was calling began to dawn on Roxanne. "Look, this case has gone high profile with the killing of a sergeant on duty. Communications want me on TV tonight. We've lost our primary investigator and we're short already. I need someone with experience, and you're right out there, where it's all happening. How's about it? Come back to work? MCU, temporary secondment, just for the duration of this one?"

"I'm due back in the detachment second week in December," she reminded him.

"Hey, we can work something out if this case lasts longer," he said. Dee hollered from her car seat, tired of sitting still and no attention. "That's a noisy kid you've got there."

Roxanne scrambled to find something to amuse her—a biscuit, a toy.

"I've got babysitting three days a week. How's about part-time?" she asked.

"Not good. What if something comes up when you're not around? You've got to be available."

Roxanne took a deep breath. She knew that she was not going to let this opportunity slip through her fingers.

"I'll figure something out," she said.

"Okay. I'll get the paperwork underway. You'll work out of the Fiskar Bay detachment?"

"That's correct. There's office space upstairs." She'd used that space herself, years ago, when she'd investigated her first case in the Interlake.

"Okay, we're on. You start as of now. I'll email you the paperwork. You'd best get here, to HQ, pronto, though. There's a constable called Nolan James assigned to this case as file coordinator, but he could use some experience out on the job. Put him to work. And you'll need to sign out a firearm. We don't want you dead too," he joked, as if it was funny.

"Keep us in the loop," he added, eager to go. "I'll be keeping a close eye on this one."

"Have you put out a call for any information about Meagan Stephens?" she asked.

"Sure. Nothing useful so far. You take care now. Welcome back on board. Stick your head round the door when you're here at HQ and say hi."

Dee had mushy biscuit all over her hands and face. Roxanne carried her into the house and cleaned her up, then called Vera Klassen.

"I can keep her until three tomorrow," Vera said. "Then I need to get Armin to the dentist."

It wasn't ideal, but it would do. Roxanne still needed to sort out the babysitting issue, but for now, she wanted to get back to the woods where Rob Marsden lay and see the crime scene for herself.

10

IDENT WAS ON its way to Cullen Village but hadn't arrived yet. Ravi Anand had returned to the office, leaving part of his team behind to guard the crime scene.

The trees stood close together, making it impossible to rig a proper tent. Anand's team had done what they could with tarps, tying them to branches for cover. Marsden lay on his back. He hadn't been attacked where he was found. Marks on the walking path showed the assault had happened there. He had then been dragged into the trees, out of sight. His wet sweatshirt and pants clung to his body, the soles of his runners were caked with dirt, and his dark hair was plastered to his scalp. His eyes were open. A bright red mark on his forehead showed where he had taken a heavy blow.

"That might have killed him, but it looks like he was hit sideways as well," Aimee Vermette said. "The side of his skull, above his ear, is bashed in. Have a look."

She said she thought it looked like a metal instrument been used—a tire iron, perhaps, or a crowbar. She was probably right, Roxanne thought, but they would have to wait for the autopsy results to be sure. Marsden was stiff, dead for hours; he must have lain here all night.

"He was facing whoever attacked him," Aimee continued. She and Roxanne had squatted down, either side of the body. "Someone followed him along the path and must have called to him. Caused him to turn around."

That person had to know who Marsden was. Whoever had followed him had intended to kill him, so the killer must be someone Marsden had met before. Roxanne stood up again and stretched her legs.

Constable Lucas Bell introduced himself. Roxanne recognized him as the young officer who had stood guard beside Cooper Jenkins's body. Now he was assigned a similar duty. It often took months for a rookie to encounter even one murder victim, but this was his second in just a few days.

"Going to be a big case, ma'am," he said, eyes wide. He looked impressed when he heard that his future boss had been seconded to the Major Crimes Unit for now.

"Call me Sarge," she told him, glad to have her job title back.

Aimee had Rob Marsden's car fob and phone. His billfold held plastic cards, including his ID, about thirty dollars in cash and a photograph of a smiling woman and two children. The boy had two front teeth missing, so he must be about six and his sister, a couple of years older.

Roxanne held the phone up to the deceased's face to see if facial recognition would unlock it. The screen lit up.

Marsden had called home late yesterday afternoon. He'd also texted with a woman who was other than his wife. After that, he had called Inspector Schultz after hours, just long enough to leave a message. There was a text to Constable Nolan James asking him to look into Willa Stein, one of the lifeguards who had worked with Meagan Stephens. Her family owned the cottage where the group had stayed and partied. The text also mentioned another lifeguard, Owen Bradshaw. Marsden had wanted information on the Andreychuks as well. Bradley Andreychuk was a known felon, he wrote. Was there any connection to a Cory Andreychuk?

Roxanne couldn't keep the phone. Forensics had first claim on it, but she borrowed the car fob for now and sloshed back through the puddles to the car park.

Constable Sam Mendes stood by Marsden's Tahoe and grinned when he heard that Roxanne was back at work.

"MCU, temporarily," she told him. "Ravi Anand's still your boss. But I'll be moving into the office upstairs."

There weren't many walkers out and about on this rainy day, but cars were prowling by with people making sure they got a good look. A cluster of vehicles was parked outside the post office and another at the grocery store. Someone waved. Even with her red hair covered by a rain hood Roxanne Calloway was recognized.

Mendes lifted the tape barrier. Roxanne opened the car. There was a paper bag in the passenger footwell. It held a burger wrapper from a fast-food outlet at Fiskar Bay. A box with scraps of limp salad lay inside, along with a sandwich wrapper from Tim Hortons and an empty water bottle. Marsden must have picked up most of his food and eaten it in the car. A disposable coffee cup sat in a holder beside a pair of sunglasses. He hadn't needed them when he went jogging, so it must have been evening when he set off. His jacket lay on the back seat, nothing in the pockets except Kleenex and an almost full container of peppermint Tic Tacs. His outdoor shoes lay on the floor, side by side.

The glove box held car insurance papers and a key card for a room at the Fiskar Bay Hotel. An envelope held several receipts. He had filled up at the highway gas station and bought the Tic Tacs there. The inside of the car was fairly clean. Roxanne pocketed the hotel key card.

He'd locked his gun, in its holster, inside the trunk, with a box of ammunition, when he went for a run. He must have believed that he was safe. Roxanne was not armed and she was tempted to borrow this one, but that would be a breach of protocol. She needed to get a gun of her own, soon as.

A white van and a car pulled up beside the police cars. Dave Kovak and the Ident team had arrived. Roxanne knew Dave well. They had worked together on different cases throughout the years.

"Can't stay away, can you, Roxanne?" Dave was opening the trunk of his own car, getting ready to suit up in protective gear. Two technicians were at the van, doing the same.

"I'm official!" Roxanne couldn't help smiling. "Schultz called me. Temporary secondment to the MCU."

"Really? Well, good luck with this one." Dave frowned. "I don't like the look of it though, Roxanne. Coop Jenkins was a good cop, did solid work back in the day. So was Marsden. Both those guys always had their eyes and ears open. Whoever killed them both is either clever or unpredictable. You're going to have to be careful."

"I think it's someone local," she said, sidestepping his warning. "The summer visitors have gone home except for the weekends. This is the middle of the week. And look at the weapons that have been used. A shotgun took out Coop. Most local farmers have one. And Marsden's head has been smashed in with something heavy, metal probably, something a guy might have handy in his truck. I think this is someone seizing an opportunity, acting on impulse. A person like that's going to make a mistake, sooner or later. That's when I'll get them."

"Just make sure they don't get you first." Dave was dressed all in white now, ready to get to work.

"Marsden didn't think anyone was after him. I won't make that mistake," she responded. "I've seen the body already. And I've checked the car. I've got the key card to his hotel room. I'll go look there. Want me to bring back the card?"

"No," he said. "The hotel staff will let us in."

"Are you done with Coop Jenkins's truck?"

He was. He had the key for it with him in his car. Someone would need to come up to Cullen Village and pick it up.

"Give it to me and I'll let Coop's daughter know." It was a good reason to call Hailey Jenkins and tell her that she, Roxanne, was now officially working the case.

THERE WASN'T MUCH to see at the hotel. The room had two beds, both made up. An overnight bag sat on one of them. Marsden had hung a change of clothes in a closet. Toiletries were still in the bathroom. There was no sign of a laptop or a tablet. He must have relied on his phone for internet access and calls while he was out of town. His files and work computer would be at HQ.

It was almost three by the time she was finished. She drove back through Cullen Village and south to the Klassen house. Her daughter was fastened into a wooden kitchen chair, one with arms, with an assortment of kitchen utensils to play with. She was banging a metal spoon on the top in front of her. Vera was lifting jars of tomato sauce out of a large pan of boiling water, her face pink from the steam. She froze and canned enough vegetables to last all winter.

"Your girl's been good," she said. "But she does need watching now she's crawling."

"Tell me about it." Roxanne went to unstrap her baby. The back door opened. Armin Klassen was a tall man, weathered and tanned from being outside most of the summer. He left tall rubber boots at the door and hung a waterproof jacket on a hook, went to the sink in his socks and turned on the taps so he could scrub his hands. He had big knuckles; there was dirt under his nails.

"Rain's stopped," he said. "It's muddy out there."

"Go change, Armin. We're going to the dentist. You have to get a tooth filled," Vera reminded him. "Roxanne's been over at the beach, looking at the body of that cop they've found."

Roxanne hadn't told her that. The news must be spreading already.

"I'm officially back at work. Investigating this case," she told them.

"That so?" Armin Klassen dried his hands.

Vera lifted Dee out of the chair. She looked happy, well cared for.

"I'm hoping Roberta can babysit three days for me." Roxanne took her baby. "Mondays, Tuesdays and Fridays. Could you cover some other days for me?"

"Maybe. What do you think, Armin?" Vera asked as he walked out of the kitchen.

"A bit of extra cash is always useful," he said without looking back.

"How about I do Thursdays? I'm here anyway while people pick up their veggies. I might manage another day occasionally."

That worked for Roxanne. Tomorrow was Thursday.

"All day?" she asked. "Nine to five?"

"Sure." Vera carried Dee's bag through to the porch while Roxanne lugged her daughter.

Chest freezers containing vegetables and farm chickens lined the wall closest to the house. Soon a deer or two would be added. Like many farmers, Armin Klassen went shooting each fall. They all had shotguns, like the one that had killed Coop Jenkins. Vera pecked Dee on the cheek and squeezed her little hand when they reached the door.

"See you tomorrow, baby," she said and waved goodbye. Dee waved right back. Roxanne's baby was going to be in good hands.

Outside, Roxanne could smell wood smoke. Someone must have a fire going nearby. She looked south and saw the sunflower field in the distance, rank upon rank of flower heads drooping as the afternoon light.

She went home, still thinking about her new assignment. By the time Matt arrived, Finn with him, she had set up an office in the corner of the kitchen where she could keep an eye on Dee and try to get some work done while she was in the house.

Matt did not share her enthusiasm for her appointment.

"Marsden's been killed and Coop Jenkins got shot? And you're going to take their place, Roxanne?" He watched her throwing a salad together. Dee was playing on a rug in the living room, Finn keeping one eye on her, the other on a video. He tolerated his new little sister.

"I'll take care. Marsden wasn't expecting anyone to come after him—if he had, he wouldn't be dead. And I'm already working the case. I agreed to help Hailey Jenkins, remember? I wasn't just going to sit back and let this happen around me. You know that.

But this is way better. I get access to forensics, resources, backup. An office. A raise. I just have to tell Hailey."

"What about Dee? Who's going to look after her?"

"Roberta Axelsson will take her for three days. Vera Klassen says she'll look after her on Thursdays. That leaves Wednesdays. I can work here or make that my day off."

"What about weekends?"

"I was thinking you'd be home." She began slicing a tomato for the salad. "You can help out, can't you? If I get this solved soon, it won't be for long."

"You know what? Whoever is doing this is dangerous and it's all happening far too close to home. I get it that you feel a need to find who killed Cooper Jenkins and it's maybe best that you're back working with the RCMP, instead of messing around on your own. But look what's happened to Jenkins and that sergeant. He was MCU, right? I don't like this one bit."

He pushed his thick hair back off his forehead, then he put his hands on his hips. "But hey, we've been here before and there's no stopping you, I know that. You'll do what you need to do, danger or no danger. I just don't want that kind of trouble coming close to here, near our kids. So here's what we'll do. I'll get Julie Ann to clear all my appointments for Wednesdays so I'll be in the office. Dee can come to work with me, those days.

"You work out of the detachment, Monday to Friday. All of this stuff—" Matt nodded at her computer, in the far corner "—has to go. Keep this job away from home and try to make weekends as normal as possible. We go to Finn's hockey games, we get together with friends, like we usually do. I know you'll end up working some of those days, but see if you can keep that to a minimum. Okay?"

"Okay," she agreed. "Thanks, Matt."

That had gone more easily than she had expected. If Matt was willing to take care of their daughter on Wednesdays, help out with the kids on the weekend, this would work.

She had planned to call Hailey Jenkins and make other calls after supper but that wasn't going to happen tonight. She needed to get to HQ soonish and would call Hailey, to share the news about the new job and let her know her father's truck was available. Then the real work would begin.

Where was Meagan Stephens?

Everything had started with that missing girl. Find her and she should find the killer. She needed to find Meagan's boyfriend. The Andreychuk place was where she would start.

11

ROXANNE CALLED RAVI Anand as she drove the short distance between her house and the Klassens's farm the next morning, on her way to drop off Dee.

"You're coming here?" he asked. "You'll be setting up an office upstairs?"

"Not yet, I'm going to go call on the Andreychuks first. I could use someone as backup. Is there anyone you can spare?"

Young Lucas Bell was the only constable available, but that was okay. All she needed was an extra uniformed presence. She might want to bring Cory Andreychuk in for questioning, and having a police car waiting and ready would be useful.

Hailey Jenkins was next. She said she'd try to find a ride out to the Interlake so she could get Cooper's keys and take his truck home. If she succeeded, they would have a chance to get together later that day.

Hailey had listened quietly to the news that Roxanne was Marsden's replacement, that she was back working as an active member of the RCMP.

"Shit," she had said. "Does that mean you're going to stop telling me anything, like the rest of you cops?"

"I'll do what I can," Roxanne had said, her tone noncommittal. She'd promised to show Hailey the place where her father had died, if she could get out here. Otherwise, they'd find some way to get the truck to Winnipeg, but she hoped she might see Hailey later in the day. She did want to keep in contact with Coop Jenkins's daughter.

The news of Rob Marsden's death was all over the internet. His wife, teary and angry, had been interviewed outside their front door. Roxanne had watched. She was young, pretty, obviously in shock, describing Rob as a wonderful dad and a good husband. Roxanne wondered if that was true. She knew from looking at his phone that Rob had been on more than friendly terms with another woman She was a civilian on the staff at HQ. Inspector Schultz had sent out a memo advising discretion on that subject, so it must have been talked about at work.

The rain was gone and the sky was blue, but it was cool enough to wear a jacket. She handed Dee off into Vera Klassen's welcoming hands, then headed straight to the Andreychuk farm. Lucas Bell was waiting at the end of the dump road. His car followed hers.

She pulled in as close to the house as possible, parking beside a large Ford truck. Lucas parked on her other side. Two blue heelers and a Jack Russell terrier barked and growled at the cars. Constable Bell stepped out of his vehicle, unfazed by the heelers. She got out as well.

"Hey you," he said to the black and white Jack Russell. "What's the barking about?"

He squatted. The terrier approached, curious. His heeler mates slunk further away, hackles up, more suspicious. Judith Andreychuk appeared in the doorway to see her dog, Charlie, having his ears rubbed by a young cop in uniform. He was fresh faced, red cheeked, grinning up at her.

"I used to have one of these," he called to her. "He liked to play soccer. What's this guy's name?" The heelers had crouched down between the cars and their owner, guarding her.

"Fuck's sake," Judith Andreychuk shouted, still on the doorstep. "What d'ya want? If this is about that cop that got himself killed yesterday, forget it. I told him, Cory's not here. He's in Brandon."

Roxanne stepped forward. "Sergeant Calloway," she introduced herself. "Major Crimes Unit. I have some questions for you."

A man appeared in the doorway behind Judith.

"What's going on here?" he asked. Ed Andreychuk was broad and tall enough to fill the doorway. He had a shaved head and a full beard. His wife stepped down a stair to make room for him as he took his place, gripping the doorframe with massive hands. He and Judith dressed alike in denim and jeans and wore grim expressions. The pair of them could have passed for siblings.

Roxanne stepped closer, with Lucas Bell following just behind her. The Jack Russell darted to the door and nestled between Judith's feet. She wore dingy white fluffy slippers; her husband wore only boot socks.

"Sergeant Marsden visited you yesterday?" Roxanne asked.

The woman placed her hands on her hips. "Didn't stay long," she said. "Wanted to know where Cory was. He took a truckload of household goods to Brandon, I told him. Cory's staying over. He's been gone a couple of weeks, almost. He's not here."

"Can we talk inside?" Roxanne asked.

"What for?" Judith asked. Ed Andreychuk stayed silent and watchful, as did his heelers, who remained positioned between Roxanne and the couple.

"We're investigating a double murder," Roxanne reminded them, "and a missing person."

"That so?" The husband leaned forward, still anchored to the door. "What makes you think we've got anything to do with that? We live quiet out here, don't we, Jude? Bother nobody. Do good work, you ask around."

Roxanne ignored this.

"Are you going to let me in so we can talk, or will Constable Bell have to drive you to the detachment in Fiskar Bay so I can question you there?" she asked, stepping closer to the foot of the steps and looking up at them. The couple made a formidable twosome. One of the dogs growled, low in its throat.

"Let them in, Jude," the man said. Then he yelled at the dogs, "Hey, you two, get down." They obeyed but remained watchful. He stepped back just enough to let Roxanne and Lucas through the door. Lucas stood about six feet tall, but Ed Andreychuk still loomed over him. They followed Judith and her terrier into the living room.

Roxanne had been here before, many times: five years ago when John and Maggie Andreychuk had lived here, later when Brad had taken over. It hadn't changed much, just looked more worn. The décor was brown, even the ceiling, nicotine stained from years of cigarette smoke. Only the framed photographs that Ed's Aunt Maggie had treasured were gone. Now there were empty cream-coloured rectangles on the walls, the original colour of the room.

Ed Andreychuk remained inside the door. The terrier had made himself comfortable on an ancient brown sofa that had been here as long as Roxanne remembered. It just sagged more in the middle and the ends of the arms were shinier. Jude plopped down beside him. Lucas waited in the hallway behind Ed, listening.

"When, exactly, was Sergeant Marsden here?" Roxanne asked. She had not been invited to sit.

"Let's see. Tuesday?" Jude Andreychuk scrunched up her face like she was trying to remember.

"What time of day?"

"Don't remember."

"Morning or afternoon?"

"Dunno." Roxanne noticed Ed Andreychuk smirk, enjoying the show. She turned her attention to him instead.

"Cory Andreychuk is your nephew?" she asked.

"Sure is." The voice was bass-baritone and rumbled up from Ed's expansive belly. He wasn't fat, but there was a bit of a paunch under the black T-shirt he wore below his jacket. She couldn't read the decal on it but it seemed to feature a skull. "He helps out. Drives a truck for me."

"He lives with you?"

"Well, yeah. For now. When he's here."

"He knew a girl called Meagan Stephens?"

"Who? The lifeguard?" He looked surprised.

"Whaddaya mean, knew? She dead too?" Jude snapped.

"We don't know. Haven't you heard? There's a missing person notice circulating, asking for information about her." Roxanne let that news sink in, then she said, "Maybe we'd best take Judith and Ed here in for a formal interview, Constable. We're not making much progress here."

"Whatever you say, Sarge. Step aside, sir." Lucas pushed past Ed.

"Okay, okay." Jude reached out and rubbed the top of her dog's head. "Grab a chair. Eddie, you too."

Ed Andreychuk did as he was told. It was clear Jude was the one in charge here. He sat at a large wooden table with a glass ashtray in the centre. Roxanne watched him pull a packet of cigarettes from his pocket and light one, just as his relatives, John and Bradley Andreychuk, had done many times before. A strong sense of déjà vu washed over her. Even the chair she sat in was familiar: large, brown, a partner to the sofa. Lucas stayed on his feet, inside the door.

"Sometimes Cory brought his pals over after work. They'd light a fire out back. The lifeguards were there, sometimes." Jude did the talking.

"Was Meagan Stephens his girlfriend?"

"Don't think so. Was she the dark-haired one? They just hung out together. Wasn't she with another guy?" Jude asked her husband.

"Dunno," he said, his tone indifferent.

"Tall," Jude Andreychuk tried to remind him. "Clean shaven, blondish hair?"

"Nope." He shook his head and took a drag on his cigarette.

"Does he have a name?" Roxanne asked.

"Nah. Don't remember."

"When did your nephew leave for Brandon?"

"See here," Ed said, speaking up this time. "Cory's doing fine these days. Had a bit of trouble at home, so he came out here for a fresh start. Things have been getting busy here and I could use the help. He went to load up a house full of furniture first thing after Labour Day. I helped him do it. He was on his way, late morning, and that girl was nowhere near. I watched him drive off."

"Why's he not back?"

"Because there's another load near Brandon that needs picking up today. Has to be delivered to Winnipeg after. He's staying over, then he's driving back tomorrow."

"Did a man called Cooper Jenkins come here, asking about Meagan, a week ago?"

"Never heard of him," Jude cut in.

"You don't know who that is?"

"No. Told you."

Coop's name hadn't been released. The RCMP had only reported finding human remains and were treating the case as a suspicious death. Still, Roxanne caught a glance exchanged between Jude and her husband. They knew more than they were saying.

"A man in his sixties, driving a green Silverado?" she reminded Judith.

"Nah." Her hand stayed on her dog, stroking his fur.

"He's an ex-cop. He was looking for Meagan Stephens," Roxanne told them.

"You talkin' about the guy that got shot? The one that you found on the weekend? Over in Pete McBain's sunflower crop?" Ed asked. He'd stubbed out his cigarette and was leaning forward, his elbows on his knees. "Never seen him."

"I'm asking you again." Roxanne tried once more. "When was Sergeant Marsden here on Tuesday?"

"In the afternoon," Jude finally admitted. "It was me that he talked to. He wanted to know where Cory was. Took down his phone number."

Roxanne saw Lucas reach into his pocket for a notepad. "And it is what?" she asked. Jude found it on her phone. Lucas noted it down.

"I told him Cory'd be back on the weekend," Jude grudgingly admitted. She set her phone down on the arm of the sofa and reached again for her dog, who lay beside her with his legs in the air. She rubbed his belly as if she needed the comfort of the touch. Maybe Jude Andreychuk wasn't as confident as she pretended to be. "I just spoke to him outside. He asked if we had a quad. A Polaris. Ours is a Honda. He didn't stay long after that."

"Where were you, the rest of yesterday?" Roxanne asked Ed.

"Just here. I did a dump run for an old couple at Cullen Village in the afternoon. They can tell you."

"And after?"

"Went for a beer at the hotel, but I didn't see that cop that got killed."

"A Tahoe SUV?" Roxanne asked, but he shook his head again. He'd only had one beer, talked to a guy about a job, then he'd come home for supper. Who was drinking with him, she asked? Just the usual guys. There hadn't been anyone there he didn't know, he said. He'd never seen any sign of that cop.

It was time to leave. Roxanne got up to go. "If you remember anything, call and ask for me," she said. She didn't expect they would.

She and Lucas walked to their cars. The heelers closed in, crawling on their bellies. Jude and Ed Andreychuk watched from the doorway, the Jack Russell snuggling close to Jude's furry feet.

"Can we talk, Sarge?" Lucas asked, quiet enough that the Andreychuks wouldn't hear. "I've been checking this couple out."

"See you back at the detachment," she said. "We can talk there."

She followed his car. It only took fifteen minutes to reach Fiskar Bay. Ravi and Jan Bjornson looked pleased to see Roxanne, without a baby this time and in an official capacity. Todd Brewster nodded his head from behind the desk. That was progress.

The room upstairs was large, with empty tables and a few stacked chairs. They pulled down a couple and sat near a window that overlooked the front street.

"Do you believe them?" Roxanne asked. Lucas sat up straight, eager to make a good impression.

"Kinda," he admitted. "I've been asking around. They're truckers, old bikers, so people don't trust them much but they're getting a reputation for doing good work. They're reliable, show up on time, charge reasonable rates. Folks say they like Cory. He's a nice kid. You didn't ask them where they came from? Why they're living in that house?"

"No," she said. "They're probably caretaking for Brad Andreychuk while he's in jail."

"Ed drove a truck all through the pandemic. He was part of the convoy," Lucas added.

That was a protest that had besieged the federal government in Ottawa for a while. Many truckers listened to the radio while they drove and some channels were rife with conspiracy theories. They had had it hard, moving from one locked-down town to another and in the end their frustration had erupted.

"The Andreychuks were living near Ste. Anne at the time," Lucas continued, referring to a small town southeast of Winnipeg. "They fell out with their neighbours and decided to sell up. They thought that they'd move west, but they've told a couple of folks around here that if the moving business works out they might just buy a place of their own and stay. They kind of like the neighbourhood, so far. Maybe this'll change their minds."

Lucas had curly, dark brown hair. He was smiley, young and fresh-faced. It was a face that people might trust.

"One thing's for sure. They knew who Cooper Jenkins was and Jude Andreychuk didn't want us to know that. Y'know what I don't get? Why would anyone kill him if he was only asking about a girl that's run off with a boyfriend? It's got to be something way more serious than that. Do you think Jude Andreychuk knows more than she's letting on? Why's she asking if Meagan Stephens is dead, too? Was that a hint?"

"We'll need to find out, constable," Roxanne smiled. Lucas Bell had potential. She couldn't second him to her team, though. He lacked experience and Ravi Anand had need of him, but he was smart and he was curious. "Keep your eyes and ears open, will you?" she asked.

"Shall do, Sarge." He trotted off downstairs, visibly pleased with himself, looking inches taller.

12

HAILEY JENKINS HAD texted to say she'd be outside the Airbnb her father had rented near Cullen Village by noon. By the time Roxanne arrived, a car was already parked beside the Silverado. Hailey and another woman about the same age stood at the door of the house, speaking with an older woman with grey hair, dyed pink, cut stylishly short at the back and sides, with the longer top gelled into a sweeping, curved crest. She wore silky wide-leg pants and a loose top in deep shades of purple and dark red.

Andrea Carlson had gathered the few belongings Cooper had left behind and was handing over his overnight bag and black bomber jacket. "There's nothing to see," she was telling them. "I've cleaned up already. New renters are arriving tomorrow."

"I need to look inside," Roxanne interrupted her. "Sergeant Calloway, with the Major Crimes Unit."

"You people have searched already," Andrea objected, "but if you must."

She stood aside and let Roxanne enter the house. Hailey and her friend followed her.

The owner was right. The inside of the house was spotless, any evidence that Cooper Jenkins had been present wiped clean away. It was recently furnished, most of it from IKEA, Roxanne thought. Newly painted white walls were decorated with brightly coloured artwork. It did not look the least bit like the traditional farmhouse it must once have been.

"You know I'm your neighbour?" she asked Andrea Carlson, who hovered at a doorway, her foot tapping, making her impatience clear. "I'm Roxanne Calloway. I live three roads over from here." She pointed in the general direction of her own house.

"Where Matthew Stavros lives?"

"We're partners."

Andrea's expression softened. "You are? We know Matt! He represented the couple we bought this property from. Lovely man. Alan and I were actually thinking of switching our business over to him now that we're living here." She smiled and extended a hand tipped with purple nails. "How nice to meet you."

"I usually run the RCMP detachment that serves this area," Roxanne told her. "But I'm working this case for the Major Crimes Unit right now." She looked out the window at the old hip-roofed barn. It was painted a traditional red and appeared to be in decent shape.

"Really? How interesting," Andrea replied, continuing to make polite conversation. Hailey and her friend had disappeared down the hallway. Andrea ignored them. "Appalling thing that's happened to Mr. Jenkins. Alan and I will do all we can to help, but I'm not sure how. We barely saw him."

"Does Pete McBain rent your outbuildings as well as your pastureland?" Roxanne asked.

"He does not. I have plans for those spaces and for this house," Andrea said, growing more animated. "It's going to be a special place for artists, writers—creatives like myself. We might even display work in the barn, maybe hold small concerts."

She wore round, tangerine-coloured glasses that magnified her hazel eyes and drew attention away from the rest of her face. It felt a bit like being stared at by a goldfish.

"And you own a quad?"

"We keep it near our house. You're welcome to look any time, Roxanne," she said, making a point of using the name and still sounding friendly. She didn't know the make. Her husband took care of things like that. They had returned to the front door.

"Good," Roxanne replied, matching her tone. "I'll let Matt know we've met. Maybe we can get together sometime?"

Andrea Carlson seemed pleased.

"Let's have drinks?" she said. She locked the house behind them. "Bye for now! Talk soon!" She walked to the path that led through a stand of trees to her new home, waving a hand in Hailey's direction as she went.

Hailey Jenkins had wandered through the house, peeking into each room. She must have seen enough. She was already outside, and her friend was getting into the car, ready to leave. Hailey was dressed in her usual black and grey. The boots on her feet had heavy soles and a hooded jacket was zippered up. She had tucked her long, dark hair behind her ears and her face, heavy with makeup, was a pale mask. Roxanne joined her as she climbed into her father's old Silverado and started it.

"How much gas is in the tank?" she asked.

Hailey checked the gauge. "It's more than half full. I'll find out when Dad last filled up and let you know."

Chances were, Coop had done that before leaving the city. If so, he hadn't driven much around this district.

Hailey's friend, Roxanne learned, lived in the same complex and was one of the few friends that had a car. She'd offered to pick up Liam from kindergarten so Hailey could spend the rest of the afternoon at Cullen Village.

"We help each other out that way; I already owe her," Hailey said.

So, Roxanne thought, she had a reciprocal child care arrangement with her friend and wasn't completely tied to home after all.

"Why don't you follow me to my house?" she offered. "It's as good a place as any to talk and it's close by."

Roxanne drove via the Carlson house. Two cars were parked on the freshly asphalted driveway. Out back, there was a shiny new metal shed and a Quonset hut. Farther out, she caught a glimpse of beehives. There was no sign of a quad. The house was a long bungalow with stuccoed walks. Nothing about it suggested the walls were made of straw bales.

"NICE PLACE YOU'VE got." Hailey removed her boots and jacket once they arrived at Roxanne's. She wore a double layer of thin socks underneath. The dogs sniffed at her feet but she didn't seem to mind. She patted their heads then parked herself on a stool at the kitchen island. No, she didn't want lunch. Coffee would do. Black, two sugars.

"Am I going to have to work on this by myself, now that you're back with the RCMP?" she asked, her hands knotted in front of her.

"This isn't a bad thing," Roxanne said, as she poured hot water through a filter. "It puts me right at the centre of the investigation. I get to know everything that's going on. Now that Rob Marsden's dead, this case has priority so I'll get all the resources I need to help solve this case. And I want to know what happened to your dad just as much as you do."

"Yeah, but it changes things," Hailey grumbled. "Before, we were on equal footing. Now we're not."

"I suppose," Roxanne replied. "But we're after the same thing. I need to find out who killed Cooper. He must have thought Meagan Stephens had just run off—he was out here asking questions, and he was on the right track. Finding that girl is the key to this case. That's what he was doing when he was killed. Sergeant Marsden, too."

"Guess so." Hailey's black-painted fingernails drummed on the countertop. Roxanne filled a couple of mugs.

"I've been doing some snooping of my own." Hailey stirred sugar into her coffee. She lifted her mug and swept some of her hair back. "Once Liam's in bed it's pretty quiet around my place. I can talk, online."

"Who did you reach?" asked Roxanne.

Nils Svensen, she replied. He was Meagan's swimming coach.

"Good-looking guy. Norwegian. You know the type. He's tall and blond, looks like he's super fit," Hailey said. "He told me he doesn't coach Meagan anymore, but she used to teach beginners on Saturdays. Said it was a pain when she didn't show up. She was supposed to be back for the start of the fall classes. Still, he didn't sound all that upset."

She sipped her coffee.

"He said it was time Meagan got a life of her own. She had to fight just to go to university, y'know. Her parents wanted her to go to Bible college, meet a nice young man, and get married. But she wanted to study marine biology. It took ages to get them to agree.

"They had some money banked for her education, but in return, Meagan had to stay home and cook supper, get the other kids to bed while her mother taught music lessons. She had to go to church all the time—Bible study, choir, even taught Sunday school. Between all that and her studies, she didn't have much time for herself.

"Nils said she had a couple of friends that had gone to school with her and who had swum with her for years, but Meagan didn't get to go to parties or sleepovers. Now that they're all at university they don't see much of each other."

He'd heard that the province was hiring lifeguards for the summer, so he'd shown the ad to Meagan. She had jumped at the chance. She'd said she'd tell her parents that the experience would look good on her resume. Maybe that was why they had let her go.

"They must have been close friends," Roxanne remarked.

"Nothing like that, I don't think, but he'd been her coach for years. He said it was time for Meagan to break free. Thinks she maybe couldn't face the thought of going back home once the summer was over, not once she'd started to have a life of her own. He was sure that she'd run away with someone, but now there's been people killed, he's not so sure. He sounded worried.

"I also managed to get hold of Willa Stein on WhatsApp," Hailey continued. "Her parents own the cottage where she and the other two beach patrol members were staying. She's a big, strong-looking girl—a phys-ed type. And she sure can talk."

Willa had said Meagan was real quiet at first, but it didn't take long for her to come out of her shell. Like Nils, she wouldn't be at all surprised if Meagan had quit school and gone off on her own. She'd changed her mind about doing marine biology. She'd told Willa that she'd settled on that because she'd seen it on TV and she could swim. It looked interesting, but now she knew there were other choices she could make. It sounded like she'd been cooped up at home most of her life. Susan Rice, the yoga teacher, allowed her all the freedom she wanted. Let her do whatever she pleased, lent her a bike so she could get around, and didn't fuss if Meagan stayed over at Willa's place. Meagan had told her that she wasn't sure what she really wanted to do.

"Willa said Meagan was pretty clueless when she first arrived at the beach. Friendly, though, kind of like a big puppy dog. She got excited about everything; it was all new to her. She couldn't believe Susan Rice had Buddhas and things like that in her house. She liked doing crafts. They all got homemade thank-you cards from her when it was time to pack up and leave.

"Meagan was worried that if she told her parents she didn't want to do marine biology anymore, they'd send her to Bible school instead. That was what they had wanted in the first place. They were the ones paying, so they could insist. Willa and the other lifeguards told her she could move out on her own. Do a general degree, get a student loan and find a part-time job, but Meagan wasn't sure. Willa said she acted like she was going to go back, but in the last few days, she got really quiet."

"Did she have a boyfriend?" Roxanne asked.

"Sure had. She was real pretty, you know." She was. They had both seen Meagan's photograph. "She hung out with Owen Bradshaw, one of the other lifeguards, at first. Willa says she knew nothing about birth control. She had to tell her to go see a doctor and get herself on the pill. Owen had a massive crush on her.

Couldn't believe it when she dumped him. But he's gone off to B.C., to do grad studies. He was long gone by the time that my dad died."

"Was there anyone she mentioned called Cory?" Roxanne asked.

"Yep, there was—but he was just friends with everyone. Willa thinks Meagan was actually more interested in another guy, someone older. Willa's friends with his sister. Her last name is Klassen."

Roxanne almost choked on her coffee.

"I know that family," she said. "They live not far from here. Vera Klassen, the mother, is taking care of my baby daughter right now. There's also a brother. Did you get to know him?

"No." Hailey set down her empty mug. "What's he like?"

"I've only met him in passing. I pick up vegetables at their place all summer, and he's been there occasionally," she said.

The Klassens worked in their gardens every morning and again in the evenings. Afternoons, when she usually stopped by, seemed to be their downtime. She only ever saw Vera when picking up a bag of vegetables from the porch. The Klassen kids could have been inside resting or out visiting friends.

"The sunflower field where we found your dad isn't far from their house. How about we go there now? I'll show you the Klassen place as we drive past."

NO ONE WAS around as they passed the farm. The heads of the sunflowers were beginning to droop in the afternoon heat. They parked by the roadside and crossed the ditch on foot. Hailey was uncharacteristically quiet as they walked through the grove. She paused in the clearing and looked down at the spot where her father had lain. Then she lifted her head.

"He came that way?" She pointed back along the track.

"It seems so. We haven't found any other tracks."

"So he was chased in? Hunted down?"

"We don't know that yet."

"It wasn't a random shot? Someone out hunting geese who made a mistake?"

"Not likely. He took a direct hit, and a stray shot from out in the open wouldn't have reached him in here."

They both glanced back down the leafy avenue. The sun didn't penetrate this part of the grove, but at the far end, golden fall sunshine spilled through.

"Could he have been dead when he got here?" Hailey asked.

"It's possible. They could have brought his body in on the quad and left it here."

"So they didn't want him to be found? Just left him to rot? Let's get out of here—I can't stand this place." Hailey had heard enough. She strode off along the quad's path and walked into the sunlight.

She paused, staring across the field at the Klassen house. "When do you pick up the baby?" she asked. "I wouldn't mind meeting those folks."

"I'm not sure that's a good idea," Roxanne replied. "I don't want to set off any alarm bells."

"Hey." Hailey marched toward the car in her heavy-soled boots, looking like a spider with big feet, her jacket flapping behind her. "I'm just a friend, visiting. No big deal, right? Once I know where to find the brother that Meagan knew, I'll go talk to him. Maybe I'll check back with you about what I find. Okay?"

Roxanne relented. "All right," she said, and drove to the Klassen house.

13

VERA WAS SURPRISED to see Roxanne at her door so early in the afternoon.

"This is Hailey, a friend from Winnipeg. She wanted to meet Dee."

It was as good an excuse as any. Roxanne didn't mention the Jenkins name, just in case Vera made the connection. Not that she suspected Vera was involved in the murders, but she didn't want word to spread around the village that she was meeting with Coop Jenkins's daughter. And if Vera found out, she would talk.

Vera said Dee had just gone down for a nap. It would be a shame to wake her, but it wouldn't last long. Roxanne knew Dee would be wide awake again in half an hour. She peeked in at the sleeping baby, who was out cold, breathing steadily, her mouth slightly open.

Vera had unearthed an old crib and set it up in a bedroom next to a single bed with a flowery bedspread. The curtains were floral too, and there was a pink skirt draped around a white dressing table. A small desk and chair sat in the corner, with bookshelves above them. Photos hung on the wall. One showed a high school girls' hockey team, another a group of teens in graduation gowns hamming it up for the camera.

"Ella's gone off to university?" Roxanne asked, back in the kitchen.

Vera said proudly that her daughter was in her first year of political science, living in residence at the university and considering a career in overseas development. Hailey Jenkins stood in the middle of the farm kitchen. Roxanne could see Vera eyeing her, clearly wondering why she was friends with a woman who dressed like that. To Vera, Hailey looked unhealthy and didn't seem like Roxanne's type at all, but she remained politely hospitable.

The bottled tomato sauce from yesterday sat in a neat, shiny row on the counter. The sink was full of small cucumbers, about to be pickled. The door to the large, glassed-in porch stood open. Bins overflowing with vegetables and big blue bags ready for pickup were stacked beside the freezers. Squash and cabbage spilled out of the containers, along with bunches of feathery dill that scented the kitchen. A few empty bins were stacked nearby, showing that several people had already stopped by. One of the full bags was for Roxanne and Matt.

"What's your son doing these days?" Roxanne asked, as she pulled out a chair and sat at Vera's table, a long rectangle of scrubbed wood.

"Nick?" Vera lifted a cookie tin off a shelf. "He's done his first degree, in agriculture. Now he's in environmental studies. He's interested in sustainable living, like us. We're hoping he'll take over the farm here, eventually, but he's helping out right now at Armin's brother's place, south of Winnipeg. Jakob had a heart attack. It's taking up a lot of Nick's time and that's a bit of a problem. He usually helps Armin out here with a lot of the heavy lifting and digging. Nick's got some good ideas. The heritage tomatoes we grow are his."

Roxanne knew what she meant. Every week this year, the vegetable bags included tomatoes in all shapes, sizes, and colours. Some were purplish-green and looked unusual, but they tasted great.

Tea was made, and oatmeal-raisin cookies were arranged on a plate. Hailey helped herself to one. Vera approved of that, though she still seemed wary of this unexpected, darkly dressed guest. At last, she sat down at the table across from Hailey and sipped her tea.

"So Nick was here this summer?" Roxanne asked. "Would he know the beach patrol kids?"

"You mean that Meagan girl? The one that they're saying is missing?" Vera put down her mug and reached for one of her own cookies.

"Just wondering," Roxanne remarked, trying to keep the conversation relaxed and easy, only a conversation between neighbours. Of course it wasn't, but Vera didn't seem to suspect a thing.

"She's really disappeared? Has that got something to do with the man that got shot in the sunflower field just down the highway?" Vera looked puzzled.

A wail from the bedroom interrupted them. *Bad timing*, Roxanne thought as she went to pick up her daughter. By the time she'd changed Dee and returned to the kitchen, Vera had found a small notepad—the kind she used for household lists—and was writing in it.

"All the young people around here spend time together," she said. "Here are Ella and Nick's numbers. You can ask them yourself if they knew that girl. Ella worked as a waitress in Fiskar Bay this summer—she might have met her too. You should talk to her."

They watched as Vera tore the scrap of paper from the pad and slid it across the table toward Roxanne.

"You need to collect your vegetables. Do you want to take Dee home with you, since you're here?"

It was clear that it was time to go. Vera had finished her tea and must have work that needed doing.

"Thanks, Vera. Can I bring her back next week? Pay you by e-transfer, monthly?"

Roxanne was relieved to see her neighbour nod. She needed to have her babysit.

Roxanne lifted the baby into her arms. Vera smiled at Dee. "Bye, baby," she said. Hailey grabbed the bag of vegetables. As they stepped outside, Roxanne glanced back and saw Vera watching them go before quietly closing the door.

"Where's her husband?" Hailey asked.

"Armin avoids having to talk to all the visitors that drop by on Thursdays. He's a quiet kind of guy."

"But she'll tell him we were here?"

"He might know already. I wouldn't be surprised if he's watching us from over there, from inside his barn."

Hailey looked around the yard. A converted stock barn, now used for cleaning and storing vegetables, stood nearby. Beside it were a tractor with a front-end loader and an ATV. An open-fronted woodshed was stacked with split logs, ready for burning through the winter.

Roxanne had just finished buckling Dee into her seat.

"Copy that information for yourself." She handed the paper with Nick and Ella's phone numbers to Hailey. "If you go talk to them, will you get back to me?"

"Suppose so." Hailey grinned, that same laconic, sideways smile that Roxanne remembered so well on Coop. "And you'll pass on anything you find out?"

"I'll tell you as much as I can." Roxanne avoided a direct answer.

Hailey looked at her sideways. "Hey, I've told you lots," she said. "Taken you to Dad's place, stuff like that. Fair exchange, eh?"

"I can pay you for information," Roxanne offered.

"So I'd be like your paid informant? I'm not sure about that." Hailey buckled up. "I'd as soon not take your money. We were going to trade. Either we share or we don't."

"Don't you need it?" Roxanne asked.

"Not right now. There's another couple of surveillance jobs I'm doing. And a bit left over from the money the Stephens family have paid. My dad's left me everything, so I'm going to be okay for a while. It'll give me time to figure out how I manage this business without him. I can get out and about sometimes now that I've got wheels, though."

Roxanne recognized that stubborn tone: Hailey had inherited her dad's independent spirit.

"Now that you're officially in charge, maybe you could hurry things along at the morgue?" Hailey demanded. "Get Dad's body released sooner rather than later?"

Roxanne shook her head. "I'm the investigator, that's all," she said. "The morgue takes its own time. So does the lab."

"You're just a cog in a great big machine, aren't you?" Hailey said, mocking her.

They had arrived back at the Carlsons' rented farmhouse, the green Silverado still parked out front. She unfolded herself from the car—long arms, long legs, as spidery as ever, with heavy boots anchoring her feet.

"So this is it? We can't keep each other up to speed like we said we would?"

"I'll tell you what I can, Hailey. Like I have today. But some of it's confidential."

"Well then. There's the cop talking," Hailey muttered, slamming the car door behind her. She shoved her hands into her pockets and stalked off toward her dad's truck.

Hailey Jenkins was quick to take offence. The visit had soured suddenly, and now Roxanne was heading home hours earlier than she'd expected. How much more work could she get done from the house with Dee at her elbow, before Matt and Finn arrived home?

ANDREA CARLSON WAS making her presence known in the Interlake's artistic community. She still maintained a studio in Winnipeg's Exchange District, but she planned to give that up by next summer and move everything to her new studio here. With some luck, the barn conversion would be done by then. She'd ordered windows. A plumber had installed water pipes and sinks. The farmhouse that they had converted to an Airbnb would provide accommodation for visiting artists or other guests—people who wanted to do an arts retreat.

Today, Andrea was visiting Sasha Rosenberg. She admired Sasha's metal sculptures. They were so adventurous, she said. Perhaps she would commission one for a garden that Alan was planning, near the barn, a place where people could walk and meditate. She was thinking about building a labyrinth.

"We have so many ideas!" Sasha and her friend, Margo Wishart, listened as Andrea enthused. Margo, who taught art history at the university in Winnipeg, had connections that could prove useful. Andrea was thrilled to meet her and hoped to get to know her better. She spoke passionately about her mission: to reawaken the creative spirit that exists in all of us.

"That is what makes us fully human," she declared. "What our school system does such a good job of suppressing," she added pointedly.

Andrea had strong views on that. She regularly led workshops in schools, funded by the provincial arts council. Now, with the opportunity to offer similar workshops for adults, she saw a chance to expand her impact. She would help people recover their full creative potential and reconnect with their true selves. As she spoke, her hands moved constantly, rings glinting on nearly every finger, her eyes magnified behind bright orange frames.

"Interesting," said Margo.

There was just enough room in Sasha's tiny house for them to sit around a small table. The room was its own kind of art gallery, the walls and surfaces displaying drawings and paintings made by local artists and crafters, interspersed with objects that Sasha found on the beach. Visitors dropped by in the summertime. Sometimes they made a purchase.

The window behind them overlooked a long garden that led to Sasha's own converted outbuilding, one much shabbier than the one Andrea Carlson envisioned, the studio where Sasha welded metal into sculptures and formed clay into mugs and bowls. Her basset pup was out on the grass, attempting to play with Margo's dog, Bob. He was stretched out in the sunshine, tolerating the attention but refusing to move from his comfortable spot.

"Roberta Axelsson says that Cooper Jenkins was living in the farmhouse that you're renting out," Sasha said.

"You know who he was?" Andrea blinked her fishy eyes, surprised by the change of subject.

"Margo knew him."

"I never met him but I heard about him." Margo put down her mug, one of Sasha's own creations. "He worked on a murder case with Roxanne Calloway a few years ago."

"Didn't you help solve that one, too?" prompted Sasha. Margo had been involved in several of Roxanne Calloway's investigations.

"Just a little. You've met Roxanne?" Margo asked. "She lives near you."

Andrea settled back in her chair and sipped from her own mug. There would be other opportunities to talk with Margo and Sasha about art and her plans, she was sure, and this new topic did interest her. "I saw her just today. She was with Cooper Jenkins's daughter."

"Was she now?" Margo's eyebrows rose. Both Margo and Sasha had learned that Roxanne had been rehired by the RCMP's Major Crimes Unit. Their good friend Roberta Axelsson had shared the news that she was now babysitting Dee three days a week so Roxanne could get straight back to work.

"Susan Rice was telling me that Roxanne has been at her house, asking what happened to that young lifeguard who was staying there this summer. She's the girl that the police are searching for," Margo added.

"Meagan? She's not back at university?" Andrea set down her mug.

"You know her?" asked Margo.

"You hadn't heard?" Sasha chimed in. "She left Susan's house with her suitcase on Monday evening of the September long weekend. She hasn't been seen since. So," she added, "we think that Coop Jenkins was out here looking for her and that's why he's dead."

"Oh." Andrea Carlson was momentarily silenced by the news.

"But you knew her?" Margo Wishart pressed. "How did you not know she's gone missing?"

Andrea explained that she and Alan had been busy settling into the new house and preparing to sell their place in Winnipeg. They hadn't met many people in the area yet. But she had run into Meagan once, at Susan Rice's house.

"Susan and I share an interest in meditation," Andrea said. "She was showing me her collection of singing bowls."

Meagan had said that she was interested in learning how to paint.

"She'd had hardly any art education at all," said Andrea. "All they did in the school she went to was colour pictures of Jesus. Staying within the lines." She sniffed in disapproval. "So I invited her to come over and visit one afternoon. We played with acrylics. Some collage. She has quite a good eye for colour. So she came over occasionally after that, when she had a day off. Rode over on a bike, all the way from Susan's. She helped us out a bit, in exchange for art classes. She just wanted to mess around with crayons or some acrylic paint sometimes. I don't think she'd ever had fun like that before.

"She said she was so sorry she'd have to give it up when she went home at the end of the summer. I gave her the names of a couple of people who teach workshops. Suggested she might want to take an art course at the university, but she said she wouldn't be allowed to do that."

"Maybe she's run away," said Sasha.

"Do you think so? I hope she's all right." Andrea Carlson twisted one of her many rings. "I do hope nothing awful has happened to her. Is it possible that she's dead, too?"

14

"ANDREA CARLSON IS such a flake."

Sasha Rosenberg dropped by her friend Roberta's house the following morning. Roxanne's daughter bobbed up and down on Roberta's arm, excited to see Sasha's puppy. She put the baby in a playpen that Roxanne had brought over so Roberta could contain Dee, who was beginning to crawl, but stubby little fingers were soon poking through the mesh and being licked.

"I wonder how much it costs to set up a place like hers?" Sasha's income was barely enough to get by on. The basset puppy had been an extravagance, paid for, in part, by the metal flower baskets that she had made for the Carlsons. Envy was making her irritable. "She's going to call her studio 'Honeypot House.' What kind of a name is that?"

"They're keeping bees, aren't they?"

Dee had discovered that throwing toys over the mesh to the puppy was great fun. Roberta rescued them from his sharp white teeth and tossed them onto the counter for washing while she talked. Dee yelled in protest; Roberta picked her up.

"That's his hobby, not hers. You know Andrea teaches art workshops in schools? Talks to the kids about colours and feelings. Happy orange, sad blue. Then they draw themselves and colour them however they feel. That's all there is to it! Teachers love her and she gets paid good money for doing that."

Sasha had never applied to do that kind of work. She couldn't figure out how to make it happen, not with clay and metal.

"You could take in mugs or bowls. Get the kids to glaze them and bring them back when they're fired," Roberta had once suggested. Dee continued to complain. Roberta gave her a cracker to keep her happy, but that was tossed straight to the puppy. She got up and walked, the baby on her hip. Sometimes that helped Dee to doze off.

"What? Lug boxes full of mugs home and back? You know what they'd weigh? And some of them would get wrecked on the trip!" Sasha replied. The truth was that she didn't want to have to teach anyone, especially a classroom full of kids, paycheque or not.

She had searched online to find out what else Andrea Carlson did. That had annoyed her even more. Sasha and her artwork only appeared on Facebook, but there was Andrea, everywhere, on Twitter, Instagram, TikTok. She had hundreds of followers.

"She's got a website, too," Sasha said.

She had tried that once. She'd used a free web-builder and it had not been successful. Andrea's, however, looked professional. There was her face, beaming out from the screen with her bio. Examples of her work in splashy colour. A blog. She delivered workshops at a well-known art centre in town and had offered some online during the pandemic. Those had evolved into weekly offerings, on Zoom. "You should see how much she charges! And people pay for it. It's all such easy, basic stuff. How does she get away with it?"

"Don't worry," Roberta said. "People are still going to come and see what you are doing." The baby's head had begun to loll against Roberta's shoulder, eyes almost closed. Roberta knew why Sasha was so irritated. Andrea Carlson's new business posed a threat to Sasha's own. "The things that you make are different from hers. Maybe some of her visitors will drop by your place, too. This might work in your favour."

"Andrea knew that Stephens girl. The one that's gone missing." Sasha leaned against the sink, her arms folded.

"I know. Margo called me last night and told me." Roberta sat down, Dee finally asleep in her arms. "I mentioned it to Roxanne when she dropped off Dee this morning. I hope I haven't got Andrea into any kind of trouble."

Egg cartons were stacked beside the door. Some of her customers picked up their orders, while Roberta delivered the rest. If there were rumours circulating about Andrea Carlson and her husband, Roberta would hear them soon.

THE CARLSONS HAD also been the main topic of conversation in the Calloway/Stavros household the night before.

"They haven't exactly reached out to meet their neighbours," Roxanne said.

"They're still city folk." Matt was slicing up the Klassens' fresh beets for borscht. A pot of stock simmered on the stove. A bunch of dill lay on a board, ready to be chopped. He liked to play chef. Dee was close by, banging a rattle on the tabletop of her high chair. Finn wasn't home. He was at a friend's house in Fiskar Bay and would need to be picked up later.

"They'll find out that they need to know who lives around them," Matt added. You never knew when you might need a helping hand living out in the country. When a tree fell and blocked your driveway or a snowblower failed to start on a blowy, snowy day, it was your neighbour that you called.

"You know the Carlsons? From when they bought the farm?" Roxanne asked.

He looked up from chopping. "I acted for the owners," he said. "It's a couple of years since that happened. The Carlsons aren't my clients."

"They're planning to switch over to you now that they're living out here." The rattle landed on the floor. Roxanne picked it up, rinsed it off and handed it back to Dee. "What else do you know about them?" she asked.

"That sounds like a work question." Matt smiled at her, teasing.

He told her what he knew as he chopped and stirred. Alan Carlson had worked in government. Matt didn't know what department, but it must have been a senior job, one that provided a decent pension. The Carlsons owned a house in an older Winnipeg neighbourhood that had become popular with young families. It would sell for a good price, and Andrea had already inherited and sold her parents' house.

The rattle landed back on the floor. Dee yelled for it to be picked up. Roxanne lifted her out of the chair instead and bounced her on her hip.

Alan was building a garden, Matt continued to say while he dumped beets into the pot. He was learning about beekeeping. Andrea was setting up an art centre. They wouldn't make much money off of either business, but they didn't need to. The Carlsons were quite comfortably off.

"We should invite them over," he said. "The weather's supposed to be fine on the weekend. Still warm enough to have a barbecue." Matt loved to fire up his big gas barbecue and turn burgers and sausages over the flames. They could have a bonfire too.

"You'll ask them?"

"Sure," he said, and walked to the sink to wash his hands. They were stained bright red, like the soup he was making. "Then you can ask them whatever it is you want to know."

IT WAS NOW Friday morning, and Roxanne was on her way to Winnipeg to visit HQ and meet Constable Nolan James, the file coordinator assigned to her team. She had ordered supplies for the unused room upstairs at the Fiskar Bay detachment, intending to turn it into a functioning office—just as she had done years earlier. While in the city, she also hoped to check in on Nick and Ella Klassen. If all went well, she might be lucky enough reach them before Hailey Jenkins did.

Constable James had followed Rob Marsden's request and checked out Ed and Judith Andreychuk's background, but he hadn't uncovered anything Roxanne didn't already know. Meagan Stephens's photo was attracting attention online, but not of the helpful kind. It was mostly speculation, false leads, and a waste of time, he told her. He'd followed up on a few of the calls, but so far, they were all dead ends.

"Sergeant Marsden thought she'd run off with a guy." He leaned back in his chair, arms folded. He was a slim man, much smaller than Marsden and good-looking, likely biracial, with thick, dark eyelashes. He kept his eyes on the screen more than on Roxanne.

His office was just a cubicle, containing a desk and a computer, with no spare chair. As file coordinator, his job was to gather information, not to go out and interview people. He said he'd do it if necessary, but she could tell he was reluctant. Constable James was a desk man. She recognized the type. The RCMP needed members like him. People skilled in online surveillance and with the patience for it were in demand. There was no shortage of work in cybercrime.

But what she needed in Winnipeg was a boots-on-the-ground investigator. She regretted having blown it with Hailey. Not that Hailey had much experience with in-person interviews either. Like Nolan James, she preferred working at a desk and communicating via screen.

Maybe the long pandemic lockdown was partly to blame. It had given people like Nolan and Hailey a chance to work from home and they had discovered that they preferred it that way.

Nolan James said he'd try to speak with the lifeguards who had worked with Meagan at Cullen Village—he could do it online, and she settled for that. He pulled up a photo of the beach patrol sitting at a picnic table beside the hut where they worked. They were in uniform, smiling for the camera. Meagan Stephens was certainly pretty. Willa Stein looked bigger, stronger and fairer. They all looked fit. The oldest one, Owen Bradshaw, had dated Meagan when she first started at the beach. The other was named Joe Russo. He'd graduated this year and was still in Winnipeg. His family owned a well-known Italian restaurant and gourmet food store in the city.

"Find out about Bradshaw," Roxanne said. "Meagan was seeing him for a while. She dumped him fairly quickly but apparently he still liked her a lot. He's in B.C. He must have gone there after that last long weekend at the beach. Maybe she persuaded him to take her with him." It was a long shot but worth the try.

Coop Jenkins's body could now be released, Nolan said. The autopsy report revealed nothing unexpected. The shotgun blast had struck his heart and lungs; he would have died within seconds.

"His daughter's been informed?"

"Not my job, ma'am," he replied. He was right—the news should come from her or from the medical examiner's office. "They're busy. Sergeant Marsden's body hasn't been examined yet," he added.

She left him to his work. Nolan James was efficient, but he worked strictly by the book. He'd be useful, she knew, but she still wished he were more willing to leave his desk.

Inspector Schultz was out at a meeting. Once she'd picked up her supplies, signed some papers for payroll and got herself equipped with a new gun, she had plenty of time to go find Nick Klassen.

HE SHARED A house near the university with three other students, in a riverside suburb. The neighbourhood was desirable but larger houses like this one were often bought and converted into student rentals, which did not make the local homeowners happy.

Nick was lean but muscular and tanned from working outside all summer. He checked her ID before letting her inside.

"Some woman's been here already this morning," he said. "She said that she was a private investigator, but she didn't look like one so I didn't talk to her. And now you're here?"

"Meagan Stephens's family hired a PI to help find her when she went missing. That's probably why she wanted to talk to you,"

Roxanne said. She didn't see any need to spoil Hailey's chance of any interview that might follow.

"I know that some guy got shot near where my parents live and a police officer's been killed. Is that's what you're here to ask me about?"

There was a worn leather couch in the living room and a couple of huge, mismatched armchairs. A coffee table held scattered papers, dirty glasses, and a couple of empty beer bottles. A large-screen TV dominated the room.

"Finding Meagan would help us," Roxanne sat on the edge of one of the chairs. It looked like it would swallow her. "You knew her?"

He'd sat down at the far end of the sofa, keeping his distance. His hands rubbed his knees. They were worn hands, used to hard work, like those of his parents. One day he'd probably have the same enlarged knuckles as his father. He took his time answering.

"I met her earlier this summer," he replied. "I haven't been around Cullen Village much lately. My uncle is sick and I'm helping out at his farm south of here. I haven't been able to get up home as much as I'd like and when I am, I need to work with my dad."

"But you know who she was?"

"Sure. She was okay. Young. She's the same age as my sister."

"Did you ever party with the beach patrol?"

"I don't have time these days. Look, Sergeant, I'm too busy for this. I've got a farm to take care of, my mom and dad need help whenever I can get up to their place. I'm having a hard time keeping up with my course work. I may have to drop my year, the way things are going. I haven't had time to hang out with the kids at the beach. You need to ask someone else about this."

"Did you ever meet someone called Cory Andreychuk?"

"Never."

"Willa Stein?"

He laughed, showing white, even teeth. "Everybody knows Willa," he said. "She's been coming out to the beach every summer since we were kids. This has got to be her second, third time on beach patrol. Now that's who you should be talking to, not me. Willa will tell you what you need to know. Look, I've got to get going. Are we done here?"

She was. Roxanne took her leave and went in search of his sister. Finding parking on the university campus took some time, and the residence where Ella Klassen lived was a few minutes' walk away. A girl on the same floor, dressed in yoga pants and a tank top and looking like she had just been exercising, told Roxanne that Ella was in class.

"There was someone else here asking for Ella, not so long ago. Said she was a private investigator, but Ella was gone already."

It was just as well that the main leads in this case were closer to home. Roxanne turned the car and headed north. Why, she wondered, was Meagan Stephens's disappearance still a mystery? Someone had to know where she was. Willa Stein was her best bet. Cottagers like her stayed at the lake until Thanksgiving weekend in October. With a bit of luck, Willa would be at her family's cottage this weekend. If Matt agreed to watch Dee for a while, Roxanne would try to talk to her, and then she might finally get some answers.

15

MATT STAVROS WAS happy to spend Saturday morning at home with his daughter. He planned to do some yard work—rake leaves, split and stack logs—but if Dee wasn't in the mood to cooperate, he'd postpone it. With Dee off her hands, all Roxanne had to do was drop Finn off at his friend's place in Fiskar Bay. Finn had his own plans: a full day of video games, and he wouldn't need a ride home until suppertime. The rest of the day would be hers.

It was a fine, sunny morning, the trees still holding their leaves, bronze and orange and brown, the occasional green spruce stencilled among them. By the time she and Finn were heading for the door, Dee was in her stroller, ready to spend the morning outside. She barely turned her head as Roxanne said goodbye. All her attention was focused on her adored daddy.

Roxanne dropped off Finn, then went straight to the detachment to set up her new office. Lucas Bell walked through from the lunchroom and volunteered to help her carry the boxes upstairs.

Todd Brewster was manning the front desk.

"You're supposed to be out on patrol," he reminded Constable Bell, his junior in rank.

"Not for another twenty minutes." Lucas manoeuvred a large box around a bend in the staircase and disappeared from sight. Roxanne had found a box cutter. She split open a cardboard lid and lifted out a laptop. Another box held a printer.

"Want me to help you set those up?" Lucas offered. He could do it when he came back from patrol, he said, keen to help, but the laptop was already set up and ready to go.

"I've been checking on the Andreychuks some more," he told her. "Not Brad. Ed."

"Really?" she said. "Tell me."

Ed Andreychuk had served time years ago, before the pandemic. He'd been involved in a ring that smuggled immigrants into Canada using his trucking business as cover. They were dropped off just across the U.S. border, where they could walk across open fields and enter Canada illegally. Ed would pick them up on the Canadian side. He'd also been caught smuggling goods across the border and had ties to the drug trade.

"So," said Lucas Bell, all bright-eyed and eager to please. "What if he's part of a trafficking network? What if that's what's happened to Meagan Stephens?"

"Interesting idea," Roxanne agreed. "I'll keep it in mind." It was too bad Constable Bell wasn't available to assist her. He was enthusiastic, a go-getter. Maybe she could still find a way to put him to use. "You're out on highway patrol all day?" she asked.

He had five more minutes before he had to go, but she could see him perk up, wanting to know what she had in mind.

"How about you keep an eye open for a big moving van going to the Andreychuk farm?"

"The one that Cory Andreychuk's driving?"

"That's it. It probably won't show up until late this afternoon, but if you see it, call me."

"Shall do, Sarge." A big toothy grin lit up Lucas's face. It made him look even younger than he was. She watched him trot off down the staircase, back to being an ordinary traffic cop, but today he was one with a mission.

As soon as Cory Andreychuk got home, she planned to bring him in for questioning and have both the house and the moving van searched.

Ravi Anand was at home when she called him.

"Cory's back from Brandon and dropping off a load of furniture in Winnipeg before he returns," she said. "It'll be late afternoon at best before he's home. I'm getting a search warrant. I might need to bring Ed and Jude in for questioning too."

Ravi said he'd be at the office by three. He'd see her then, and they could decide how much support she'd need.

Setting up her temporary office didn't take long. Before long, Roxanne was on the road to Cullen Village, searching for the cottage owned by Willa Stein's family. It was an old summer cabin built on stilts, with a screened front porch. Soon it would be boarded up for the winter. The cottage sat halfway down a street that led straight to the lake, visible at the end of the block. A small Kia Rio was parked in the driveway, but there was no sign of Willa.

The door was unlocked. That was nothing unusual, especially among families that had cottaged here for generations. They liked to maintain the old traditions even though crime was more prevalent and the summer months busier. Roxanne stepped inside. There were signs of a recent party and an attempt to clean up. The kitchen counter was stacked with dirty dishes and empty beer cans, but the living room had been tidied and vacuumed.

A wooden shelter by the back door, likely meant for firewood, was instead piled high with empty cans and wine bottles. A few had once held vodka or tequila. Behind an old garage, a green canoe lay on its side.

"You looking for the Stein girl?" An elderly man peered over the fence.

"Have you seen her?"

"Not this morning. She had someone over last night. Not the usual crowd, though."

"So she didn't have a party last night?"

Not yesterday, the man said, but there had been a doozer last Saturday. Lots of noise. That happened on lots of weekends. There were neighbours that complained, but he just put in his earplugs and went to bed. He'd liked a party himself when he was her age.

"Could she have gone for a walk?"

He didn't think so, it was more likely she'd gone swimming. She did that, most mornings, as long as the weather held. She'd be back. That was her car in the driveway, so she couldn't be far away. Would she like him to let her know when she showed up? She was Sergeant Calloway, wasn't she? From the RCMP? Roxanne had been recognized.

"Is this official police business?" he asked. "About those two murders? And the girl that's gone missing? The one that was working with Willa over at the big beach all summer?"

"Did you know her?" asked Roxanne.

"Seen her. A nice-looking girl. I knew who she was from her photo, the one you've got out on the internet. I've seen her out here." He pointed at the unkempt grass in the Steins' backyard. "Dancing around that firepit, not so long ago. Was hardly wearing nothing." He almost leered then seemed to remember he was talking to a policewoman and straightened his face.

"When was that exactly?"

"Let's see. Maybe September long? Just before they all quit for the summer."

"Can you be sure? It's important," Roxanne said.

He screwed up his face, trying to remember. Yes, it was that weekend. Saturday or Sunday. He wasn't sure which.

Had anyone visited recently?

It had been quiet since then, but someone had definitely stopped by last night. He didn't know who it was. It was before nine, and already dark. He'd only seen the headlights when the car pulled in behind the Rio. He went to bed by ten, and the car was still there at that time.

She handed him her card. If he remembered anything else he thought was important, he would call her?

"Will do, officer." He straightened up and looked at her as if he were about to salute. Maybe he'd once served in the military. "Want me to let Willa know that you've been here looking for her?"

"No. Just let me know right away that she's here. And you won't say a word to anyone else about this, will you?"

"Gotcha, Sarge." He winked at her.

Until the end of summer, this street would have been lined with cars belonging to cottagers and holiday renters. But this Saturday, only one other driveway was occupied. The street was quiet. Roxanne walked down to the lakeshore at the end of the road, looking for Willa Stein.

She saw a small patch of beach and a swimming pier, but no sign of a swimmer. Returning to her car, she drove to the main beach in the centre of the village instead. There, she crossed a stretch of grass beneath golden, leafy trees to the hut used by the beach patrol. It was locked and shuttered. A wind was picking up, and a few leaves were falling. The weather was changing. Out on the lake, waves had begun to form, though the bay remained sheltered. Roxanne scanned the shoreline—there wasn't a single person in the water.

Willa Stein could be anywhere. Maybe her elderly neighbour had it wrong and she had jogged, just as Rob Marsden had done, at the south end of Cullen Village's long beach. Maybe she was drinking coffee in someone else's cottage.

Roxanne went back to her car.

Lucas Bell's suggestion that Meagan had been trafficked was an interesting one, a long shot, but if the Andreychuks were dealing with their cousin, Brad, it could be possible. Was Brad linked to a trafficking circle and manipulating his family from his jail cell?

Were the Andreychuks continuing the family business while Brad was locked up? Had Meagan Stephens been drugged and transported west in the back of Cory's moving van? He could have handed her off to another truck travelling west, somewhere along the Trans-Canada Highway, anywhere between here and Brandon. Had she already been handed over to a pimp, put to work on the streets of Vancouver, drugged and made addicted to keep her compliant?

Had Cooper Jenkins encountered Ed Andreychuk before, when he was a detective, working for the City of Winnipeg Police Service? Had he been recognized, out here near Cullen Village? Was that why he was dead? She had so many questions that needed answers.

She left a message for Nolan James at HQ in Winnipeg to check all police records pertaining to the Andreychuks. An out-of-office message bounced back. He'd reply on Monday. She could wait. Perhaps Willa Stein would have shown up by then. She turned the car around and headed back to Fiskar Bay, picked up a large coffee and one for Todd Brewster, who was still working the front desk. He grudgingly thanked her.

A short while later, she was seated at her new workstation in the corner of the big room, near the window that gave her a view of the street and the parking spaces out front. She tapped away at the laptop. Police files and social media yielded all kinds of useful information. It took less than an hour to find some answers.

Ed Andreychuk had served two sentences, one for bringing a family across the border and another for possession and trafficking of drugs. He'd done time in a "correctional centre," not the big penitentiary that now housed his cousin and other, more dangerous, convicts.

He and Jude had previously lived on a farm just south of Winnipeg, a property that had once belonged to Jude's family. During the pandemic, Jude had been a vocal member of the anti-vaccination movement, and both she and Ed took part in the convoy to Ottawa protesting the federal government's restrictive public health measures.

She dug deeper and uncovered more details. Ed and Jude had left the farm shortly after returning from the convoy to Ottawa. Some of their neighbours hadn't appreciated their involvement in the anti-vaccination movement—or the stream of big rigs that turned down their road to stay overnight. Jude and Ed had posted large placards at their gate demanding *FREEDOM!!!* and flown big Maple Leaf flags. Those drew complaints too, along with snide remarks at the grocery store and gas station. Eventually, they decided to leave and try their luck elsewhere. In the meantime, they had free lodging at Ed's cousin Brad's place in the Interlake—three years to look after the property while Brad served the rest of his sentence. Plenty of time to figure out their next move and put down fresh roots.

Roxanne couldn't find any connection between the Andreychuks and Cooper Jenkins. It was too bad she and Hailey weren't speaking; this would have been a good lead for Hailey to pursue.

ED ANDREYCHUK HAD hauled a truckload of household junk to the dump that afternoon for a couple in Cullen Village who were downsizing. He drove off the highway and onto the road that led home in time to see a police car cruise past the house.

"The cops have just been by," he told Jude, kicking off his boots at the door.

"Yeah." She turned away from the window. "I saw him. Just one cop—the young one who was here when that woman sergeant showed up. He drove by again about half an hour ago, coming from the other direction. Looks like they'll be paying us another visit soon."

The police were still looking for Cory, they figured, but Ed and Jude might get hauled in too. It didn't take them long to decide what to do. Ed and Jude had like-minded friends who lived just off the Trans-Canada, west of Winnipeg, with a large yard. Jude called them. They owned a motorhome, parked out back, and could camp there for a couple of days. They had to be back by Monday, though. There was work needed doing.

Jude called Cory while she packed. He was already in Winnipeg, nearly finished unloading the van full of furniture. She told him he could join them or stay somewhere else, but it was best if he stayed away from the farm for another week. Ed would need to pick up the big van. They planned to meet at Headingley, just outside Winnipeg, where Cory could swap the van for the truck.

Within an hour, they were on the road: Ed in the motorhome with their two heelers, Jude following in the truck with her Jack Russell riding shotgun. The cop in the cruiser had gone east the last time he passed by. They headed in the opposite direction.

The house and outbuildings at the farm were locked up tight. So were the cars. Their alarms were set. Jude wished she could see the look on that red-haired woman sergeant's face when she found out she couldn't get in. Not that it mattered—the whole place was clean as a whistle.

16

THE ANDREYCHUKS WERE long gone, along with their truck and their dogs, by the time Roxanne and her team arrived. The house was locked up and there was still no sign of the elusive Cory.

"Do you want us to search anyway?" Ravi asked, but Roxanne shook her head. Ed and Jude might just have gone visiting. Cory could have decided to stay in Winnipeg for the night. Aimee Vermette would soon be on patrol in place of Lucas Bell. She could keep an eye on the farm and let Roxanne know if and when any of them appeared.

There was no word from Willa Stein's elderly neighbour, but that was okay. The Andreychuk line of inquiry seemed more promising. She just needed to wait for them to return, which she was sure would happen. Ravi headed back to the detachment, and Roxanne went home. The dogs bounced down the driveway, pleased to see her. Dee waved from her stroller on the veranda. Matt was putting his axe away in the shed and looked glad to see her. He needed to visit a fisherman's house to buy fresh pickerel cheeks. The barbecue planned for the evening was off—the sky was overcast, the wind picking up, and rain was on its way. Matt had changed the dinner menu.

Roxanne resigned herself to being mom for the rest of the day. She checked her email as the hours passed. There was still no word that anyone had arrived at the Andreychuk farm by the time their guests rolled up to the door.

"You're quite the chef," Andrea Carlson said that evening, sitting at Roxanne and Matt's dining table. Outside, rain battered the windows, but a fire blazed in the woodstove. Dee had settled down for the night and Finn had opted to eat in his room and spend the evening with his friends online.

The Carlsons had brought a jar of their own honey as a house gift. Andrea had designed the label, with the name of Alan's brand-new apiary. The Honeypot—the same as her studio.

"It's not very inspired but it is appropriate," she said. "We're both making sweet things happen, aren't we, dear."

She smiled at her husband over the rim of her wineglass. They had brought an expensive bottle of French Bordeaux. They had visited France in the spring and Andrea hoped to get back to Europe next year, "The architecture and the art are so inspiring!" but Alan wanted to build more beehives and grow his garden. "We can still manage a couple of weeks in Italy," she said, continuing to smile winningly at her distinguished-looking husband.

Alan had a thick head of hair, iron grey but silvery at the temples, a well-lined face with a slightly aquiline nose. He kept his lips closed when he smiled. Roxanne could imagine him in a well-cut suit, a senior civil servant, a man who spoke carefully and knew when to keep quiet. She couldn't picture him as a gardener, but that was what he now aspired to be. He had dug a large garden plot behind their new house, he said, and planted some potatoes. There was still some sprawling late zucchini. A couple of pumpkins would be ready in time for Halloween. Next year he'd have a full country garden, grow enough to fill their freezer for the winter.

"Just like the Klassens do?" asked Roxanne.

"You know them?" Thick eyebrows winged over cool grey eyes. He didn't need glasses or perhaps he wore contacts. This evening, Andrea sported yellow frames to match a long linen dress, a muddy golden colour with big pockets. A bronze-coloured woven shawl was draped around her shoulders.

"They're good neighbours," Alan Carlson was saying. Armin Klassen had been helpful. He had an interesting collection of heritage seeds. But it was his son, Nick, who was the most informative.

"He's very savvy when it comes to agriculture and he has access to labs at the university." Nick had brought over a tiller to dig out the garden plot for them and figured out how to get the pH balance of the soil just right.

"We pay him, of course," Andrea chipped in. "He's still a student, you know. They can always use a little extra money."

"Meagan Stephens is a student too. Didn't she do some art classes with you?" Roxanne asked.

"She did!" Andrea frowned for a moment then smiled again. "A lovely girl. So intelligent and curious. She came to visit me so she could explore her creativity, but it turned out that she was interested in everything we were doing. She helped Alan separate the honey from the combs. She was with us one day when there was a swarm, wasn't she, Alan?"

Alan nodded in agreement. "They had settled quite high up in a tree near the farmhouse," he explained. "I lent her beekeeper clothing and she shimmied right up a ladder. Shook the branch and the bees fell right out." He couldn't have done it himself, he admitted. His knees weren't reliable and Andrea had no head for heights. "Meagan did exactly as I asked her and got the bees into a box. She was very resourceful."

"Is there any news about her?" Andrea asked, her voice full of concern. "It's been almost three weeks since she disappeared, and there's still no sign, is there? I've seen her photo out in all the media—have you had any sightings?"

"Sorry, I really can't say." Roxanne decided not to answer. She popped a piece of fish into her mouth.

"Have you sold your property in the city?" Matt took the hint and changed the subject.

Not yet, they said. But they were looking for a small condo, a crash pad if they wanted to go to the theatre and stay overnight.

They'd sell their house then. Perhaps they could use Matt's services when that happened?

The rest of the evening passed smoothly enough. The Carlsons left a little before ten. It was still raining.

"Our turn next," they said as they hurried down the steps to their car, protected by a brightly coloured umbrella. Roxanne and Matt waved goodbye from the shelter of their veranda. The dogs ran out into the downpour, quickly peed, and came back up the steps. Matt opened the door so they could scoot back inside.

"Andrea's the one with the cash," he said. He'd run into Pete McBain when he'd been buying the fish. Pete made a point of knowing who lived in his neighbourhood. "She comes from a moneyed family and she was the only child so she inherited everything. Pete says that Alan was pushed to take early retirement. He was encouraged to leave his job."

"Why was that?" Roxanne closed the door against the wind and the rain. The house was quiet with their guests gone and Dee asleep. Finn had said goodnight and gone to bed as well.

"Something to do with a complaint from a woman employee. Inappropriate behaviour from a few years back. There'd been rumours, for years. They tried to hush it up."

"Isn't that typical?" It annoyed Roxanne when she heard of that still happening. "You knew that and you still invited him here for dinner?"

"I'd asked them already. It was too late to cancel. Didn't you want to talk to him anyway?"

"Well, yes, but you did too," she reminded him. She was still more interested in what she had just learned. "Alan's got a reputation for messing around with other women and pretty, young Meagan Stephens was helping him with his bees? Up a ladder? With him down below?"

"There's something for you to think about, but not right now, Sergeant." Matt scooped her into his arms. "It's time for bed," he said. "How about you just forget about that job of yours for a while."

HAILEY JENKINS HAD received an invitation from the Stephens family to come to church that Sunday morning.

"We are going to offer up special prayers for Meagan's return," Carrie Stephens had said when she called. "People are inviting people who knew her from outside the church. Your father died while he was searching for her, and we thought you might like to attend in his place."

Hailey looked at herself in the mirror, realizing her dark, edgy style wasn't helping when it came to questioning people. She'd noticed how suspicious Nick Klassen had been when he opened the door to find her on his doorstep, dressed in her usual black. Wearing all that eyeliner had definitely been a mistake. Ella Klassen had been out when Hailey called, but the students on her floor had looked just as wary. Getting their trust meant she needed to change her appearance.

She took Liam to the thrift store and told him he could spend ten bucks on a new toy. Meanwhile, she rifled through the racks and found a pair of navy polyester pants, a jacket with fancy buttons to go with them, and a white blouse, with a neat little collar. A beige raincoat was a real find. She'd look like a real sleuth in it, she thought, then went to search the shoe section for something with a small heel, something dressy looking but ones she could run in, if she needed to.

The next morning, she put on her new clothes. She had already stripped off her nail varnish, fastened her hair up and applied some lip gloss—nothing else. No eye makeup at all.

"You look pretty, Mom," Liam said as he lugged his almost new remote-drive car to his friend's house where he'd be staying for the morning.

The church, like the Stephens's house, was in the south of the city, close to the highway that circled Winnipeg. It was a large, new building with a huge parking lot, almost full of cars. A young man in a high-vis jacket directed Hailey to a vacant spot.

Inside, under a vaulted ceiling, pews were arranged in three sections, forming a large semi-circle. The pews were padded, Hailey was glad to see. She found a seat near the back.

A wooden altar and choir seats faced the congregation. On either side of a retractable screen were two stained glass windows: one showing Jesus surrounded by children, the other depicting lilies and a cross. The screen displayed upcoming church events, including Mother and Child Mondays, choir practice, and a housing committee meeting. A clock counted down the minutes until the service began at eleven. Visuals were controlled from an open booth located behind the congregation.

The room was almost full. Soft electronic music played quietly, although the church had an organ at the front. Five minutes before eleven, Carrie Stephens entered through a side door, took her place on the organ bench, pulled out the stops, and the instrument wheezed into life. The choir members processed down the aisles as powerful music filled the church, taking their assigned seats. A pastor in white robes followed them. The words to a hymn appeared on the screen; the congregation stood and sang.

Hailey hadn't attended church much. Her grandmother had taken her occasionally when she was little. This service followed the familiar pattern of hymn singing, Bible readings, and prayers. The preacher was more enthusiastic than those Hailey remembered—less severe and more cheerful in his delivery.

Hailey surveyed the congregation. Families sat with their children. She looked for a single father with four children, ranging from young ones to teenagers and noticed one sitting in the front pew. That had to be John Stephens, with Meagan's brothers and sisters. A blond-haired man, seated at the other side of the aisle, resembled Nils, the swimming coach, but she had only seen him on Zoom and might be wrong. About halfway through the service, everyone sang a hymn about Jesus loving little ones and all the children were led out for Sunday school.

Shortly after, Meagan Stephens's smiling face appeared on the big screen.

"We meet here today to ask for God's help in bringing our friend and daughter, Meagan Stephens, safely home," said the preacher. He wore a body mic that made his voice reverberate throughout the cavernous church. He talked about hope, but Hailey noticed a few eyes being discreetly dabbed.

"God takes care of those who have faith in His goodness," the man preached, "especially in times of tribulation. We must trust that no harm has come to our beloved Meagan, that she is in safe keeping." He led them in prayer, then the choir stood. The song they sang was not a hymn but one that Hailey recognized: "Bring Her Home," from *Les Misérables*, the gender changed to reflect a lost girl. Carrie Stephens played the organ and the fervent words filled the church.

Afterwards, coffee was served in a wide entranceway. John Stephens and his family were surrounded by well-wishers. Hailey couldn't get close to them but she added her name to a book of attendees, so that Carrie and her husband would know she had been there. There was no sign of Carrie.

Catching the eye of the man she thought might be Nils Svensen, she introduced herself.

"I didn't recognize you," said Nils. "You look completely different from what I remember on screen." He introduced the smaller, dark-haired man at his side. Hailey recognized Joe Russo's name.

"You were the other lifeguard at Cullen Village!" she said. "I need to talk to you."

Nils and Joe were members of the same swimming club. They trained together, swam competitively. It was Joe who had told Nils about the job that summer at Cullen Village that Meagan had applied for and got. Both he and Nils were friendly, more than willing to talk. Maybe, Hailey thought, her new look was working for her.

"Want to go for lunch?" Joe asked. His family's restaurant was in Winnipeg's Little Italy. He texted them and asked them to hold a table.

Half an hour later she was eating pasta and salad, a glass of red wine at her elbow.

"The old guys in my family import grapes from Italy so they can make their own." Joe Russo had black eyes and curly black hair. He'd liked Meagan, he said. She was fun but she hadn't been interested in him. Hailey wasn't surprised. She watched him and Nils exchange looks. They were more than swimming partners.

Meagan had been Owen Bradshaw's girl at first, but he hadn't lasted long.

"He's in Vancouver, isn't he? Could Meagan have hitched a ride with him?" she asked.

"Not a chance. He chased after Meagan for a while. Couldn't get it through his head that she was done with him, but he got over it. I've got his email address. Do you want it?" Joe took out his phone and sent it. "She hung out sometimes with a local guy called Cory Andreychuk. You should go and talk to him." Joe didn't have contact information for Cory.

"Did she drink?" Hailey asked. "Do drugs?"

Sure, a bit. Cory usually had some dope on him but Joe didn't think Meagan cared much for it. She just liked to party and have fun.

"We didn't see so much of her the last few weeks," he said. "She'd ride off on her bike once we finished for the day. Said that she had somewhere else to go."

The patrol took down the flags warning of water conditions and locked up at eight each night. During the first few weeks, Meagan often returned to the cottage where they were staying after that. Sometimes she even spent the night, but by mid-August, that had mostly stopped.

"I think she was seeing someone else," Joe said. "Could be Cory or one of his buddies. Lots of people came to Willa's parties, locals as well as cottagers. Meagan got to know a lot of guys."

Had she ever said she didn't want to go home at the end of the summer?

Not to him. He'd assumed she was going back to Winnipeg when the job was over, that she'd go back to school. He had no idea where she had gone.

After lunch, Hailey hurried home. She was going to be late picking up Liam. It was unfortunate she'd have to stay home the rest of the day, but she was eager to change into her own clothes. The new outfit worked well for the job, but the shoes had to go—they'd given her a blister on her heel. She just wanted to look like herself again.

17

THE FISHERMAN WHO had sold Matt Stavros the pickerel cheeks went out in his boat early Monday morning. His was the only vessel out on the water, south end of Cullen Bay, as the sky lightened to grey. There was no more rain and the wind had dropped, but enough of a breeze remained to kick up small waves and rock his boat. No matter. John Thorstensen had been fishing this lake all his life and he had nets to pull in.

He had a good catch so far, some catfish, whitefish, but mainly big, fat walleye, the one they called pickerel hereabouts, the kind that fetched a decent price in Winnipeg. His final net was the heaviest so far. He saw why as soon as it broke the surface. Something large and black was stuck inside it. Then he noticed something white, at its side, with fingers. Was that a hand? He tugged on the net and a face turned in his direction. This was not good. He had caught a swimmer, in a wetsuit, long dead, by the looks of it. He couldn't tell if it was male or female.

Thorstensen was a canny man. He dropped anchor and hitched the net to the back of his boat while he considered what to do. He could drag the body up over the side or tow it behind him, so he could get it to shore, but if he damaged it the cops would give him heck. They would want to see where he had found it, too. He called 911 and told the operator what he had found, then he took the cap off the thermos of coffee he always brought with him and settled down to wait. There was nothing else he could do. He hoped that the police wouldn't take too long getting here. He needed to get back to the dock, where his bins and his truck were waiting, ready for him to load up and take his catch back home. Start gutting and filleting. Tell his missus what he had found.

The coastguard showed up first, in their inflatable Kodiak. Another boat brought the Mountie that ran the RCMP these days, the brown one with the turban, and a new guy that Thorstensen had never seen before. They took photographs of the body, his boat, the spot where he'd put down his net. "Right here. Never budged," he told them.

They dragged the body over to the Kodiak and lifted it onboard, still wrapped in his net. He'd get compensated for his loss if it was damaged, the RCMP corporal told him. He watched how they handled it. There were fish trapped in there, too. Some of them were alive and flapping and he'd never get paid for losing that part of his catch. "Right," he grouched. "How long's that going to take?"

By the time they got to the dock at Fiskar Bay, an ambulance was waiting, the new young doctor from the hospital as well. The sergeant they called Calloway, the red-haired one that usually ran the RCMP around here, was standing there too, not wearing a uniform, though. The Indian guy got out of the boat and talked to her. Coloured folk. Women. That was who ran the RCMP these days.

The harbour had almost emptied out, ready for winter. Most of the big, expensive motorboats that had been moored here all summer had been hauled away. The people who owned them had plenty of money but no idea how to live on the lake. Some of those boats never left the harbour. They used them just like cottages. The big sailboats too. Most of them had been hoisted up out of the water onto dry land to winter beside the yacht club, where there were security cameras—lots of those. The police told him he could go, just stop by the detachment later and make a statement. That was just as well. He needed to offload the rest of his catch. The harbourmaster and a cluster of fishermen were hanging around, though, at the pier that was reserved for the fishing boats.

"Who is it then, John?" they asked. He didn't know. Some cottager, maybe, stupid enough to have gone for a swim before the weather turned bad.

They watched the medics unload a gurney from the back of the ambulance. Between them and the coast guards, they lifted the body, still wrapped in Thorstensen's net, out of the boat and up onto the dock. The doctor went to look.

"Definitely dead. 9:12," said the doctor, noting the time.

Roxanne Calloway stared at the waxy, pale face of the woman—short hair plastered to her scalp, tangled in the fishing net. It wasn't Meagan Stephens.

It was Willa Stein.

"How long has she been in the water?"

"More that twenty-four hours, for sure."

"Someone visited her on Friday night. She hasn't been seen since, as far as I know." Roxanne turned to speak to Ravi.

"She must have gone for a swim deliberately, if she's in a wetsuit." Lucas Bell stood behind them, listening to every word. "Maybe she was already in the water when someone got to her."

The doctor was hunched over the edge of the gurney. "She's taken a blow to the back of the head."

Roxanne stepped closer to look. "Hard enough to kill her?"

The doctor straightened and shook her head. "I'm not sure. It could've knocked her out, then she drowned."

"But that's what happened to Sergeant Marsden, right?" came the voice of the ever-eager Lucas Bell from behind them.

"She could have hit it on something," one of the medics suggested. He stood close by and had managed to get a good look. "A rock. The end of the pier, if she jumped off it."

"Nah." One of the coast guards disagreed. "She was way out in the bay when she was found. If she'd been close to the shore, she'd have been washed up last night."

"Dunno," said a colleague. "That wind was a nor'wester. It could have blown her that far."

"We'll find out when they do the autopsy. That'll show us if she drowned or not," Roxanne said to end the speculation.

Not that it would. This discovery would be the major topic of conversation all day among all the people who worked the harbour. The body would go straight to the morgue in Winnipeg. In the meantime, she called Ident. The Stein cottage would need to be examined.

DAVE KOVAK ARRIVED with his team from the Forensic Identification Unit by late morning and got to work. The elderly man who lived next door to the Stein cottage poked his head over the fence once more. No one had been there since Friday, he was sure of that, he said.

"Sure been quiet," he said. "What's going on? This got anything to do with the kerfuffle out on the bay this morning?"

He hadn't seen it happen, but he'd heard about it. A friend who walked his dog early every morning had called to tell him. He'd also seen something online—mentions of the coast guard, a couple of RCMP officers in a boat. There was even a photo on Facebook.

"Nothing's happened to Willa?"

He sounded genuinely concerned. Roxanne didn't answer, but he had seen police in white suits enter the cottage and he could guess. His friend had mentioned a fishing boat, and something heavy pulled from the water, tangled in a net. The coast guard had taken it away. Had someone killed her? Right next door to his house, maybe while he was asleep in bed?

Maybe he'd like to be closer to friends for a day or two, Roxanne suggested. Not that she thought he was in any danger, but he lived alone. Maybe could use the company, given what had happened.

"No," he said, unwilling to leave. "This is where I stay." He continued to watch while the search got underway.

Dave Kovak shook his head. Whoever had done the cleanup job in the living room had not been careful. There were fingerprints everywhere. Willa's partygoers.

"Last Saturday night," the neighbour reminded Roxanne. "She usually comes out every weekend until October long. Her dad comes out to close the place up for the winter."

"But the beach patrol is done. They've all gone home."

"Willa's friends with all the local kids, not like a lot of cottagers. She's spent all her summers out here since she was little. Her parents let her have the run of the place these days. They're both busy folk. I hardly see them anymore. Willa's been having parties here since she was in school. She acts like she owns it. She told me she was glad she liked beach patrol job because she could stay all summer. She never wanted to leave."

"Thank you. That's good to know," said Roxanne and saw him look proud, glad to have helped.

"Any time, Sarge."

The little Rio yielded little information. It was registered to Willa and she'd driven it through the car wash fairly recently.

"We'll run all the fingerprints through the system," Dave assured her. "Something might show up."

AIMEE VERMETTE CALLED in from the highway. The Andreychuks had arrived back in their yard just after lunch, driving a big motorhome and a moving van. She could see no sign of Cory.

"I've got another job for you," Roxanne told Dave. He rolled his eyes. He'd thought the Ident team would be wrapping up soon and heading back to Winnipeg, but that was not about to happen.

Then she called Ravi at the detachment. "The Andreychuks are back. I need to bring them in for questioning."

"Really? Cory was in Brandon Friday night, wasn't he? He couldn't have killed the Stein girl."

"That's right," she said. "He's not here, but his aunt and his uncle are. I want them put in different rooms until I've finished checking out the house. Cory, too, if he shows up."

Only Jude Andreychuk was home. The moving truck was gone. "Ed's out on a job."

She stood in the middle of her doorstep, arms folded. As far as she knew, Ed was somewhere between Poplarwood and Fiskar Bay, with a load of live chickens. He'd headed out to pick them up as soon as they got back. She didn't know where Cory was, either. They'd met up with him just outside Winnipeg to exchange the moving van for his truck.

Cory had his truck back now. He was somewhere in the city, but she didn't know exactly where. He hadn't said when he'd be back.

Jude wasn't impressed when white-suited forensic specialists tumbled out of a van that had pulled into her driveway. Neither were her two blue heelers. They prowled at the edge of the yard, hackles raised, growling. But she glanced at the search warrant and stood to one side so they could enter the house. "You won't find a thing," she told their backs as they disappeared down the hallway.

She wasn't keen to hand over the keys to any of their various outbuildings. The garage, the barn, and their vehicles, including a big motorhome, stood out in the yard. It was the size of a touring bus, with sliders on the sides to make it wider when it was parked.

"Fuck's sake," she muttered and pointed to the wall inside the door. Clusters of keys hung on a rack of small hooks, screwed into the wall.

"That many, eh?" Dave Kovak took them all. Some had key tags; some were for house locks. Smaller ones must be for padlocks. Jude stayed on the step, gazing into the distance, making it clear she had no intention of helping identify them.

"How about you lock up those dogs?" Dave asked her.

"What for? They ain't bothering nobody. And Charlie's got his buddy back." Lucas Bell was chucking sticks for the Jack Russell. They asked where she tethered her dogs. Reluctantly, Jude led them round the back of the house.

"Charlie doesn't get tied up, ever," she said.

"I'll keep an eye on him," Constable Bell offered. He had been assigned to remain on site while the Ident team worked and Jude was taken to the detachment for questioning. Todd Brewster drove off with Jude Andreychuk in the back of a police car.

Roxanne went inside to take a look. She started in Cory Andreychuk's room. It was neat, pretty basic, and sparsely furnished, with a bed, a chair, a dresser. It held a few articles of clothing. He must have taken most of his belongings with him. There was no evidence of drugs in the room. The rest of the house was clear of them, too. One of the other bedrooms had been converted into an office, where she noted a small safe.

"We'll take that and get it opened," said Dave, "unless you can get Jude to tell you the code." He confiscated a computer. There was a receipt book and a work log on a shelf. The Andreychuks were doing okay, workwise. Their moving business was solidly booked for the next couple of weeks and after.

They went to the back door. The heelers stood and watched, ears alert, tongues hanging out.

"This is going to take hours," said Dave, surveying the car graveyard. "You could hide drugs anywhere out there. Choose a wreck, any of them, and stash it in the trunk, or inside the upholstery." They walked through the outbuildings. The workshop was full of tools. Car parts littered workbenches and the floor. Old tires were piled out behind it. "This was Brad's business, right?"

"His official one. He used to hide stolen goods in what was the machine shop."

They walked over to it together. The building had once housed farm machinery, but all of that was long gone. Now, it held a stock trailer, an older van, and a couple of Skidoos. A large empty space suggested where Ed and Jude likely parked the motorhome. Roxanne paused outside, squinting. The sun had come out, brightening the landscape. In a nearby field, freshly cut hay lay in big round bales, scattered across the grass. They probably belonged to Pete McBain.

The stock barn held additional vehicles, including another truck and a trailer. One space was large enough to accommodate the big moving van now parked out in the yard. Near the door stood a tractor and a quad. It was a Polaris, not a Honda, as Jude had told her earlier. Maybe she had lied? From here, it would take less than five minutes to reach the highway, and from there it wasn't far to the Klassen house, then on to the sunflower field. A quad could have made the trip easily.

"Okay," said Dave. "We'll check it thoroughly. If there's any trace of Cooper Jenkins on it, we'll find it. Otherwise, we'll be here the rest of today. Maybe tomorrow too, unless we get lucky."

Roxanne planned to call him later to find out what, if anything, they'd uncovered after she interviewed Jude. Ed as well, if traffic patrol managed to spot him. He was the one she really wanted to talk to. Him, and Cory Andreychuk. Cory had to have known Willa Stein.

18

THE INTERVIEW ROOM at the RCMP detachment in Fiskar Bay had been freshened up during Roxanne's tenure, but it remained grey and bleak. All it held was a table and four upright chairs. A recording machine sat on the table, and above it, a single barred window let in some light. Most of the illumination, however, came from harsh fluorescent strips overhead. Constable Brewster escorted Judith Andreychuk inside. She lowered herself into one of the chairs, planted her feet firmly on the floor, and crossed her arms, her expression as grim as her surroundings. Her jaw was clenched tight, and her lips were nearly invisible.

Roxanne sat opposite her and pressed the start button on the recorder.

"Brad Andreychuk is your husband Ed's cousin?"

"Sure is."

"And he lets you stay at his place for free?"

"What makes you think that?"

"Because we have access to your bank accounts," Roxanne told her. "You don't pay rent."

"That right?"

Jude shifted on the hard wooden seat. It was a tad small for her. She then unknotted her arms and leaned forward, bringing her large face closer to Roxanne's. She wore no makeup, and her hair was pulled back tightly with a plastic hairband stretched from ear to ear, keeping every stray strand in place. Jude was a no-nonsense kind of gal.

"See here, we're doin' him a favour. Ed and me, we're keeping his business running for him while you guys have him locked up. We get any cash we make and that's diddly squat. But you'll know that already, won't you, since you've been looking?" Her upper lip curled into a sneer. "He should be paying us for keeping an eye on the place, if you ask me."

"And what is Brad's business?" Roxanne asked.

"Scrap metal. Spare parts. You've seen it, what else would it be?"

"He didn't just deal in scrap," Roxanne remarked. "He fenced stolen goods."

"Well, yeah, but that was Bradley, wasn't it?" Jude sat back and stretched her legs out under the table. There wasn't much room. Roxanne had to move her own feet back, out the way. "We don't do nothin' like that."

"Someone's getting drugs to him while he's inside."

They had checked. The federal penitentiary where Brad was safely locked up was less than an hour's drive away. Drugs circulated and Brad was suspected of being a source, but the staff hadn't found any on him yet.

"Ain't us."

"Ed visits him regularly, once a month."

"Sure he does. They're first cousins. He reports in. Tells him how things are going, like what we've bought and sold. Ed picked up an old Chevvy last week."

"You've got contacts in the drug trade. Ed's been charged and convicted before now," Roxanne reminded her.

"That was years ago." Jude yanked her feet back, leaned forward again, steely eyes drilling straight into Roxanne's face. "He did time for that. Been clean ever since."

"He did some people smuggling too," Roxane reminded her. "That was only five years ago."

"Lookee here." A hand emerged from under her arm, and a finger stabbed the tabletop. "It's all done and over. We sold up, decided to get away, and make a clean start. Ed learned his lesson. Okay?"

"So you've moved into Brad Andreychuk's place? Brad's a known felon. How's that going to help Ed stay clean?"

"Sure he is, but Brad's kin, right? And the place needed lookin' after."

"You said before that your quad was a Honda, but it's not. It's a Polaris."

"Guess I got that wrong, didn't I? Sorry. They all look the same to me."

Jude heaved herself around on the hard seat again. She tucked her hands into the pockets of her jean jacket this time. She looked more worried now that she'd been caught out in a mistake. Less pugnacious.

"See, I want to head out west, Alberta maybe. But Ed, he's not so sure. We've both got family in these parts. The Andreychuks aren't all bad. You know Brad's brother, Jeremy? He's done well for himself. Got a good job, a wife and kids, a nice house. Maggie and John, their parents, salt of the earth they were. Never put a step wrong."

She was right about that. Roxanne remembered the Andreychuk parents. They'd been a tough pair, but they'd always played straight.

"We've done good these past coupla years. Built up a reputation. People need stuff moved and we do it. We show up on time and we don't break the china. We move livestock and get their beasts to the feed lot in decent shape. That's what Ed's doing right now. Delivering chickens to the abattoir. You ever tried cleaning out a truck after it's been full of chickens? We're good, hard-working folk and people round here know that. You bringin' us in here, takin' our place apart looking for whatever it is you're lookin' for, that ain't good for business."

"All right," Roxanne agreed. "Why is Cory living here with you? Doesn't he have other family or friends in Winnipeg?"

"See here." Jude leaned in again, assertive once more. "Cory's okay. Got in with a bad crowd at school, happens to lots of kids. He doesn't see any of them these days."

"Who's he visiting in Winnipeg right now?"

"He's got a sister, doing okay. She's just finished nurse training. Don't you go messing him up. Cory's like a son to us. Ed's learning him the trade and he's doing just fine."

"He knew Meagan Stephens and she's gone missing. A private investigator's been shot, an RCMP sergeant's been killed, and now we've found a girl that worked alongside Meagan as part of the beach patrol this summer, dead, out in the water."

"What?" She and Ed had been away. She hadn't heard that news.

Roxanne told her. Jude rubbed her jaw, her mouth slightly open, clearly astonished. Then she fired back, "Couldn't have been us, could it? Or Cory? We were miles away."

"She might have died Friday night. Before you and Ed left."

"Geez. You're dead set on pinning this on my guys." Jude stared at Roxanne for a moment, then lowered her chin, furrowing her brows and tightening her lips as she thought. "Maybe we need to get a lawyer," she finally said. "Not that we've got anything to do with this."

Matt Stavros couldn't represent her, given his connection to Roxanne, but a husband-and-wife legal team practised in nearby Poplarwood.

"Nah," said Jude. "I don't want some Mickey Mouse country lawyer. We know a good guy in Winnipeg that'll help us out."

The one she mentioned practised criminal law. He was tough but he hadn't kept Ed out of jail last time, or his cousin Brad. He wasn't available but he'd send a colleague, they were told. It would take a couple of hours for him to get out to Fiskar Bay. Todd Brewster led Jude away to a cell. They could hold her for now, so she couldn't go near her house. Nothing had turned up there, so far. The quad had only been driven by one person, probably Ed. There were no other prints on it.

There was, however, a call from another RCMP detachment. A lone patrol had stopped Ed Andreychuk while he was driving a load of live chickens to an abattoir in Gunstone, a small town northwest of Winnipeg. The birds needed to be delivered alive and in decent shape. Leaving them in the back of a truck for long without food or water was not an option. Because of this, a police car was escorting him. Todd Brewster was sent to pick Ed up as soon as the delivery was complete.

Constable Brewster drove down the long, straight road. He was not impressed. Why did he have to waste a whole afternoon on this errand when the real action was at the Andreychuk place? Why was that rookie, Bell, there instead of him? And why couldn't the team that tracked down Andreychuk just bring him to Fiskar Bay, instead of Brewster having to fetch him? Maybe the farmer should have found someone else to deliver his chickens. This was soft policing—playing nice.

Brewster had got to sit in on that interview with the Andreychuk wife, but that had gone nowhere. Weren't they looking for a murderer? A serial killer who had taken the life of an RCMP sergeant, no less? There were probably four deaths connected to the case. The Stephens girl had to be a goner. It had been three weeks since anyone had seen her. Her picture was all over the internet, but every tip they'd received so far had been a dead end. Brewster had heard his share of those calls He'd been stuck, listening to attention-seekers for what seemed like hours, every one of them a waste of time.

Maybe they'd find her body out among those car wrecks at the Andreychuk farm. Then Calloway could stop pussyfooting.

Up ahead, he spotted a combine harvester hogging more than its share of the road. A couple of cars were approaching from the opposite direction. Todd turned on his flashers. The oncoming cars slowed and pulled onto the shoulder to make room. The combine shifted over, and he zipped past. That was how you got things done. Red lights loomed ahead where the road met a main highway. He kept the flashers on, hit the siren, and watched as traffic stopped to let him through. Then he turned south. In another ten klicks, he'd take the turnoff to Gunstone. He'd be there real soon.

Gunstone had four streets running north to south, with a couple of cross streets intersecting them. A gas bar with an attached convenience store sat on one corner, and the abattoir was located at the southern edge of town. Todd spotted a large van parked right at the abattoir's entrance, with an RCMP car pulled in beside it.

Todd parked on the other side of the squad car and walked to the abattoir door. An older guy in an RCMP uniform hurried out and almost banged into him. "Bastard's gone," he blurted. Todd looked along a corridor and saw a door at the far end, half open.

A big guy in a rubber apron and boots came in behind Todd. "So?" he called to a younger man, behind a counter. "You got keys to that van? I've gotta get those birds out of there and it's all locked up."

They had no keys. They must have disappeared along with Ed Andreychuk.

"Get me a bolt cutter, Aaron, will ya?" the abattoir worker demanded.

"Wait up, right there." Todd Brewster stepped in and blocked his path. "What exactly happened here?"

"He drove right up to the door, blocked the way in, then took off down that hallway and out the back," the older RCMP officer explained. "Someone must have been waiting for him."

Brewster went to check A road ran behind the building and a small parking bay led to a loading dock. Two cars were parked there. A wooden shelter beside a BFI bin held garbage cans. Across the road stood two houses. Beyond that, it was open prairie—flat and empty, with barely a tree in sight.

The older cop walked up behind him. "Checked already," he said. There was no sign of Ed Andreychuk.

"You let him keep his phone? So he could call someone and get them to come and pick him up?"

"Hey," replied the other cop, looking up and down the empty road where nothing was moving in the afternoon sun. "All I was told was to follow a guy delivering chickens and hold him here for you to come and get him. What's he supposed to have done?"

"That's the guy who's probably been killing folks out near Fiskar Bay. The one that took out that sergeant from the Major Crimes Unit."

"Shit, someone should have told me." The other cop was unapologetic. "The guy was that dangerous and nobody said?"

A woman emerged from one of the houses opposite. She had her hair pinned up under a pink chiffon scarf and wore carpet slippers. A ginger cat followed her. She waved. They walked over to meet her. The cat sat in the driveway, watching, its striped tail swishing back and forth.

"You're looking for the man who ran out the back door just a few minutes ago?" she asked, pointing toward the rear of the abattoir. "There was a car parked along the road, just around the corner," she added, indicating the nearest intersection.

The abattoir's back door would've been clearly visible from that spot and it was also in full view from her living room window. She'd wondered why the car was sitting out on the street when there was plenty of space in the parking bay.

The driver must have seen the man run out the back door. By the time he reached the roadside, the car had gunned around the corner and screeched to a stop in front of him. He jumped in, and it sped off. From there, the road led straight to the highway. That's the way they had gone.

"It was a Toyota. A sedan, not a big one. Dark coloured, black maybe or blue." She had managed to get a good look at the person in the front seat. Someone young, wearing a ball cap. A fast driver.

Todd walked back through the abattoir to his car. Poultry cages were being unloaded from the back of the trailer, the hens clucking softly, on their way to the chopping block.

He called the Fiskar Bay detachment and spoke to Sergeant Anand.

"Tell Calloway that Ed Andreychuk's disappeared," he said. "He was gone by the time I got here. Some young guy was waiting in a car and helped him get away."

19

ROXANNE LOOKED OUT the upstairs window of her makeshift office in Fiskar Bay and noticed Councillor Pete McBain walking up to the door of the Tim Hortons coffee shop on the corner opposite. She hurried downstairs and across the road. Pete was already at the counter, paying for a coffee and a sandwich, when she walked in. A cluster of older men sat around the largest table. They lived in a Plus 55 retirement home nearby and this was their regular afternoon haunt.

"Afternoon, Sarge," one of them said. Pete turned to look. She noticed that he was wearing a business suit, as if he was about to go to a meeting.

"Hey, Roxanne. Heard they've got you back on the job—officially. That didn't take long."

"Well, yeah. I need to ask you something." Roxanne kept her voice down so the old guys wouldn't hear. "Have you got a minute?"

"Ten, if you're lucky." Pete checked the time. "I'm meeting a guy here real soon."

"That'll do." They walked to a small table by a window as far away from the group of men as possible, knowing full well that their conversation was being noticed and commented on.

"Bad news about the girl that John Thorstensen's just fished out of the water," said Pete. "She was on the beach patrol, like that other one that's missing too, right?"

"Her parents have owned a cottage at Cullen Village for years. Name's Stein. Did you know them?"

"Nah. They were cottagers and lived down at the village." He had grown up around Fiskar Bay and had partied closer to home when he was younger.

"The parents are hardly ever there," Roxanne told him as they prised open the tabs on disposable coffee cups. "The daughter pretty well had the place to herself all summer. A couple of the other beach patrollers were boarding with her."

"The patrol's gone, though, right? Summer season's done."

"Yes," Roxanne agreed. "But the Stein girl still came out on the weekends."

"How'd she end up in the water?"

"We don't know yet. The coast guard says she could've been dumped off the pier near her home. The current from there would've carried her down to the end of Cullen Bay, where we found her. But it's also possible she went into the water farther out in the lake, maybe taken there by boat. Of course, it might not be anything like that. It could've been an accident. She might have gone swimming, been caught in a current, and hit her head. We still don't know if that's what killed her, or if she drowned."

"Not good," said Pete, swallowing a mouthful of coffee. "Go talk to Mike if you need to know which of the local kids showed up at her parties. You know he's working on that big new building down near the harbour? He'll be quitting work around four."

"Good suggestion." Roxanne noticed a dark blue Toyota Corolla drive by, heading toward the RCMP detachment. A car like that had picked up Ed Andreychuk outside the abattoir at Gunstone. She quickly got to the real reason she wanted to talk to Pete.

"Do you own the old Andreychuk farmland?"

"Yep. Bought it off of Brad, along with his dad's herd of Black Angus."

"What about the barn?"

"Brad won't sell. Won't let me rent it either, but that's okay. I'd rather winter my beasts closer to home."

"Why do you think he needs to keep it for himself?" asked Roxanne.

"Storage, probably. Your guess is as good as mine, Roxanne, but you know Brad. He'll have his reasons." He looked knowingly over the rim of his coffee cup.

The Toyota had stopped outside the detachment door. A young woman in jeans, a plaid jacket and a red ball cap got out. So did Ed Andreychuk.

"Well, look who that is," said Pete.

Roxanne chose not to comment. Ed and the young woman had gone inside the detachment. She'd catch up to them, but she had one more question to ask Pete.

"How close is the Carlson land to the Andreychuks'?" she asked as she stood to leave.

"Right up against. They don't want to sell yet but they'll change their minds, sooner or later. Then I'll have that whole patch."

"Can you run a quad straight across both sets of fields?"

"To my sunflowers?" he said, realizing what she was asking. "They'd have to cross three back roads but there's nothing much else in the way. You could do it on a diagonal."

"Cut straight over the Andreychuk farmland to the house that the Carlsons rent out as well?"

"Yeah, you could, now that I'm done haying."

"You were finished by the time we found the first body?"

"Sure was. Got it done by the end of August this year. Here comes my guy." A black Audi drove down the street and into a parking space outside. Roxanne no longer had Pete's attention. She took her leave.

Roxanne made sure to walk back across the road at a steady pace, as if she was in no hurry. The old guys were watching her go and they'd be speculating about why she had hurried over to the RCMP detachment so soon after Ed Andreychuk had been dropped off.

The girl who had arrived with Ed was Tanys, Cory's sister. She'd picked up her uncle from the abattoir in Gunstone earlier that day.

"He was in a panic. Thought you wanted to nail him for all those murders," she said. When she took off her red ball cap Roxanne could see neat dark curly hair underneath. "He asked me to come and get him so I did, and then I talked some sense into him. 'See,' I said to him, 'If you act like you're guilty, they're going to believe it.'"

So she had turned the car around and brought him right here.

Roxanne took her into the interview room. Seated in the chair opposite, her legs crossed, Tanys looked a lot more comfortable than her aunt. She seemed perfectly at ease.

"My Uncle Ed doesn't look like it, but he's really a big softy when you get to know him. Kind as they come. Look how he took Cory in and gave him a chance to get back on his feet. And everything was going fine until that Stephens girl ran off and people started dying around here. There's no way Eddie would hurt anyone. He can't even watch a dog being put down. Jude has to take care of all that. And empty the mouse traps. He just can't bear to see those little furry dead bodies."

"He's served time," Roxanne reminded her.

"Yeah, because he got sucked into something. Truckers like him had a bad go of it, you know, during the pandemic. There was nowhere for them to stop off to eat or pee even; nowhere to shower when they were days out there on the road. They listened to a whole lot of conspiracy stuff on the radio while they were driving. Problem is, Uncle Eddie's a bit gullible, if you ask me."

"He got caught with drugs before the pandemic."

"And he's served his time for that. Learned his lesson the hard way. Since he and Jude moved up here, they've done real good, and now you're messing it all up for them. He's doing great. There's jobs lined up for the rest of this month that he needs to get to. And now there's a truck and trailer need to be picked up from Gunstone as well. You'd no need to be interfering with him out doing a job. You've got nothing on him. You need to let him go."

The thing was, she was right about that. Dave Kovak called, and Roxanne took the call from the farm. His unit had found absolutely nothing to incriminate Ed Andreychuk, his wife, or even Cory. The barn was clean and so were all their vehicles. So was the house.

Now his team was combing through the car graveyard, popping open trunks and hoods. Still nothing. They could do a deeper search, but that would take more time and money, and Inspector Schultz had already shut that down.

They had found no sign of a body, and it was the murders they'd been tasked with investigating, not some small-time drug operation. As far as Kovak and his Ident team were concerned, they were done.

"Where's your brother?" Roxanne asked Tanys, noticing one sneakered foot tapping up and down. The girl was either impatient to end the conversation or more nervous than she let on.

"Dunno," she said. "Probably at his girlfriend's."

"Do you know her?"

"We've met. They've been together more than a year. And before you ask, she just moved into a new apartment, somewhere near downtown. I don't know the address."

"But you've got her phone number?"

Tanys did not. "I'm not that close to her." If Cory wasn't answering their calls it wasn't her problem. "He's probably as scared of you as Eddie is."

Roxanne let all three Andreychuks go. The Winnipeg lawyer wouldn't be needed after all. She stood at the office window, watching Tanys squeeze her large aunt and uncle into her Corolla and drive off.

She didn't believe half of what Tanys had told her. There had to be a better reason why Ed needed to flee Gunstone and why Tanys came to rescue him. And why was Cory still so hard to find?

The reason Ed had taken off was more likely drug-related than connected to the murders. He could have had drugs on him. There might even be some in that Toyota right now. Or perhaps he and Cory had met up and passed them along before Tanys brought her uncle back to the Interlake. That might be why Cory was still staying in Winnipeg. Maybe Brad was involved after all.

Cory had had a girlfriend all along, so there was no strong attachment of that kind to Meagan Stephens. She was nothing more than a passing summer acquaintance. Roxanne could insist on picking him up to find out what he was up to, but she knew he couldn't be the killer; he'd been miles away the entire time. It looked like a dead end.

Not that she lacked other leads to follow. It was ten minutes to four. There was just enough time to catch Mike McBain before he finished work for the day.

Roxanne walked over to the building site. She needed the exercise and it was a great afternoon for it, the sky blue, barely any wind. The big old elms that lined some streets were still well-leafed but many of them were turning yellow, and a mountain ash that she passed was laden with red berries, like the trees that Matt had planted near their own house to commemorate his aunt Panda and her dead partner. Lots of berries signified a harsh winter ahead, she had been told. She hoped that wasn't true.

She passed Matt's law office. His car was gone. He must be out visiting someone. Finn was going to his friend's house after school. Matt had said he'd pick him up later. She only had an hour before she needed to pick up Dee at Roberta Axelsson's house. Soon she turned onto the street beside the harbour where the big new seniors' residence was going up.

Mike McBain's red truck, marked with distinctive black stripes, was parked beside the road at the end of a long driveway. Roxanne approached a tall wire fence. The gate was open, but a sign instructed visitors to check in at the office, which appeared to be located in a long grey temporary shed.

The new building stood seven storeys high, a concrete shell, the lower levels with doors and windows installed, the upper ones wrapped in orange tarps. A large red crane stood between it and the office and a couple of men were manoeuvring a Bobcat back and forth, shovelling sand. They wore hard hats and high-vis jackets.

She heard a loud whistle from up above. Mike McBain waved to her from a gap in the tarpaulins, way up high.

"Hey, Sarge, what's up?" he called down to her.

"I need to talk to you," she yelled back up.

A man opened the office door. "McBain's working," he said. "And you can't enter this site without permission, ma'am."

"He's just about done for the day, isn't he?"

Roxanne didn't need to pull out her ID or insist on talking to Mike. He was already texting to say that he'd be at his truck in ten minutes. She walked back down the driveway and waited in the sunshine. An eagle flew overhead, its white head clearly visible. At the harbour, a truck was pulling a yacht on a trailer, its sails furled and wrapped tight, ready to be stored for the winter. A couple passed by with a dog, looking curious about why she was standing there. They must have recognized her. Mike was already striding down the driveway with his friend Vassily in his wake. Both still wore vests with bright green fluorescent stripes and orange hardhats.

"What can I do you for, Sarge?" asked Mike.

"I need to ask you about Willa Stein," Roxanne said.

"It really was her? We watched them lifting the body out of the boat down at the harbour from up there this morning." He pointed to the top of the building. "Heard it was maybe Willa afterwards. Hey, how's about we go for a beer?" That wasn't what Roxanne would have chosen but she went along with the suggestion. She wanted to keep this conversation friendly.

"A quick one," she told him.

Vassily hesitated. "I go home now, Mike," he said.

"Hey, it'll just be the one. Give me your hat." Mike opened the truck door and chucked the hats and vests into the back of the cab. He gave Vassily a ride to and from work, he told Roxanne. Vassily didn't have much choice. He could have walked home but his apartment was at the other end of town and he didn't want to offend his friend Mike. He tagged along.

The hotel was only half a block away. They walked to it, Mike doing most of the talking.

"Good you're back. Same kind of job as Izzy's, right?" If his sister couldn't work the case, he'd as soon it was going to be Roxanne, he said. "The Sarge here's solved loads of murders," he told Vassily. He ordered beers for himself and Vassily and a soda for Roxanne.

"Suppose you can't have one. Don't want folks saying you were seen drinking on the job, middle of the afternoon, do you?" said Mike as he paid for the drinks.

They sat outside on the deck. It was still just warm enough, as long as they wore their jackets and no one else was there to overhear. A boardwalk ran along the beach and the water sparkled all the way to the horizon.

"You went to Willa Stein's parties?" Roxanne asked.

"Sometimes. They've been going on for years. Everybody did."

"Who's everybody?"

"Well, let's see. Those other beach patrollers, for sure."

"She had one last Saturday night. The beach patrol was gone by then. Did you go?"

"Stopped by for a bit, didn't we Vassily?" Vassily didn't say anything.

"Who else was there?"

Mike rubbed his chin. "Don't quite remember. I had a few."

"Do you remember?" she asked Vassily. He shifted in his seat. He had barely touched the beer.

"They are Mike's friends. I do not know," he said, avoiding looking at her.

"It's important to find out," Roxanne persisted. She needed some names. "It's not only Willa Stein that's dead. You know that one of our sergeants has been killed, and that man you both found among the sunflowers was looking for Meagan Stephens, the other beach patrol girl that's still missing. You must have talked to someone at the party."

Just a couple of guys they worked with, Vassily stated. They hadn't stayed long. Vassily had caught a ride home with them. Left while he could.

"Meagan used to show up at all of Willa's parties," Mike said. "Dancing around like a maniac. Great girl—loads of fun. Then she just kind of stopped showing up, a while before she disappeared."

"Was she seeing someone else?" Roxanne asked.

"Probably. She was real cute. But I don't know who it was, so don't ask me."

Roxanne was getting nowhere. She hurried back to her car and arrived at Roberta Axelsson's house just as Margo Wishart and Sasha Rosenberg were leaving after their afternoon Scrabble game. With Dee present, it had been hard to focus. Now Sasha's puppy had run out the door and was chasing a hen across Roberta's yard. Dee squealed with laughter as Roxanne took her from Roberta, watching Sasha trying to catch her pup. Roberta rushed off to rescue the bird, leaving Margo alone with Roxanne. They hadn't talked for a while.

"You're back working full-time and it was another one of the other beach patrols, a girl called Willa Stein, that was found in the lake this morning?"

"That's right," said Roxanne. "Did you know her?"

Margo shook her head. She'd just said hello to the patrol occasionally when she walked by them with her dog.

"They looked so young and healthy," she said. "And now two of them are gone?"

"Meagan Stephens might still be alive," said Roxanne. "We haven't given up hope. Not yet."

But it had been nearly three weeks since anyone had last seen Meagan, and with each new death, that hope was fading.

20

THE CITY OF Winnipeg Police Service picked up Cory Andreychuk at his girlfriend's house in the small hours of the following morning as part of a city-wide drug raid. They found fentanyl, carfentanil and cocaine stashed in a locked box in the cab of his truck. The raid was linked to a national drug network that was being investigated by the RCMP, and the two forces were collaborating. Cory was being held for now in a city cell.

An inspector from the drug unit called Roxanne soon after she had dropped Dee off again at Roberta Axelsson's house.

"You ordered a search of the Andreychuk farm yesterday?" he asked. Roxanne pulled onto the shoulder of the road so she could reply.

"That's right," she said. "As part of a murder investigation that's happening out here. Dave Kovak's team carried it out. They didn't find a thing."

"You know Bradley Andreychuk? We're pretty sure that he's up to his ears in this drug business. Ed, his uncle, used to shift drugs for him when he was out on the road trucking, and we think Brad's moved him into his house so Ed can manage things while he's locked up. That's mostly a fresh batch from Vancouver that Cory's picked up, somewhere on the highway between here and Brandon. We're pretty sure that Cory and Ed help ship the stuff up north."

"Is this related to the case that Izzy McBain's working on?" asked Roxanne.

"Correct. We thought it was going in by train, but it's not. It's more likely by air." A train chugged up to Churchill, but the journey took at least two days. Most northern towns connected to Winnipeg by plane.

"If there was anything left in or around the house, Ed could have passed it on to Cory yesterday before we searched," Roxanne suggested. Ed might have taken any drugs stashed in the house or an outbuilding with him on the trip to the abattoir, planning for Cory's sister, Tanys, to pick them up there. But he had been flagged down by the local RCMP, and Tanys had ended up having to rescue both Ed and the drugs.

"Okay. We'll bring those two in." The fact that Tanys was a nurse interested the inspector as well. She could have access to prescription drugs.

"Ed is a suspect in the murders that have happened out here as well," said Roxanne. "And I should talk to Cory. He's not our killer, but he might know something. Can you leave him where he is for now? I'll be there inside the hour."

She turned around and headed south to Winnipeg. A wind had whipped up overnight, strong enough to push against the side of the car as she drove the long, open highway. A couple of fields were littered with geese, their grey wings tucked around them, black heads lowered to the ground. Clouds were thickening on the horizon and the sky was grey. Bad weather was coming. Having Cory locked up at the north side of town was a stroke of luck, however. Roxanne wasn't delayed by city traffic. Fifty minutes later she reached the city police station and was ushered into an interview room.

"You've got an hour," a uniformed constable told her, "then the drug unit's picking the little shit up."

Cory Andreychuk looked a lot like his sister, with curly dark hair, a small frame, and a quick smile. He dressed like Tanys too, in jeans and sneakers, a striped shirt over a tee.

"People think we're twins," he said, all friendly and disarming, "but she beat me to it by thirteen months."

Roxanne hadn't come to chat and time was limited.

"You passed drugs on to your uncle Ed when you returned his moving van to him and got your truck back," she said.

"Me? Never." His cheeky grin told her he was lying and that they both knew it. She could do nothing about that. He'd just deny anything she said. She tried a different tack.

"Tell me about Meagan Stephens," she said and watched him stiffen.

"She hasn't shown up yet?" he asked.

"Were you seeing her?"

"Me? No." He shook his head. "That was way back, not long after she first came to the beach. D'you know what? I think I was one of her first real boyfriends. She hung around with one of the other lifeguards before me but that was all, and he didn't last long either. She said she'd dated a couple of guys from her church but all they were allowed to do was go for a walk, with somebody tagging along to make sure they didn't get up to anything, so they didn't count. She'd never been allowed to dance before. Can you believe it? Never been to a party, even."

"Never done drugs either?"

"She wasn't all that keen, really." The question didn't seem to faze him. "Tried smoking a joint, but she didn't really go for it. She did like a beer, though. Otherwise, she was kinda into clean living, if you know what I mean. Exercising. Eating healthy."

"We've been told she liked to party," Roxanne said.

"Well, she did like dancing, once she got the hang of it. And she liked guys." Cory grinned again.

"But not you?"

"Nah! I wasn't smart enough for Meagan." He shrugged, more relaxed. "She was real brainy, you know, as well as being pretty nice looking. She'd missed out on a lot of stuff growing up. When she wasn't working the patrol she was riding around on a bike, checking things out. Gardening, yoga, vegan food, artsy stuff, you name it. She even helped some guy with his bees, she told me."

"So you still talked?"

"Sure." The grin spread all over his face once more. "We were still buddies. Why not?"

"Did she say anything about not wanting to go home at the end of the summer?"

"No. But I didn't see much of her by then."

"You traffic in fentanyl," said Roxanne. The smile disappeared. "And you belong to a drug network that ships illegal goods back and forth across the country. There's nothing to stop you drugging up a girl like Meagan Stephens and passing her along to a sex trafficker in Vancouver. How much is a girl like that worth?"

"No way." His eyes opened wide in alarm. "I never did nothing like that."

"But your cousin Bradley would. And what Bradley says goes, in your family."

A helpless, panicked look spread across his face, leaving his mouth hanging open.

"If Brad's into anything like that," he said, "I don't know anything about it. I liked Meagan. I don't know where she's gone." He sounded utterly sincere. Roxanne was inclined to believe him.

"What about Willa Stein?" she asked. "It was her house where the parties were held, wasn't it?"

"Yeah, some of the time. But there's plenty of bush parties happening other places."

Roxanne knew where some of those places were, tucked away in vacant, treed spots all the way along the shoreline to Fiskar Bay. Her team often got calls about late night noise from some of them.

"You know we found her body yesterday."

"I heard," he said, now looking genuinely worried. "Tanys texted me. Wasn't anything to do with me, though. I wasn't there. I was here, in town."

"But you know who Willa's friends were?"

"That's everybody!"

"Who did you see when you partied at her cottage?"

Cory was evasive: it was hard to remember names—most of them were cottagers already gone home and back to school.

"Mike McBain? He's local," she prodded.

"Yeah, sometimes. And the Klassens, but they never stayed long."

"Nick? And Ella?"

"He dropped by once, maybe, but Ella was there a few times."

Afterwards, Roxanne sat in her car in the parking lot as rain ran down her windshield. If she interviewed the Klassen kids, Vera would probably hear about it. She didn't want to disturb that relationship—she needed Vera as a babysitter—but she didn't have much choice.

She called each of their numbers. Both went to voicemail, but Nick called right back. He was at his uncle's farm south of the city, he said, but he could talk now.

Yes, he'd been at his parents' house on Saturday. His dad had needed a hand clearing the fall debris around the farm. He'd stayed for a quick lunch and been back in Winnipeg before four. He had gone out with friends that evening. Yes, he knew about Willa. He'd been shocked to hear what had happened to her. He'd learned about it last night online. He'd known her forever.

"It's hard when someone your own age dies like that," he said. "Could it have been an accident?"

"We don't know exactly what happened," Roxanne told him. "But we've been told that she was a really strong swimmer."

"That's true. She's lived in the water all summer long," he said. "All the years that I've known her. She's been around since we were kids."

How well had he known Meagan Stephens?

"She came over to my parents' place with Ella a couple of times. She was interested in how organic it is. Nice kid. She hasn't shown up yet? If Willa's death looks suspicious, do you think that she's a victim too?"

Roxanne could hear the concern in his voice. "We hope not," was the best answer she could give. Was there anyone else that Nick knew of, who was also friendly with Willa? Who had partied with her? Anyone that he thought could help them with their inquiries?

Nick said he would think about that. But everyone else that he knew, his age and Willa's, had moved on, was in grad school now, or working. He'd kind of outgrown Willa's parties. If anyone sprung to mind, he'd be sure to let Roxanne know.

The rain drizzling down the windshield had lightened up. The lifeguards needed to be spoken to, but she figured Hailey Jenkins was probably already on that. Maybe she could stop by Hailey's place while she was in Winnipeg, ring the doorbell, and see if Hailey was open to patching things up—and maybe sharing what she knew. If Hailey had come across anything useful, it was worth a try.

HAILEY OPENED THE door before Roxanne was halfway up the path, already damp from the walk across from the parking lot. She was dressed in her usual black, hair framing her face, long and leggy, arms folded as she leaned against the doorframe, glowering at Roxanne.

"Well, look what's here! You look soaked. I suppose I'd better let you in before you catch your death." She stood aside to let Roxanne enter.

Two small boys were playing in the living room. A table had been upended and a blanket draped over the legs.

"I'm in the office, Liam. Won't be long," said Hailey. Her son was too busy hammering something, plastic on wood by the sound of it, to answer.

Hailey sat. So did Roxanne.

"Willa Stein's drowned?"

"You've heard?"

"That why you're here?"

"No, it's not. Other things are happening out my way. We've just found out that the Andreychuks are moving drugs up north for their cousin Brad while he's in jail."

"That right?" Hailey hoisted one foot onto her knee. She wore well-worn black sneakers. "How come you're here telling me this?"

"I just thought you might find it interesting. Cory Andreychuk knew Meagan Stevens. We're thinking they might have drugged her up and trafficked her out west."

"Geez." The foot went back down onto the floor.

"I still think finding Meagan is the key to solving these murders," Roxanne continued, "but she might be long gone by now."

"You think that my dad was onto what they were doing so they killed him? Then that cop and now this other girl, Willa Stein? How come they wouldn't have trafficked her too?" Hailey made a good point.

"Willa's older than Meagan and not so naïve. Maybe she wasn't so easily taken in. Cory's sister is called Tanys. She tried to convince me that Ed's too soft to kill, but Jude, his wife, is tough and strong. She could have shot Coop. Hit Rob Marsden on the head. Willa too."

"Wasn't Willa in the water? How did she get there?"

"She was wearing a wetsuit, so either she'd just been swimming or was going to go. The water had become choppy so we can't rule out the possibility that it was an accident. The body might have banged against a rock, but Willa was a strong swimmer and she knew the lake. She'd been swimming there all her life."

"So someone could have killed her first and chucked her off one of those wooden piers?"

"Maybe. Or someone took her out on a boat and dumped her overboard. Willa had a canoe at the back of her cottage. And paddles."

"So basically you haven't got a clue and you're just guessing? I suppose you want to know if I've found out anything?"

Hailey grinned. They were back on a better footing. She described her visit to the church the Stephens family attended and about meeting Joe Russo. She'd also called Owen Bradshaw, the other lifeguard, who was in Vancouver. Owen had left Cullen Village shortly after their shift ended on the Monday of the long weekend. Since he had an early morning flight the next day, he was long gone by the time Meagan disappeared.

"Y'know what?" she said. "There's a notebook of my dad's that your guys missed. I found it under the seat of his truck, and you won't believe who shows up in it. The couple that own that B&B my dad stayed in are called Carlson, right? I think he booked himself into their place deliberately. Do you know that the guy was fired from some high-end government job because he was having an affair with some girl that worked for him?"

"I've heard something about that."

"Well, Dad was hired, back then, to watch the girlfriend's apartment. He got footage that helped expose what Carlson was doing. That woman wasn't the first victim. She was just the only one they could prove. But what if Meagan wasn't abducted at all? What if this guy messed around with her, and Carlson got scared she'd go home after the summer and blab to her parents? So he killed her and hid the body?"

"That's an interesting idea," Roxanne agreed, "but it's all speculation."

"Yeah, but it explains why she's disappeared. And maybe why my dad got shot. Carlson could have recognized Dad's name. You could find out if that other cop that got killed was poking around the Carlson place asking questions, couldn't you? And maybe Meagan had already said something about it to Willa Stein. It all fits, right?"

"I'll mention it," said Roxanne.

"You know what? This is good. I need someone to talk to now and then. Me and Dad did it all the time. We talked about how things were going, like we're doing now. Being a PI all by yourself isn't much fun."

That explained why Hailey was willing to tell Roxanne all of this. She was lonely.

"There's no reason why we can't talk now and then," Roxanne suggested. "Just run ideas past each other. It doesn't need to be anything formal."

"You don't need to be the boss of me?"

"No. I guess not."

"Okay then. We'll try it. You should put surveillance on the Carlsons." Hailey grinned her lopsided grin, the one that reminded Roxanne of Coop.

"Good suggestion," said Roxanne.

That had gone better than expected, Roxanne thought as she drove the long highway home. Hailey was a useful contact. The information about the Carlsons needed checking out, but she'd best call Inspector Schultz first. He'd need to know if she was going to treat Alan Carlson as a suspect.

21

"HOLY SHIT, I don't like the sound of this. You'd better look into it. Just don't do anything that might rock the boat with Carlson unless you absolutely have to." Inspector Schultz was back at his desk and apologized for missing her when she'd stopped by. His voice crackled over the phone, the rain affecting reception.

"Keep the Andreychuk option open, though. If they're involved in sex trafficking, it's possible they targeted Willa Stein, and maybe she fought back harder than that Stephens girl. We still haven't got the morgue results, so we can't say for sure that Willa was murdered. Not yet anyway."

If they found out Willa was dead before she went into the water, that would prove someone had killed her. Schultz planned to speak with Abdur Farouk over at the morgue himself and push things forward so they could settle that question.

Roxanne could tell he was still hoping to pin this on the Andreychuks, but they also needed proof that Ed and Judith were still involved in the drug trade. Right now, they only knew Cory was involved.

"Keep an eye on them as well and be careful how you go with Carlson. You know, I used to golf with him back when he was deputy minister? It's been hushed up that he's been messing about with women. Nobody told me that was why he quit when he did. That's government for you. How do they expect us to do our job when they don't tell us what's going on?"

And he hung up.

She passed the sunflower field, the heavy flower heads bowed low, soaked from the steady drizzle. At the corner by the Klassens' market garden, she turned off the highway. It wasn't long before she reached the Airbnb where Coop had stayed, then the Carlsons' straw house.

Alan Carlson's Lexus was the only car in the driveway. Andrea must be out. Roxanne turned up her collar against the rain and ran to the front door. She knocked loudly on a wrought iron knocker that looked like Sasha Rosenberg's handiwork. No answer. No matter. She spotted a light on in the window of the big shed beside the house.

Alan opened the door wide, his usual close-lipped, shrewd expression almost breaking into a smile. He was probably wondering why she was here, but his voice didn't show it.

"Roxanne!" he said. "Come in out of that rain."

The room smelled of beeswax and honey. An electric drum, used for separating the honey from the combs, stood near the window. Rows of wooden honeycomb frames hung on a rack. Supplies were neatly arranged on shelves. Rows of golden jars sat on a table. He had been labelling them.

"I need to ask you some questions about the disappearance of Meagan Stephens," Roxanne said.

"Is that right? Haven't I answered those already?" he asked, still pleasant but without inviting her to sit. "I'm not sure that there's much more I can tell you."

"Some points need clarifying. It shouldn't take too much of your time, but it might be best if we talk at the detachment. Then we'll have it on record."

Alan Carlson knew what that signified. She saw it in the cool look he gave her as he took off a large apron and put a sticky brush into a jar of water.

"Well then, let's go do that," he agreed. He needed to go to the house and get a rain jacket. He emerged wearing a cloth cap as well, the brim pulled down, his keys in his hand. "I can take my car? Join you there?" He followed her car to Fiskar Bay and parked the Lexus next to hers outside the detachment.

Perhaps they might have some tea to warm them up on this dreary afternoon, he suggested as she ushered him toward the interview room, acting as if this was a perfectly normal event. Afternoon tea on a rainy afternoon. Todd Brewster did not look pleased to be sent out into the wet to fetch it from Timmies.

Alan Carlson sipped his tea and never raised his voice, but his displeasure became clearer once Roxanne told him what she now knew.

He insisted he had not been dismissed from his government position; he had chosen to retire. None of the allegations against him had been proven. They were quite untrue. Yes, he had visited his colleague at her apartment because she had an autistic son in whom he took a genuine interest. That was the reason for his dropping by as often as he did. The woman had confirmed this when questioned, but in today's climate of false accusations and trial by public opinion, such slander could easily ruin a man's reputation.

He and his wife had decided that the best course of action was for him to apply for early retirement and his request had been accepted immediately. He would have left the government in a few years anyway; plans to retire were already in place. They had purchased land out in the Interlake, and their straw house was nearing completion. They had moved here to begin a new life.

"It would be unfortunate for our fresh start to be tainted by old, unproven lies," he said. He and Andrea hoped to build a new home surrounded by good friends.

What he implied was obvious. The Carlsons had been guests in Roxanne's own home. Interrogating him in an RCMP interview room was not neighbourly. But she needed to continue.

Meagan Stephens had been a frequent visitor, she reminded him.

"Meagan was introduced to my wife by the person she boarded with. And she did not visit regularly," he replied, calm yet alert.

"She helped you with your bees," Roxanne reminded him.

"Hardly. She did help out the day the hive swarmed, but mostly she was with Andrea, in the house, practising crafts. She only came out to the house three, four times, maybe? She wanted to make gifts for her brothers and sisters, I believe. You'd need to ask Andrea about that."

Had he ever met Willa Stein?

"That other girl who drowned? Never. Is that all you need to ask me? I can go?"

He left his empty cup on the table, put on his oiled waterproof jacket and his brimmed cap, looking like an old-world country gentleman.

Ravi Anand joined Roxanne as she watched him drive away.

"You think he might know something?" he asked.

"It was just an idea." Roxanne felt uneasy. "He's so smooth, has all the right answers, as if he's thought it all out before, in case he needs them."

"You think he's lying?"

"Maybe. Or there's something he's hiding."

A message had come in from Abdur Farouk at the morgue. She returned his call. Abdur was annoyed that Inspector Schultz had pressured him to rush the autopsy. Of course it had been a priority, he said abruptly. He'd just finished stitching Willa Stein's body back together.

Willa had been dead before she entered the lake, he explained. Even if she'd hit her head on the end of the pier or on a rock when she jumped, she still would have inhaled water. But that hadn't happened. The blow had come earlier, delivered by something heavy.

"You also autopsied Rob Marsden?" Roxanne asked. "He was hit in the head too."

"Yes, but he was hit from behind, first time. This woman was facing her killer. The blow came at her sideways, like the second blow that Marsden took. The person you are looking for is right-handed," he told her.

As were most people. Alan Carlson was right-handed. She remembered how he had put on his hat. What if Hailey Jenkins was correct and he really had tried to chat up Meagan Stephens? What if Meagan had mentioned it to Willa as they sat in the sunshine on a long August afternoon while children splashed in the water of Cullen Bay and there was nothing much for the beach patrol to do except keep watch, chat to pass the time of day? What if he had made a real move on Meagan; she had resisted and he had killed her? If Willa had suspected that he had killed Meagan and he had found out, he might have made sure to silence her, as well. He was still in his fifties and looked fit. He could have driven her body down to the pier and pushed her over the edge by himself if he needed to.

But if Carlson had killed Meagan, where would he have hidden her body? She recalled the dinner conversation about how he'd spent part of the summer preparing a garden—getting Nick Klassen to till the soil and check the pH balance. How easy would it be to bury a body in a freshly turned vegetable plot?

This was all speculation, all "what if," but it was possible.

Roxanne needed to get to Roberta's house and pick up her daughter. She called Inspector Schultz once more while she drove through the rain.

"It could have happened that way," he agreed. "It's easy enough to find out if there's a body in a newly dug garden. Things are quiet out there at Fiskar Bay, middle of the week. See if Anand can spare a guy to go prod around that vegetable patch in the morning. If he finds something solid buried there, we can dig it up."

Ravi would not be pleased, but it would only take an hour or two of one person's time. The Carlsons would not be happy, either.

When Roxanne arrived at Roberta Axelsson's house, Andrea Carlson was just leaving.

"Lovely baby," she said to Roxanne, seemingly unaware that her husband had been at the Fiskar Bay detachment that very afternoon. "Such a bright little girl. You and Matthew must come to our house for dinner before too long."

Roxanne doubted that would be happening anytime soon, not after she'd brought Alan Carlson in for questioning. She collected Dee and drove home, back to Matt and the rest of her family. The rain had softened into a misty haze. It might clear soon, just in time to inspect the Carlsons' vegetable patch the next morning.

LUCAS BELL WAS working the night shift, cruising the highway and glad that the rain had finally stopped. It was just past one in the morning, with several hours still ahead of him. He was bored. On a whim, he turned down the road that passed the Andreychuk house to take a look. The house stood nestled among the trees. Parked nearby was a truck hitched to a box trailer—likely the one Ed had driven to the abattoir. Ed must have been released. He was back. Both he and Jude were probably inside. The house was dark, and the dogs were quiet.

Lucas was surprised to see a car parked on the grassy verge just past the house, near a stand of trees and close to the car scrapyard. It was hidden in the shadows, out of sight from the Andreychuks' yard light.

He pulled over and killed his headlights, but not before he caught sight of a woman stepping out from the trees, wearing a dark jacket with the hood pulled up, black jeans, and dark boots. She moved toward him like a shadow. Lucas got out of his cruiser cautiously.

"Hey," she said in a loud whisper. "It's okay. Roxanne knows who I am. Hailey Jenkins, PI. Helping with this inquiry."

"There's dogs in that house," he said, also whispering. "You're lucky you didn't disturb them. You're working with Sergeant Calloway?"

"That's right. Surveillance. I'm a specialist. Major Crimes are overstretched these days, y'know?"

"Did you say your name was Jenkins? Like the guy who got killed near here?"

"That's right." The rain had stopped. Above them, clouds scuttled across the sky. Between them were stars and an almost full moon, giving enough light so that Lucas could just make out a pale face, eyes heavily made up. "I'm his daughter."

"And you're a PI? Working with Sergeant Calloway?" He took out his phone, ready to call and check. But she stopped him.

"You don't want to call her at this early," she said. "She's got a baby, so she needs her sleep. You can check tomorrow. See, I'll give you my card." She reached into a pocket.

"What are you doing out here in the middle of the night?"

"I've just placed web cams on the Andreychuk place. Roxanne knows all about it."

That wasn't entirely true. Hailey had suggested surveillance, that was all. She'd thought, after her talk with Roxanne, that she could drive out and do the job tonight, if she could persuade her friend to have Liam for a sleepover.

"What for?" he asked.

"Because the Andreychuks are dealing drugs," Hailey hissed, leaning in close so she wouldn't wake the dogs. "They pass them off to someone through their nephew Cory, who helps get them shipped up north. But Cory's in jail now, right?"

Lucas was impressed. This woman clearly knew what was going on. She had to be working with the Major Crimes Unit if she had information that current. But weren't they investigating the murders?

"They might be connected to trafficking girls," Hailey told him. "I think my dad found out about it, and that's why he was killed. I've just set up a couple of cameras to keep an eye on the Andreychuks, in case someone shows up to drop something off or pick something up. It's possible Ed Andreychuk is smuggling drugs to his cousin Brad in the penitentiary."

She knew about that too. Lucas was even more impressed. This woman knew far more than he did and she must have been given permission to have set up the webcams. She said she needed to get going, had to drive back to Winnipeg. The cameras were connected to monitors at her house, she told him. She'd be keeping watch and would let Roxanne know if she saw anything suspicious.

Lucas let her go and watched as she drove off. Should he call Sergeant Calloway about this? But she already knew—this woman was clearly working for her. He decided he'd just mention the encounter next time he saw the sergeant, so she'd know he was aware of what was happening and staying vigilant.

He turned his cruiser around and drove back up the road, past the sleeping Andreychuks and their quiet dogs. It was almost 2:00 am. Four more hours left in his shift.

22

RAVI RELUCTANTLY AGREED to send Todd Brewster to inspect the Carlsons' vegetable patch the following morning, prodding the soil with an auger. The plot, about forty feet square, was still sodden from the previous day's rain. A third of it was undisturbed, covered with pumpkins and other plants, but the rest needed to be thoroughly checked.

"Trust Calloway to dump a job like this on me," Brewster muttered as he scraped packed mud off the soles of his rubber boots onto the grass.

The job wasn't complicated—he knew what he was looking for. That Stephens girl was still missing, despite signs and messages posted everywhere. Todd had fielded his share of prank calls, listening to people spin long stories, but he was never the one to follow up on them.

"Don't they always keep the best work for themselves." Brewster thrust the rebar down into the dark, damp earth once again, still complaining to himself. He could use a break and a hot drink.

It didn't look like the couple who lived here were going to offer him anything. The Carlson guy had just stood there with his hands in his pockets, eyeing Todd like some kind of inspector. Someone had mentioned he'd been a big shot in the government before retiring. Then he wandered off into the trees. His wife had stepped outside in a floaty skirt that reached her ankles, standing silently on the back step. Big purple glasses. She looked at Todd, flapped her hands, and went back inside. Wouldn't she have known if that man had really killed the girl and dug a hole big enough to bury her?

Six feet under, right? He had to poke way down. If there was a body buried here, he hoped he would find it soon, then the MCU would send out a crew to deal with it and he'd be done. He saw the man go back into the house.

He plodded on, thrust down the auger and hauled it up, again and again, with stops to clean the dirt off his boots. He'd just started on the next section when he heard a car start at the front of the house. He straightened up and stretched. The woman drove off in a dark blue Subaru in a big hurry.

ROXANNE CALLOWAY WAS at home. It was Wednesday, the day that Matt was supposed to take Dee to work, but he had an appointment that couldn't be rescheduled at short notice. That was okay, Roxanne had said. She'd drop Dee off at the office later that morning. She didn't really mind. She needed to stay away from the Carlson dig and wait for results.

Ravi Anand hadn't been pleased about having to send a man to examine the Carlsons' garden, but he'd complied. It left him one man short, and he just hoped nothing else came up that needed RCMP attention. It was a messy job Brewster had been asked to do, and all based on a guess, wasn't it? Roxanne didn't have proof. The accusations against Carlson had never been substantiated. She didn't even know for sure if he'd ever molested Meagan Stephens.

Ravi was usually on Roxanne's side. She knew that he was frustrated, that she'd pressured him into sending his constable out to dig. Yes, the MCU should do their own dirty work, she had agreed, but that garden needed to be searched, and things were usually quiet in Fiskar Bay, middle of the week in September. He could spare one man for a morning?

"Well, let's hope it's not a waste of time," Ravi had replied.

Roxanne needed some fresh air. She put Dee into a stroller and set off down the driveway. The dogs tagged along. With no cars on the country road that ran past their house there was no need to leash them. They stayed close, sniffing along the ditch, enjoying their freedom. Roxanne began to jog once she reached the road, pushing Dee in front of her. The baby laughed—she thought that was fun. Roxanne used to run daily. She ought to get back into the habit. She should do it daily, with Dee strapped into the stroller, when she had the time, like now.

A car turned the corner up ahead, heading straight toward her. Roxanne stopped and called the dogs in to leash them. The car screeched to a halt on the other side of the road. The door flew open, and Andrea Carlson jumped out, slamming it behind her.

"What do you think you're doing?" she yelled. "You interrogated my husband, and now there's some RCMP guy trampling all over our garden, poking holes in it. And you've got cameras up in our trees spying on us?"

Joshua, the terrier, started barking furiously. Dee began to wail, startled by the noise and the red-faced, screaming woman. "Shush," Roxanne said, reaching down to scoop up her baby.

"What did you just say?" she called to Andrea as she unstrapped Dee. "About cameras?"

"In our trees, trained on our house. And one next door on the house that we rent out. That's unlawful! A breach of privacy!"

Andrea was wearing a colourful jacket over a long skirt and mauve glasses, but she was missing her usual makeup and her hair was unkempt. She must have left the house in a rush. She was still shouting. Joshua growled. Dee wrapped her arms around Roxanne's neck and whimpered, hanging on tight.

"Stop yelling! You're scaring my child," said Roxanne. "Tell me, what cameras?"

"Like you don't know!" Andrea remained loudly furious. She stayed by her car and didn't come closer. "My husband's done nothing wrong. All those accusations, that's all they ever were. What's this vendetta you're waging against us, now, wrecking our lives out here? Are you that desperate to find a killer? You'll find nothing at our house. We're registering a complaint."

Andrea yanked her car door open and jumped back inside. Roxanne held Dee close with one arm and kept a firm grip on Joshua's leash with the other. He was barking again. Maisie, the Lab, loped after the Subaru but trotted back once the car turned the corner and disappeared. Roxanne soothed her daughter. Dee still clung to her, whimpering. As soon as she had calmed her down and settled her back into the stroller, Roxanne pulled out her phone. She needed to call Hailey Jenkins. Those cameras must be her doing.

Hailey was unapologetic. Sure, she'd planted cameras at the Carlsons' place, she answered. It was against the law? She didn't know that. Oops. She was watching the feed right now. A police car was parked by the roadside and a uniformed man in boots had just walked around to the back of the house, carrying some kind of long pole. It was a shame she'd wasted a camera on the rented house next door—nothing was happening there. She should've placed that one around the back of the Carlsons' property instead, while she had the chance.

"That's your guy out back, right?"

Roxanne did not respond to that. "You should have told me you wanted to put those cameras up," she said. "We should have had a warrant. You didn't do a great job of hiding one of them, either. One of the Carlsons noticed it."

"You're kidding. Someone's got good eyes. And a good reason to be looking," said Hailey. "Didn't you know I'd put them up?"

"No, I did not. You never said."

"Well, you should have been told. I was seen. A young cop caught me over at the Andreychuk house, around one this morning. I'd just finished putting up the ones there. We had a good chat, him and me."

"I haven't been into the office," said Roxanne. "I'm at home."

"Well, that's your problem, don't blame me," Hailey said, as contrary and unapologetic as her late father. "I'm watching the Andreychuk house right now. Ed's back, did you know? He's unhitching the box trailer from the back of his truck."

"Has anyone dropped by?" Roxanne asked, curious in spite of herself. "It's around this time of the month that he usually goes to visit Brad in the penitentiary."

"Haven't seen anyone yet. I'll let you know if someone shows up. But, hey, Andrea Carlson's back at her house, in her Sube." Hailey must have all her monitors open so she could keep an eye on both houses. "She's just stomping in the door. Looks real pissed off."

Andrea must have driven to Roxanne's house as soon as she knew about the cameras. Soon her husband would be calling HQ to complain.

"You need to shut off those cameras," said Roxanne, "until we get them approved."

"Who's 'we'?" Hailey shot right back. But she agreed to do it, for now.

"Funny kind of house, isn't it?" Hailey was still looking at the screen, while she could. "Got real thick walls. I can see the window wells."

"It's built out of straw bales."

"So you could hide a body right inside one of them, couldn't you? Meagan Stephens wasn't all that big. Maybe she's not in the garden after all."

That wasn't something Roxanne wanted to hear—but Hailey might be right. Hadn't Alan Carlson helped build the straw house? Stacked bales to form the walls, then coated them with a layer of concrete? What would it take to remove a section of that outer layer, hide a body inside, pack it tight with straw again, and patch it over with fresh concrete? Was that even possible? Roxanne hoped Todd would find something in the garden instead. She really didn't want to go to the inspector and suggest they start tearing holes in the walls of the Carlsons' newly built house.

A new call was coming in. It was Schultz.

"Got to go, Hailey."

"Okay. I'll keep looking. Will let you know if I see anything interesting."

Roxanne had no authority over Hailey. What she chose to do as a private investigator was her own business, but Inspector Schultz was worried. The superintendent had received a call from Carlson complaining about breach of privacy, police harassment and damage to his property. What was this about cameras, trained on the house?

"Not my doing. Jenkins's daughter works as a PI. She's investigating on her own behalf and she put up the cameras."

"You know her?"

"We talk now and then," Roxanne admitted. "She's a useful source of information."

"Isn't she bit too close to the case?"

"Yes, but she worked alongside her father and she wants to know who killed him. The Stephens family hired them to find their missing daughter, as well. She knows what he was working on before he was killed."

"She told you she was going to rig those cameras?"

"She mentioned surveillance. That's all."

"You've told her that they need to come down?"

"I just talked with her."

"You didn't charge her?"

"No, I didn't. She's new to investigation. I think her father rigged webcams wherever he liked. Coop Jenkins liked to bend the rules and she's learned from him. It's maybe not her fault."

"You need to back off on that relationship, just to be on the safe side," he said. "Carlson was never proved guilty of doing anything wrong. He wasn't fired; he retired, and he's still got good friends that he talks to. Wait and see if anything shows up in the garden."

"I hear you, sir," she said. "But the webcams are a good idea. I'd like to reactivate them."

"Shit, Calloway. You might be right, but Carlson still has strong connections."

"Yes," she agreed. "And he's probably taken down the cameras already. But I think there's illegal activity going on at the Andreychuk residence. That site's worth keeping an eye on. I need permission to use the ones there. Can you hurry it through?"

Schultz laughed. "You're chancing it, Roxanne. But okay. Let's hope something shows up there." The garden probe could continue at the Carlsons, he told her, since it was already in progress. But that was all that must happen there, for now.

LUCAS BELL SHOWED up early for work, hoping to tell Sergeant Calloway about his strange encounter outside the Andreychuk residence the night before, but she wasn't in her office upstairs. Instead, Corporal Anand wanted to have a word with him.

"Have you discovered a woman claiming to be a private investigator, running around the neighbourhood rigging illegal cameras on houses in the middle of the night?" Anand asked.

"Well, yes," Lucas stammered, "but she said she was working with the Major Crimes Unit. I thought she was allowed."

"Why did you not include that in your report from yesterday?"

"It's MCU business. I came in early to check with Sergeant Calloway in person, but she's not here yet."

"And how do you know the woman was telling the truth?"

"She gave me her business card," Lucas said. He pulled it out from his wallet and handed it to Anand, who examined it and then kept it.

He was told that the woman had placed other cameras and that complaints had been made against the detachment. It would have helped if Corporal Anand had known about this before getting a call from the Superintendent. What Constable Bell needed to understand was that he reported directly to Anand as his immediate superior—not to the Major Crimes Unit. The detachment's lines of communication had to be followed. Those were the rules.

Lucas realized he had embarrassed his boss. He mumbled an apology and promised not to repeat the mistake.

He did as he was told, went outside, and started up a car, ready for a few more hours on highway patrol. He knew he'd screwed up, but didn't think it was that bad. He'd fully intended to tell Sergeant Calloway, and he'd been interested in what Hailey Jenkins had been doing. He was glad he'd entered her number into his phone. He might want to keep in touch.

23

AN AMBULANCE SHRIEKED down Fiskar Bay's main street just as Lucas Bell was driving out of town. The message to turn back came within seconds. There had been an accident at the building site near the harbour. Lucas was to go there instead. One of the Ukrainian workers had slipped and fallen five storeys. He was unconscious, seriously injured—broken bones, possibly a spinal injury, and a blow to the head. He needed to be rushed to Winnipeg.

Aimee Vermette arrived at the scene first. Work had stopped, and the crew stood in small clusters near the temporary office hut. Several of the men, recent Ukrainian immigrants, spoke quietly among themselves in their own language. The foreman told Aimee he had no idea how Vassily Kovalenko could have fallen. He was one of the most careful men on the crew.

But Mike McBain knew why. He stomped up to Aimee and Lucas in his heavy work boots, his hardhat placed squarely on his head.

"Vassily's been worried sick. You guys have been picking on him and me ever since we found that dead guy down near Cullen Village. Roxanne Calloway's been by, asking questions. Vassily needs to keep his nose clean if he wants to stay in this country, not that he's done anything wrong, but she's got him scared. Depressed, y'know?

"His brother's fighting in that war and he's gone missing. There's no one to look after their mother back home. He's got too much on his mind, so he stepped wrong up there on the scaffolding and lost his balance. That's all it took. Now he won't be going anywhere and it shouldn't be this way. You guys and Roxanne Calloway are kinda to blame for this."

He strutted back to the work crew. Some of the Ukrainian workers looked impressed that he'd spoken up to the RCMP. "Mike's got a sister that's one of them," a local worker muttered loudly enough for Aimee and Lucas to hear. Aimee rolled her eyes.

"Are you going to be seeing the Sarge soon?" she asked Lucas.

"I'm not telling her what he said." Lucas remembered what he'd been told about lines of communication. Sometimes the rules could work in your favour. "That's Corporal Anand's job."

"Yeah," said Aimee. "But we're the ones that heard Mike speak. It's best that one of us tells her ourselves."

The ambulance pulled away, siren blaring and lights flashing. It wasn't going to waste any time getting Vassily Kovalenko to a hospital in the city. In the meantime, one of the officers needed to climb up inside the building to take measurements and photograph the spot where Vassily had fallen.

"You'll need proper work boots," Aimee said, eyeing the shoes on Lucas's feet. "Go over to the detachment and get a pair while I take statements."

As the senior officer present, Aimee had decided Lucas would be the one to go up. That was okay with him. He was comfortable with heights, and he'd much rather be here than out patrolling the highway yet again.

While he was at the detachment, he'd also get the chance to pass along what Mike had said to Ravi Anand, just like Aimee had instructed. Lucas planned to cover all his bases—stick to the rules and do everything by the book.

HAILEY JENKINS SAT in her Winnipeg home, eyes fixed on the monitor showing the Andreychuks' front yard and front door. It was still active. Roxanne had just sent an email saying her boss was getting it approved, but she saw no reason to wait for official permission. It was just as well she was watching. An SUV had just pulled up next to Ed's truck. The man who got out was white, clean-shaven, and possibly in his fifties. He had grey hair, stood above average height, and was of medium build; he was reasonably fit. He wore grey pants, a navy bomber-style jacket, and black shoes. Hailey watched as he lifted a cardboard box from the back of the SUV, along with a smaller package.

The door to the house opened. Two blue heelers rushed out, barking as usual, but the man didn't act surprised, so this probably wasn't his first visit. A large woman was standing in the doorway. She seemed pleased to see him. So did her small Jack Russell, which stood at her feet wagging his tail. She welcomed the man in and closed the door, leaving the heelers outside to keep guard.

Hailey replayed that section of the video. The best view she could get of the man's face was from the side, but she managed to zoom in and enlarge the image. She sent both the video clip and a screenshot to Roxanne Calloway.

Roxanne was fairly sure she recognized the man's face as someone she'd seen around Cullen Village. She couldn't use this as evidence, not yet, but it wouldn't hurt to find out who he actually was. Dee was just waking from a nap and needed to be fed and changed. Once that was done, Roxanne loaded her into the car, left the dogs at home, and drove to Roberta Axelsson's house. Roberta knew almost everyone in Cullen Village; she might be able to identify him.

Another text came in from Hailey. The man had left the Andreychuk house without his packages. He'd stopped in just long enough to make the delivery.

Roberta was not home. Roxanne bit her lip. Who else could she ask? Margo Wishart wasn't as socially connected in the village as Roberta, but she might be able to help. She drove to Margo's lakeshore house. Roberta's old beige Buick was parked in the driveway and so was a dark blue Subaru. Andrea Carlson must be inside as well. Visiting right now was not an option.

Roxanne took off around a corner, so no one in Margo's house would see her drive by, and went straight to the highway. It was almost noon. She could drop Dee off with Matt's assistant, Julie Ann, and go talk to Ravi Anand, to warn him that some action was happening at the Andreychuk house.

Julie Ann was young and blonde, a true Icelander. She looked surprised at being asked to babysit. She didn't expect Matt back in the office for an hour at least, but she took Dee from Roxanne and said she'd manage.

Ravi listened, looking tired. He'd agreed to send Brewster to the Carlson garden, but the search was taking longer than expected and seemed to be a complete waste of time. And now Roxanne wanted him to send someone over to keep an eye on the Andreychuk place on the off chance she might find some evidence? Didn't she know that there had been an accident at the new building site near the harbour? Vermette and Bell were still on scene.

Roxanne hadn't heard anything about it.

"No? He fell a couple of hours ago. One of the Ukrainians, right off the fifth floor. You know him. It's Mike's Ukrainian friend."

"Vassily Kovalenko?"

"He's badly hurt. They had to rush him to Winnipeg. And Mike's been mouthing off about police harassment. He says you got the guy so worried that he's been depressed lately. Distracted at work. Says that we're to blame—you especially."

"I didn't make him fall! I just asked the usual questions. I had to do that." But Roxanne was dismayed. That kind of talk gave her and the RCMP a bad name, and she was sorry that Vassily was injured.

Ravi's curiosity did get the better of him, however. He looked at the headshot she showed him. He didn't recognize the man, but Jan Bjornson, his civilian office manager did.

"That's Emil Sorensen," she said. "He lives down at the far end of Cullen Village. He's a guard at the penitentiary."

"Really? There's the connection between Ed and Brad Andreychuk! He could have been making a drug delivery," Roxanne said to Ravi. "That house has to be watched."

"Ask Inspector Schultz to send someone. I can't help you, Roxanne. I've no one else to spare—you know that." Ravi turned on his heel into his office and closed the door.

"Don't mind him." Jan spoke quietly, sharing office gossip. "He's had a disappointment. He applied for a job running the detachment at Minnedosa, but he didn't get it. It's too bad, not that I want him gone, but you'll be back here soon, won't you?" she said.

"That's a shame. Maybe he'll have better luck next time." Roxanne knew first-hand that old prejudices still existed in the force. She'd faced it herself and knew that Ravi's turban had raised a few eyebrows in Fiskar Bay when he had first arrived. She hoped things would work out for Ravi. He deserved a promotion.

She went upstairs and called the penitentiary. It took time and some persuasion, but she was finally passed to the head of security and discovered that Emil Sorensen was due to start a shift at 6:00 pm.

Finding out what was in the packages he'd dropped off was a priority. Roxanne could hand the case over to the drug unit, but that would mean admitting the video evidence had come from an unauthorized source. The cameras were obviously still running. There was no sign of that warrant yet. What she needed was hard evidence that the guard and the Andreychuks were couriering drugs for Brad. Roxanne doubted Ed and Jude would keep the goods in the house for long. What she needed was someone to watch the house and follow them if necessary, but the detachment was overstretched. There was no one available to send. That meant Roxanne would have to do it herself for now.

She drove down the highway west of Fiskar Bay—the one that led directly to Winnipeg. It ran between the Andreychuk farm and the prison. She hoped she was right: that Ed would head out in that direction, or someone coming to collect the packages would come that way.

There was an old farm at the corner of the Andreychuks' road. No one lived there anymore. She pulled into the overgrown driveway, her car hidden behind a stand of trees. The sun was already low in the western sky, but it would be hours before dark. If she had to work late, that was fine. Dee would be with her daddy by now, and Matt could manage things until she got home. A ladybug landed on the windshield. Otherwise, everything was still.

Within the hour, a message came in from Ravi: Todd Brewster had finished poking around the Carlsons' garden. There was no body. She'd been wrong about that. But shortly afterward, the warrant for surveillance of the Andreychuk residence came through. She called Hailey.

"Great," said Hailey. "Liam's gone to bed. I'm onto it."

IN MARGO WISHART'S kitchen, Margo and Roberta Axelsson listened as Andrea Carlson stood by the window, too agitated to sit. A glass of wine in her hand, she launched into a rant about how the RCMP sergeant who lived nearby was tormenting her and her husband.

"That woman's out of control," Andrea snapped. "She's got it into her head that Meagan Stephens—the missing girl—is buried in our garden. Can you believe it? There's a Mountie out there right now, stomping around in muddy boots and making a mess."

She took a long drink before continuing.

"Roxanne Calloway has somehow convinced the RCMP that Alan had something to do with Meagan's disappearance. All because we were kind to her." Andrea turned to face them. "I tried to help that girl. She was interested in art, so I invited her over. We did some painting and collage—just a couple of afternoons, that's all. And when she got curious about beekeeping, Alan let her help when he took down a swarm from one of our trees. She loved it. She was so appreciative." Her voice cracked with indignation.

"And now? This is how we're repaid? Alan is being treated like a murderer?"

She drained the last of her wine and held out her glass for a refill, then launched right back in: Matt Stavros seemed like a nice man. He'd invited them over for dinner one night. He'd cooked it himself. That Roxanne hadn't lifted a finger to help. What on earth did he see in her? She was a cold fish. Older than him too, wasn't she? Roberta was babysitting for her? Why? Couldn't she afford proper daycare?

"She's got Dee's name on a list." Roberta came to Roxanne's defence, but Andrea ignored what she had said.

One thing was for sure. Roxanne Calloway wouldn't be sitting down to dinner at Andrea and Alan's house any day soon.

Margo looked out the window. The light was fading now, but the lake still reflected the last glimmers of it. She could make out the black silhouettes of geese resting on the silvery, still water, with more arriving to land. At least a hundred of them were gathered along her small stretch of lakeshore, with many hundreds more scattered between here and Fiskar Bay, preparing for their southward migration.

Roxanne must have her reasons to suspect the Carlsons, Margo thought. Alan wasn't yet sixty, and she knew he had been high up in government. Hadn't he been deputy minister of the Environment? He'd retired early. Once her guests had gone, Margo called a friend of hers, a woman architect who taught occasionally at the university, as she did, part time.

"Oh, Carlson!" her colleague laughed. "He's too good-looking for his own good. One of those guys who acts like he's doing women a favour if he takes an interest in her and he's been getting away with it for years. I was warned off him long ago. Not that he ever tried anything with me. I've heard he's developed a taste for younger women now, so I suppose I needn't worry," she laughed. "The story is that someone who worked with him complained. Next thing we all knew, Alan had discovered that he had an urgent need to retire early so he could go out into the country and learn about bees. He was never charged with anything, as far as I know. He got to leave quietly and keep his pension."

That explained why Roxanne was professionally interested in Alan Carlson. One predatory man and one missing student? Little wonder she was looking into their vegetable plot. Margo felt she should tell Roberta. She didn't want Roberta thinking poorly of Roxanne. The problem was, Roberta couldn't keep a secret.

Roxanne probably already knew what Margo had just learned, but still, she'd mention it when the chance came up. Email didn't seem appropriate—it was better suited to a quiet word, in person.

24

ROXANNE WAS SELDOM alone. Finn had been home all summer and Dee had needed a lot of attention. Now, she flipped between work and her domestic life. The only time she was ever by herself seemed to be when she was in the car, as she was now. It was a rare luxury. She sat behind the trees and watched the sun go down. A pair of crows flew in to roost nearby. They squawked at her but then settled onto a branch.

She should call Izzy McBain while she waited, to let her know she might have a lead on the drug case Izzy was investigating up north. It would also be a chance to bring up what was going on with Izzy's brother, Mike, and see if Izzy could talk some sense into him, get him to stop spreading damaging rumours. But for now, she put it off, choosing instead to enjoy the quiet.

The yellow glow from the Andreychuk yard shone between a row of old willows. A light had clicked on at dusk. It must be on a timer. She couldn't see the door to the house, but any car coming or going would be easy to spot. There was hardly anyone out driving this time of night, in the middle of the week; no one else on this back road. She wanted to close her eyes. She rarely got more than six hours' sleep these days, but she couldn't afford to nap right now.

It was nearly eight o'clock, just after sunset, when a truck pulled out of the yard and headed in her direction. Roxanne watched it pass and saw Ed alone in the driver's seat. He wasn't in a rush. He reached the road end and turned onto the main highway leading straight south toward Winnipeg. She waited a moment, then followed at a distance. Nothing separated his vehicle from hers. He settled into a steady speed of 109 kilometres per hour, just over the limit. Keeping up with him was easy.

"He's left the house," Hailey Jenkins said into her phone.

"I know. I'm following him right now." Roxanne watched his tail lights glowing in the darkness ahead.

"He was carrying a box, bigger than the last one, open at the top," said Hailey. "You going to be okay? Have you got backup? In case you need it?"

Hailey was right. If Roxanne needed to make an arrest she should have someone at her side. "Got to go," she said, "I'll call you later. Let you know what happens."

Ravi had made it clear that she was placing too many demands on the Fiskar Bay RCMP, but she called the station anyway. Aimee Vermette answered. Lucas was out on patrol, she said and she'd send him for now. But first: where exactly was Roxanne?

"I don't want to scare Andreychuk off," she said. "He's just turning off the highway onto the road to Gunstone. Tell Lucas to get close but not draw any attention to himself and get him to call me."

Gunstone Road ran right past the federal prison—a formidable structure built on raised ground, visible for miles and silhouetted against the night sky. The building was brightly lit, enclosed by high chain-link fences topped with coils of barbed wire. Ed must be heading there to make a delivery. Roxanne called the head of security to warn him: something might happen soon nearby. The suspect she was following was now within four kilometres of the prison.

"We're all closed up. Do you think he's got a drone?" asked the man. "That he's going to fly something over the wall?"

"I wouldn't be surprised," said Roxanne.

Ed was slowing down, turning into the driveway of a nearby marshland nature reserve beloved of birdwatchers and environmentalists. Birds would be settling for the night in its wetlands, but Ed didn't go far enough in to disturb them. He stopped the truck just off the road. Roxanne drove past him.

A farmyard appeared up ahead, with a side road leading to a barn set apart from the farmhouse. Hopefully, no one would notice her. She turned off her headlights and eased the car in behind a shelterbelt of spruce trees. Lucas called in. Aimee had told him where Roxanne was heading and he was already on the highway, just minutes away.

She nosed the car forward for a better view. The cab lights were on in Ed's truck. The passenger door stood open, and he was outside, messing about with something on the front seat. He lifted it out, and the door slammed shut behind him. In his hands, lights flashed, red and white. It had to be a drone. He was still fussing around with it.

Lucas called again. He was turning onto the Gunstone road. "Get here now," she told him. "I'll close in from the other side as soon as I see you coming." Just then she saw flashing lights rise from Ed's hands and soar off into the sky. A red glow indicated that the drone was heading directly toward the prison.

Seconds later, she heard a siren. Bright, flashing lights approached from the east as Lucas sped toward the scene. Ed Andreychuk noticed, too. By the time he reached his driver's door and opened it, Roxanne had slammed her car to a stop, blocking the road in his direction. Lucas Bell did the same from the other side.

A cloud of birds burst from the tall marsh grass, honking and quacking as they darkened the night sky. Lucas reached Ed's truck first. Ed stood at the open driver's door, hands in the air, illuminated by the cab light. Lucas made his first arrest, handcuffed Ed, and led him to the police car.

Roxanne texted her contact at the prison: a drone was on its way. The controls were on the driver's seat of the truck, where Ed had dropped them. She just hoped the package had made it— that Ed hadn't aborted the flight, and it wasn't lying in a field somewhere between here and its destination.

She didn't need to worry. Just as she and Lucas were preparing to leave the marsh and head back to Fiskar Bay to book Ed Andreychuk, her phone rang. Emil Sorensen, the guard, had stepped into the exercise yard just before the drone came in to land. They'd caught both the drone and Sorensen.

She followed Lucas back to Fiskar Bay, watched him sign Ed Andreychuk in and lock him into a cell, then they went to pick up Jude. The dogs barked as they walked up to the door.

"I can take the Jack Russell with me," Lucas offered. "The heelers can manage if someone comes by and feeds them, but that little guy's a house pet. He can stay at my place until they tell us where he should go."

"I'll be out soon," Jude told him as they shut her in the back of the cruiser. "Then I'll come and get him. Kibble's at the back door."

"You're too soft, Constable," Roxanne said, as she slammed the car door shut, but that did solve one problem. Neither Jude nor Ed would be going home any time soon. Lucas might have the dog for a while.

Once they were back at the detachment, she tried speaking to each of the Andreychuks in turn, but both clammed up. She called Inspector Schultz at home. He didn't mind being disturbed for good news.

"I'll talk to the drug unit and get those two picked up first thing tomorrow," he said. Ed and Jude wouldn't say anything about smuggling girls if it was happening too, but maybe that prison guard had heard something. Sorensen must be shitting himself. He might crack under a bit of pressure.

"Good work, Calloway!" the inspector said. "You sure you don't want to come back to the MCU full-time? We could use you here."

That wasn't going to happen—not with two kids to take care of out in the Interlake—but Roxanne was pleased to be asked. She texted Hailey Jenkins, and the reply was a simple thumbs-up emoji. That was it.

It was past eleven when Roxanne got home. Finn and Dee were sound asleep in their beds but Matt was waiting up for her on the sofa, watching TV, a dog on either side of him.

"You're home," he said, his eyes still on the screen.

"Hey, guess what happened! I nailed the Andreychuks tonight. Ed was sending drugs to his cousin in jail by drone."

"That right?" He didn't ask the dogs to move so she could sit beside him, but he did click off the TV.

"I did a stakeout!" she told him, still pleased with herself. "I haven't done one of those in years."

"Good for you," he said. "So now you're working on a drug case as well as murder?"

"It's all related, I'm sure of it." She walked into the kitchen area. Matt might not feel like celebrating with her, but she was going to have a glass of wine.

"You didn't remember that your son had tryouts for hockey tonight and you had said you would be there?" His words stopped her, just as she was reaching for a bottle of red.

"Sorry," she said. "I clean forgot."

"We managed," he replied, eyes still on the screen. "But you can't dump Dee on Julie Ann, like you did today, without asking either. I don't pay her to babysit."

"It was just for an hour."

"I got held up. It was longer."

"That's not my fault. This was your day to take care of Dee anyway." Roxanne was taken aback. She had expected congratulations, not this. "What's up with you?" she leaned onto the counter, annoyed and disappointed at his reaction. "I had work that needed doing. I caught drug smugglers tonight. Isn't that important?"

"Couldn't someone else have done that? Why does it always have to be you, Roxanne?"

He clicked off the TV and rose from the sofa. The dogs stayed where they were but watched his every move.

"This case is getting more and more complicated," he continued. "It's taking up more and more of your time. Maybe going back to the Major Crimes Unit before we'd found adequate child care wasn't such a good idea." He walked toward her but stopped at the archway between the living area and the kitchen, leaning against it with his hands tucked into his pockets.

"Roberta and Vera are good mothers who know how to raise babies," she protested, pouring herself a glass of wine. "Dee has always been in good hands. And today Dee was your responsibility. It's not my fault that you got held up on a job and weren't there when you were supposed to. Not my problem, Matt."

"Yeah, you're right. But the thing is, I've got demands on my time too. I was going to call you and ask you to pick up Finn, because Pete McBain needed to meet with me. He's buying another piece of land and had to get the offer in right away, so I needed to stay late. Instead, I had to call Pete and cancel. I told him I'd come over to his place as soon as you got home, but guess what? You didn't.

"And you know what he told me, Roxanne? He said people around town are saying you've been bullying that poor Ukrainian guy who fell off the building he was working on. That you've got him scared, that he's worried he'll be deported if he's in trouble with the law. That he's depressed. That he didn't fall. He jumped."

"What? That's not true. It was an accident." The glass of wine remained untouched. "And I didn't bully him. I just needed to ask him questions. I had to. He and Mike found Coop Jenkins's body and he was at a party in Willa Stein's house."

"Yes, but he's vulnerable, Roxanne. He's only in the country temporarily. Pete says the guy has a brother in the Ukrainian army who's gone missing, and a mother he's trying to bring over. He's under a lot of stress and Mike's been telling people you didn't go easy on him.

"You worked hard when you were running the detachment here to make the RCMP seem more approachable. *Community policing*, you called it. But talk like this isn't good for your reputation.

"It's great you caught those guys tonight, but you need to remember that my work matters too. There are other people in the RCMP. If you can't do the job, someone else will. I work for myself—you know that. If something comes up, there's no one to step in for me. I can't afford to have people saying I'm unreliable.

"And, yes, today was my day to take care of Dee. I'll talk to Julie Ann and make sure that my schedule's clear on Wednesdays from now on, but just until you're back on your real job, okay? We need to get this babysitting problem sorted out by then."

"Now, if you don't mind, I need to get to bed. I've got an early start. I said I'd meet Pete before eight tomorrow. Finn's taking the bus to school, he won't need a ride."

Matt turned around and went upstairs. His dogs jumped from the sofa and trotted up behind him.

Roxanne screwed the cap back on the wine bottle and poured the glassful down the sink. She didn't want it any more.

Matt was feeling guilty for not holding up his end of the babysitting deal, and he was dumping that guilt on her. But that wasn't her fault. He was right about Finn, though, she had screwed up by missing his practice. She'd need to make it up to him. Maybe plan something special for the weekend, just the two of them. And Dee? She was fine for now. Roberta and Vera were both good sitters. The arrangement wasn't perfect, but it was the best she could do for now.

The news about Vassily was more troubling. It was too bad that he'd fallen. She'd call tomorrow to find out how badly he was injured. He couldn't have jumped. Or could he? It had to have been an accident, she assured herself. There was a woman in Fiskar Bay who made floral arrangements. She'd pick up a bouquet and a get-well card to bring to Vassily Kovalenko's wife.

Those rumours had to be quashed. Matt was right: she had worked hard to build a good relationship with the town of Fiskar Bay. She didn't want to wreck that now. She'd be back in her old office in December, back to her real job, as Matt had called it.

She'd had such a good time tonight and had felt so alive. She'd done well; even Schultzy had said so. He'd hinted there might be a place for her back in the MCU, if she wanted it. Sure, there were risks, but investigating was what she did best.

Still, the reason she'd left all those years ago hadn't changed. All policing was dangerous, but working in the MCU meant regular contact with hardened criminals. She had a family to think about. Going back wasn't an option.

She went to the sofa and turned the TV back on. She was wide awake and needed something to distract her if she was going to fall asleep. Even so, the night had gone well. She couldn't help thinking Matt could have been a little more appreciative.

25

THURSDAY MORNING WAS more hectic than usual, Matt hurrying out the door to meet Pete McBain before eight, Finn getting ready to leave for school on the yellow school bus. Matt had been sound asleep by the time Roxanne had gone to bed and now he was being polite. That was fine with her, she told herself. At least he wasn't criticizing her. He'd get over it, she was sure. Matt could never stay in a bad mood for long. Finn seemed to be his usual self.

"Sorry I missed the tryouts," she said.

"It's okay. I'll be on the team for sure. No big deal," he replied, hauling on his backpack. So what had Matt been complaining about?

"How about we do something together on Saturday," she said. "Go to Winnipeg and watch a movie? Just the two of us?'

"Nah." He shoved his feet into his runners. "I said I'd go to Noah's. We're doing a science project."

"Okay. Maybe another time."

"Sure, Mom." He disappeared out the door. Finn was growing up and didn't miss her one bit, she told herself. Matt had got that wrong too.

She yawned. She hadn't got enough sleep last night, but Dee needed to be readied and packed up for a day at Vera Klassen's. When she got there, jars full of pink jelly stood in a row on a counter near the stove.

"Crab apple. I'll send some home with you. I potted it last night. Didn't want to be messing about with hot jam when missy here is in the kitchen," Vera said, reaching out to take Dee. The baby stretched towards her, all smiles, happy to see her. Why was Matt complaining? Vera provided perfectly good care. It was too bad she was only available one day a week.

Roxanne got to Fiskar Bay, wondering what kind of reception she'd receive from Ravi, since she'd borrowed Constable Bell last night without asking him, but he seemed cheerful as well. The Andreychuks were about to be driven off in a van sent by the drug unit. Brad might be kept in jail a little longer because of this, and out of Ravi's hair. That was always a good thing, he told her.

"Lucas Bell had a good experience last night," he added. "I read his report." So Roxanne was forgiven for taking Lucas away from highway patrol.

"Sorry you didn't get the Minnedosa job," she said. "You didn't ask me for a reference."

"You were off duty." He tucked his hands into his uniform pockets and rocked back on his heels. "They needed one from my immediate superior."

"Well," she said. "That'll probably be me next time. I'll make sure it's a good one."

She called the florist and ordered a bouquet of cut flowers. As soon as they were ready, she picked them up and brought them to Zlata Kovalenko's door. Another woman, also a recent Ukrainian immigrant, answered. She explained she was looking after Zlata's son while he was off school due to his father's accident. She didn't invite Roxanne in, instead standing just inside the doorway. All the Ukrainian immigrants were shaken by what had happened, she said. Zlata was in Winnipeg, staying at the hospital. She hadn't left Vassily's side. He'd needed surgery on his leg and had multiple fractures. Recovery would take a long time, and he might have to walk with a cane. He wouldn't be able to work as a labourer anymore. Zlata didn't know how they'd manage financially. The woman wasn't particularly friendly, but she accepted the flowers and said she'd make sure Zlata got them.

"And tell her I am sorry," Roxanne said.

"Yes." The woman looked sternly at her. "I will do that," she said as she closed the door.

Roxanne could tell she was being held at least partly responsible for what had happened to Vassily. She shouldn't have apologized. She'd only meant she was sorry he was hurt, but her words could have been misinterpreted. She wasn't responsible for the accident—she was sure of that. She should track down Mike McBain, find out exactly what he and others were saying. But the building site was shut down for the day because of the accident, and Mike was probably still at home, asleep. She'd have to wait to talk to him.

In the meantime, a message had come in from the drug unit. The Andreychuks were still staying silent, but the prison guard, Emil Sorensen, had responded well to the suggestion that cooperating might reduce his charges. They told him they'd do what they could to keep him out of jail if he came clean. He'd definitely lose his job, but since this was his first offence, he might get off with community service. After all, he'd only made deliveries. He confessed to what he did. He was sent a message online, telling him where to pick up the drug packages, then he passed them along to Brad's relatives at the farm. Ed would fly them over the prison wall at night, when the yard was empty and things were quiet. Sorensen would retrieve them and pass them on to Brad.

He freaked at the suggestion that there was far more to Brad's business than moving drugs around. Stolen goods? What about girls? Sex trafficking? No way that was going on, he insisted. He'd have heard. Some of the inmates knew that he did the odd job for Brad, helped keep them supplied with dope, and they told him lots in return. Wanted to keep on his good side. He was sure he'd have heard if anything like that was going on, for sure.

Roxanne hung up. If Sorensen was telling the truth, then the Andreychuks hadn't sent Meagan Stephens out west into the sex trade.

But what if she'd found out about the drugs? That would have been a good reason to silence her for good. There were plenty of places to hide a body, especially in the car graveyard behind the farmhouse. Ed could call a scrap disposal company to haul away a load of cars. They'd be crushed flat and Meagan could disappear forever.

She went to her upstairs office and called Inspector Schultz once more.

"What's up now?" he asked. He was busy.

She told him. They needed to do a deeper search of the Andreychuk farm. It was entirely possible that Meagan Stephens's body was hidden there. Those cars that littered the yard needed to be taken apart, not just looked over as before. All the outbuildings and the house itself needed to be thoroughly re-examined too.

"You sure, Calloway?" he asked. Reluctantly, he pulled up photos of the Andreychuk site. "Look at it—cars, busses, vans. Got to cover two, three acres? That's going to take days. Is there anywhere else they could have put her?"

In the bush, maybe. Or the lake. But animals dug up bodies unless they were buried deep and the lake washed them up, as it had done with Willa Stein. Remains usually surfaced and Meagan had been gone now for more than three weeks.

"There's still the Carlson house."

She heard the inspector sigh, but she went on, describing how its thick walls were built by stacking straw bales and encasing them in concrete. Alan Carlson had bragged about helping with the construction, so he'd know exactly how it was done. It might be possible to break through a section of the hard outer layer, hide a body inside the straw, then fill it back in and patch it over with fresh concrete.

"Meagan wasn't big," she reminded him. "It's a good way to hide a body."

"What about body fluid? It's going to leak," he snapped, looking for problems.

"Couldn't you wrap it in plastic? I'm not suggesting that we need to tear down whole walls. Can't Ident use thermal imaging to see if there's anything buried inside one of them?"

"Nope. Can't see through concrete."

"How about sniffer dogs?"

"Dunno, I'll ask." His voice grew quieter as he considered the plan. "Carlson's going to make hell if we go back and start bashing holes in walls, then come up empty," he argued. "But if that's what happened, the wife must know about it. He'd have needed a sledgehammer to smash concrete and make enough space to hide a body. That would've made a mess."

She could hear him warming to the idea.

"Tell you what—go pick her up and talk to her. Find out what she knows. That could save us a pile of trouble."

"If I get inside the house I'll try to have a quick look at the walls and see if they've been tampered with." Roxanne grabbed her jacket and her car keys. "See if there's a recent patch somewhere."

"Yeah, yeah. That as well."

THE SKY WAS grey, with a dark band of clouds thickening to the west. She hoped it wouldn't rain again. Alan Carlson's Lexus was parked outside their house, but there was no sign of Andrea's blue Subaru. It was Andrea that she needed to talk to. Where might she be?

She went to her usual source for local information. Roberta Axelsson might know how Andrea spent her Thursday mornings. She was in luck this time. Roberta was loading bags of egg cartons into the back of her car ready to go make deliveries, but she knew where to find Andrea.

"She'll be at yoga class," she said. "Why do you want to talk to her? Is it true that you had the police over at their house all of yesterday digging up their garden? What are you looking for?"

"I can't stay and talk right now." Roxanne avoided answering. That was okay, Roberta said, she needed to be gone, too. But Roxanne could tell that she was dying to know.

Andrea's car sat on the roadside outside Susan Rice's yoga studio, behind Margo Wishart's Honda.

Shoes were lined up along the hallway outside the studio door. Inside, the lights were dim. Susan's class—six women—were stretched out on mats with their eyes closed. Susan sat on a cushion, gently running a polished stick along the edge of a metal bowl. A row of similar bowls, varying in size, was arranged on the floor before her. A clear, ringing sound vibrated through the room. When Roxanne opened the door, light flooded in and everyone's eyes popped open.

"Sorry to interrupt," Roxanne said.

Susan set the rod in her hand down.

"One moment, Roxanne," she said, then turned back to her class. "We need to adjust slowly. Breathe deeply, ladies, and you may open your eyes."

But the permission came too late. Everyone had already turned their heads toward the intruder, eyes wide open. Among them was Andrea Carlson, the most colourful in the group, wearing pink yoga pants and a lime green top, her hair wrapped in a multicoloured scarf. She squinted at Roxanne, clearly curious.

Susan guided the group through a series of stretches to help them return from their relaxed state. They followed along, but Roxanne could tell the whole room was alert and aware of her presence. She stood quietly by the door until the exercises were finished. Most of the class knew that Roxanne worked for the RCMP. She might be here on police business.

Finally, Susan spoke the closing "Namaste" and rose with her usual fluid grace. She turned on a light on a nearby table, and a murmur of voices began to rise.

"I just need to talk to Andrea," said Roxanne. She didn't like to single the woman out, but she didn't have much choice. The class would watch to see who she left with anyway. Heads swivelled from her to Andrea.

"Right now? Can't it wait? I've got to get to Winnipeg." Andrea frowned.

All the women were taking their time, changing their shoes and reaching for their jackets. They chatted about an upcoming event at the Rec Centre, about a sale coming up at the Legion, but Roxanne could tell that it was an excuse to stick around. They all wanted to know why Roxanne was here and needed to talk to Andrea. One of them was Margo Wishart.

Margo caught Roxanne's eye and lifted an eyebrow, just as curious as the rest of them. Susan was arranging her singing bowls by size on a shelf by the wall. Andrea strolled over to the clothes rack, grabbed a shiny green rain jacket, and walked over to where Roxanne stood by the door.

"I need to speak with you, now," Roxanne said. "We can go to the detachment and talk there."

"Can't do," Andrea objected. "I've got an hour at best, then I've got to head out for Winnipeg, and I need to change." Then she smiled. "How about we go to my house instead?"

"We just examined your garden, and I've already had to ask Alan some questions. That's not a good idea," Roxanne said, trying to avoid conflict. And she needed to talk to Andrea alone.

"No problem," Andrea replied, now quite friendly. "Your guy aerated the soil for free. Alan says it'll do the garden good. Don't worry about him—he'll be busy potting honey, and we'll have the house to ourselves."

Some of the women began drifting toward the door, realizing nothing exciting was about to happen.

"All right," Roxanne agreed. If Andrea was willing to be pleasant, she'd play along. That might work to her advantage, too.

At the very least, it would get her inside the straw bale house for a proper look. "I'll meet you there."

As she left the yoga studio, Margo Wishart followed her. "Roxanne!" she called. "Got a moment?"

It didn't take long for Margo to pass along what a colleague had said about Alan Carlson. He had a long-standing reputation for paying inappropriate attention to women he worked with.

"Just thought you should know," Margo added as they watched Andrea's car disappear around a corner.

"Thanks. Keep that to yourself, will you?" Roxanne said. Margo was one of the few people in the village she trusted to keep quiet.

As she followed Andrea, Roxanne turned over what Margo had told her. Alan had been a deputy minister in the provincial government. If the rumours were true, many women would have worked under him, and stories about his behaviour had apparently been commonplace. It had gone on for years before anyone made a formal complaint and that, Margo said, had been quietly dismissed. Could Andrea really not have known?

Now Roxanne wished she had insisted they go to the detachment for a formal interview. Still, visiting the house would give her a chance to inspect the walls, she reminded herself.

Rain began to drizzle down her windshield as she parked between the Lexus and Andrea's Subaru. The front door opened as she dashed toward it, collar tucked up against the drizzle.

"Come on in where it's dry." Andrea Carlson welcomed her in. "Alan's here after all. He's making us an espresso."

26

ROXANNE LEFT HER wet shoes at the door and padded inside in her stocking feet. Andrea took her damp jacket and hung it on a hook beside her green raincoat.

"Come say hello!" she chatted as if this were an everyday social visit. "Alan's in the kitchen."

The entrance hallway opened into a spacious, open-plan area that combined the lounge, dining room, and kitchen, stretching from the front to the back of the house. The furnishings and fitments, of wood, steel, and glass, were elegantly tasteful. At the far end, behind a granite counter, Alan Carlson was grinding coffee beans.

"Latte? Cappuccino?" he called to her, apparently as much at ease as his wife. Andrea must have called him from her car to warn him that Roxanne was coming, so here he was. She would not be talking to his wife alone after all.

"Just black," Roxanne replied, hiding her annoyance. At least being here gave her a chance to look around inside the house. She glanced about. The interior walls had been drywalled; only the exterior ones—the thick, straw-filled walls—caught her interest.

"I've never been inside your house," she said, a comment any first-time visitor might make, though hers was deliberate.

"Then Andrea must give you the grand tour," Alan replied in the same casual tone, loading the espresso machine, still playing the part of a friendly neighbour. That suited Roxanne just fine. Now she had a perfect excuse to look around.

The front and back windows were deeply recessed, while the long side wall running the length of the room had none at all. That wall was painted a deep, greenish grey, with half of it covered in horizontal planks—old wood in different textures and tones, the nail heads still visible, giving it a rustic look. Those planks could be removed and replaced without leaving a trace. It was too bad she couldn't take a photo for Ident. The rest of the paintwork was white. Artwork hung everywhere, all contemporary, all bright.

"Those are mine!" Andrea pointed to three of the largest, painted in splodges of reds, yellows and purple. They were each big enough to hide something suspicious, but they were higher on the wall. It would be difficult if you needed to lift a body, but maybe doable if there were two of you.

The back door led out onto a deck. She and Andrea looked out into a thin drizzle. There, she could see the large vegetable garden. The rain would help to wash away all the muddy boot prints left on the grass, from yesterday. Andrea didn't mention it, or the possibility of going outside. If Roxanne wanted to walk around the house and view the walls from there, she would have to bide her time, wait for a dry day when the Carlsons were both gone. They were often away, in Winnipeg. She just needed to find out when and come over here for a walkaround.

There was a toilet at the back as well, with another windowed wall. It was too small to conceal a body. But the room that ran parallel to the main living space, on the opposite side of the house, was Andrea's art studio and it had another long, windowless wall. That one held her supplies: cupboards beneath the worktops, shelves above, all crammed with pots and jars. Clearing it to expose any wall space would be time-consuming, but the clutter could also hide something quite effectively.

"Coffee's ready!" Alan called from the kitchen.

"There's just bedrooms upstairs. Nothing very exciting." Andrea walked back into the living space. That was as much of the house as Roxanne was going to see this morning.

"Don't you have an office here?" she asked Alan. He passed her a mug. Brown sugar and cream sat ready on the vast countertop.

"It's over in the honey house." He was still fussing with the coffee machine, making an espresso for himself. "Andrea works here and I work there. That way, we each have our own space. Works for us."

"Is that a straw house, too?"

"Absolutely," said Alan Carlson.

So, another place to hide a body, one where few people went other than Alan himself. Andrea had picked up a tall mug filled with latte.

"I've got to leave inside half an hour," she remarked brightly. "And I need to go change. Can I leave you two to chat?"

That wasn't what Roxanne had planned at all. Was Andrea avoiding been questioned by her? If so, what did she have to hide? Meantime, Alan walked over to a woodstove and lit the kindling already laid inside it. Flames flickered up behind the glass door.

"We may as well make ourselves comfortable," he said and walked to a capacious sofa covered in pristine white fabric, red and orange cushions scattered along its back. There were no pets in the Carlson house, no animal fur or muddy pawprints. Unlike Roxanne and Matt's home, this house was immaculate. Andrea's bright pink legs disappeared up a wooden staircase. "See you in a bit," she called down to them.

"Now, Roxanne," said Alan Carlson. He laid a small cup down on a round coffee table. "What makes you so curious about our garden and our house?" He moved one of the cushions out of the way so he could sit back. It was a pointed question, but he remained relaxed.

"Just eliminating possibilities," Roxanne replied. "You told me and Matt that you helped build this house yourself?"

"I did, but I'm not much of a carpenter." He lifted his coffee. "I'm learning. I have to, if I'm going to run an apiary."

"But building a house of straw is unusual, isn't it?"

"You do know I was involved in environmental issues when I was in government? I'd heard about houses like these and I did my research. They're amazingly well insulated and it's natural fibre. I wanted to set an example, Roxanne. I was able to lend a hand in building it, if that's why you're asking. With mixing the concrete too, although I didn't apply it. I left that job to the professionals." His smile was condescending. He had guessed what she wanted to know. Had he done that deliberately, or was it just coincidence? She couldn't tell.

Roxanne crossed one stockinged foot over the other in front of the fire. It was beginning to warm up.

"How is it that you always worked behind a desk and now you're doing something so practical? It's a big change, isn't it? From deputy minister to building beehives?"

"You want to know what really brought me out here?" He set down his espresso and looked directly at her, handsome and ready to charm. "I'll tell you, in confidence, Roxanne. I know you've heard the rumours about why I resigned, why I made unexpected changes in my life. To Andrea's, too. I know you suspect there might be some truth to them, that perhaps I had something to do with the disappearance of that Stephens girl. That's why you've had someone poking around our garden—it's obvious. And now you're here to interrogate my wife. You're asking about the construction of my house. Let me reassure you: there's no dead body buried in the walls."

He'd anticipated it all. He smiled again, lips narrowed, much as he might have done many times while sitting behind a government desk, delivering a polite but firm disappointment.

"I didn't leave my job for that reason. I left because of a health diagnosis. Leukaemia. Not too far along yet, but it will probably kill me sooner rather than later. So Andrea and I decided to make the best of the time I have left. I might get a few good years in yet, and I do come by my interest in beekeeping honestly. My grandfather kept hives. I used to help him, when I was a boy.

"I don't want people knowing that I am ill," he continued without emotion. "You can tell Matt if you must, but that is all. Given both of your professions, I'm sure I can trust you both to be discreet."

"I am so sorry."

"Andrea and I have nothing to hide," he continued, "but perhaps I can help you with your inquiries. If you are still looking for Meagan Stephens, you should go ask our other neighbours, the Klassens. That girl was not the slightest bit interested in me, nor me in her, I can assure you of that, but I know she visited their farm. She told us all about it, how she knew Nick and his sister Ella as well."

"Why didn't you mention this before?" Roxanne asked.

"Why should I? You didn't ask and they're good neighbours. Armin tilled that garden for me. I'm getting heritage seeds from him to plant in the spring. Nick is knowledgeable when it comes to agricultural research. He's working his uncle's farm too, you know, one near Steinbach. He's got plans for it. He's told me. He has a freer hand than he does up here, where his father is still in charge, but he still comes by as much as he can. Armin's getting on in years and needs his help now and then.

"I don't choose to point fingers, Roxanne. I've been on the receiving end of those myself, as you are aware. It was quite amusing watching that constable out there getting his feet dirty for nothing, but if you are thinking of breaking down my newly built walls, which you are, I believe…?" An interrogative brow was lifted in her direction. "That is another matter entirely. And there is the matter of those other deaths. You know our land borders on the Klassens'?"

"You rent it out to Pete McBain. He grazes his cattle on it."

"Not this year. He used that field for hay, and the crop's already been taken off—it's bare now. There's a stretch of woodland behind it that leads over to the old farmhouse we own next door."

"The one that you rented out to Cooper Jenkins?"

"Precisely. There's nothing but open fields between that house and the sunflower field where you discovered the body. And the Klassens' house and gardens."

"Are you suggesting that the Klassens might have been involved?" She found that hard to believe. Vera and Armin had lived here for years and were helpful neighbours. Right now Vera was caring for her own daughter.

"Not at all." He was too smart to agree. "But if you are going to subject my wife and me to this kind of close examination, you should perhaps be doing the same to them. I think the rain's gone off." They both looked in the direction of the big front window. He was right. "Let's go for a walk. I want to show you something."

She agreed to go. It wouldn't hurt to look.

Andrea came clattering down the stairs as they put on their jackets.

"You told her?" she asked. "About the cancer?"

"I had no idea," Roxanne said.

"We'd like to keep it that way." Andrea was dressed up for a trip to the city in a scarlet coat with matching lipstick. "I can't stand it when people act like they're sorry for us."

"I'm taking Roxanne for a walk, to see where our field and the Klassens' join up." Alan said lightly.

Andrea was wrapping a purple scarf around her shoulders. She patted it into place.

"You know there are paths through our woodland, right? You've probably seen the one between our house and the place we rent out next door—the farmhouse where that man who was shot was staying? Well, the barn is behind that farmhouse, and the woods stretch from there all the way to the next road, passing right behind the Klassens' field. Alan can show you.

"I went for a walk there that Monday evening of the long weekend, three weeks ago, just before it got dark. You can see the Klassens' house pretty clearly through the trees, even some of their garden. They had a bonfire going out back. Nick was there, and so was a girl who looked like Meagan Stephens. I'm pretty sure it was her. She was laughing, and he had his arm around her.

Alan Carson took over the story. "That was right before she went missing. It's not our garden you should be digging up, Roxanne. There's plenty of room to bury a body at Klassens', and they've got the right equipment, too. A tractor with a front-end loader? That would scoop out a deep hole, no trouble at all."

"Why haven't you mentioned this before?" Roxanne's mouth had gone dry.

"No need." Alan dismissed that question. "That's all Andrea saw, and you know that the girl was still alive on the day she's talking about. She wasn't declared missing until several days after."

"You knew we were looking for her. We've posted her picture online. If what you're saying is true, you're the last person to have seen her, Andrea."

"Not at all. We assumed Armin or Vera would have told you." Alan answered for his wife.

"I hate to say it—the Klassens have been so kind and helpful to Alan and me—but honestly, they're the ones you should be questioning, not us," Andrea added.

"Let me show you," Alan offered again.

"No," Roxanne said. "I'll go look myself."

She found it hard to believe what she was hearing. Was this a way to deflect her from searching the Carlson house any further? On the other hand, she couldn't ignore what Andrea had said, that she had seen someone who looked like Meagan, with Nick Klassen, the night before she disappeared.

"You need to cancel your trip today," she told Andrea. "Neither of you is to leave this area until I say so."

"Are you crazy? Haven't you heard what I just said?" Andrea stopped at the door. She had turned the handle, ready to go.

"Are you charging us, Sergeant?" Alan appeared calm but she could hear an annoyed edge creep into his voice. "Do we need legal advice?"

"Not if you have anything to hide. This is just a precaution. You need to stay home today."

She stepped outside, little doubting Alan Carlson wouldn't hesitate to file another complaint against her. Inspector Schultz would be calling soon. She continued on into the wood, regardless.

She walked briskly through the wooded patch between the Carlsons' house and the rented farmhouse next door, then circled around to the barn. Inside was a quad, she reminded herself, one that might have been used to transport Coop Jenkins's body to the sunflower field just three fields away. Ident had searched the farmhouse already but only to check for evidence that Coop had been there. They'd have had no reason to examine the barn and other outbuildings back then. It could have been missed.

The woodland was exactly as Andrea had described. About six hundred feet of dense brush with a well-maintained path ran its length, beside the field. There were clearings along the way where you could easily enter and exit the trees. The poplars were shedding yellow leaves, which were damp and scattered across the path, sticking to her shoes. Still, the path remained largely clear of roots and easy to walk.

A break in the trees opened onto a mown field. Rows of round hay bales were stacked at either end, ready for Pete McBain to collect. The Klassens' market garden was clearly visible, laid out in well-maintained patches. Most of them had been dug over, but tall corn stalks still stood, along with thick clusters of green leaves where various squashes grew. She thought she spotted orange pumpkins peeking out among them. Two big plastic shelters arched over some sections of the garden. Behind the house was a patch of green grass with a large firepit surrounded by wooden chairs. A barbecue stood near the wall of the house. Andrea Carlson could have stood exactly where Roxanne was now, hidden among the trees on a summery evening, watching without being seen.

She saw Armin Klassen walk from a large shed, pass his tractor, and enter the house. Roxanne set off across the field. It was a shorter, quicker route than returning to the Carlsons' for her car. She needed to clarify what the Carlsons had said. The Klassens had to be questioned.

Right now.

27

ARMIN KLASSEN SAT at the kitchen table with a bowl of borscht in front of him, its deep red surface streaked with a splodge of sour cream forming pink and white swirls in the middle. Dee was perched in an ancient high chair, an old-fashioned terrycloth bib tied around her neck. Her mouth was stained crimson with beet juice. She banged her fists on the tray in front of her, yelling at Vera, who sat beside her, for more food.

"Roxanne! I wasn't expecting you! We're just having lunch." Vera stated the obvious. She held a bowl and a small spoon in her hands. Bread buns, a slab of butter, wedges of dill pickles and cheese slices, neatly arranged on a plate, were laid out on the table.

"I was over at the Carlsons' house, then I went for a walk through their wood over at the other side of the field. It comes so close to your house, I thought I'd come over to say hello. Hi, baby!" Roxanne's daughter beamed up at her, then switched her attention right back to Vera. She opened her mouth for another mouthful of mashed beet.

"Let me do that. Yours is getting cold," Roxanne volunteered. Vera's soup sat in front of her, uneaten.

"But you'll have some yourself?" Vera got up to go fetch another bowl. Dee chewed, pink juice dribbling down her chin. Roxanne took a vacant chair on the other side of her daughter and wiped Dee's messy face. She picked up the bowl of pureed soup and a small spoon.

"Who's she?" asked Armin Klassen, pointing his own spoon in her direction.

"That's Roxanne. Dee's mommy." Vera looked his way and stopped ladling. "You know Roxanne, Armin! Sergeant Calloway? She's in the RCMP."

He peered across the table, then appeared to make the connection.

"Police have been messing about over at Selinskis' place," he said, still using the old name for the Carlsons' land. "What's all that about?"

"I can't say right now." Roxanne spooned more food into Dee's hungry mouth, puzzled. Why did Armin not recognize her? They had been neighbours ever since she moved in with Matt almost three years ago. She'd been in charge of the local RCMP for the past six years and was, by now, well known in the community.

"Better not wreck any of that bush other side of the field." Armin had torn open a bun and was buttering it. "We need that windbreak."

"I don't think that will happen." Roxanne was fairly sure of that. The ground in the woodland hadn't been disturbed, not as far as she had seen. She doubted that a body had been planted there. She dropped another spoonful of red mush into her daughter's open mouth and watched Dee clamp her lips tight. It was like feeding a baby bird. "You know there's a pathway through it?"

"That's always been there. The Selinskis always made sure it was well cleared. They used to walk over here to play cards on Saturday nights." Armin seemed to recollect what he was talking about now. It looked like forgetting who she was had just been a temporary blip.

"Andrea Carlson says she came through there Monday night of the long weekend and saw you all having a bonfire."

"That right?" Armin bit his buttered bun.

"We weren't here that night." Vera put a bowl in front of Roxanne. "Nick and Ella had a barbecue. They asked their friends over. Here's your soup."

"Do you know if Meagan Stephens was there?"

"Meagan?" Armin looked confused.

"You remember, Armin. One of the lifeguards. The pretty one with the short, dark hair. The one Roxanne's been looking for." Vera took her place at the table again. Armin didn't reply. He turned his attention back to his lunch.

"So you knew her?" asked Roxanne.

"To look at, that's all. She was just one of the kids that hang around in the summer." Vera answered for both of them.

"So she would have been there that night?"

"I don't know. We went over to Poplarwood to visit my cousin. Left the young folks to enjoy themselves," Vera replied.

Armin added cheese to his bun. He said nothing, but Roxanne could tell he was listening. Andrea Carlson had never claimed to have actually seen Armin and Vera that night, but Roxanne pressed on.

"Meagan knew your son, Nick?" she asked.

Dee interrupted, shouting something that sounded more like "DADADA!" than "MAMAMA!" as she demanded more soup.

"Pass her a crust of bread." Vera tore another bun apart and handed a piece to Dee. "It will keep her busy. Look at those shiny new teeth!" She pointed at the two small white stumps in Dee's lower gum as Dee chewed.

"The woman that lives over at the old Selinski place is spying on us?" Armin asked.

"Andrea Carlson. You tilled their land, remember? Alan Carlson's talked to you about getting his garden ready. Nick's been helping him, too." Vera jogged his memory once more.

Armin was definitely becoming forgetful, but only for a second or two. It was mostly names, nothing unusual for someone his age. Vera must be at least twenty years younger than him. That made sense. Their children were still in their twenties.

"Hey, that's what you do when people need a hand, don't you? Even if they're city folk who don't know how to do anything right.

It's called being neighbourly, that's all. We've never had them sit down to eat with us."

Armin sounded irritable as he made his point. Sharing a meal at their table, as Roxanne was doing now, was a privilege only extended to people they considered friends.

"Those folks won't be here long," he predicted. "Won't last past the first winter, you'll see. And they shouldn't be saying things about us to the likes of you."

Roxanne saw Vera look more anxious, but she was almost done asking questions.

"If Meagan was here that Monday night, maybe Nick gave her a ride back to the city the next day," she suggested.

"I don't think so." Vera swung her head round to face Roxanne. "Nick took Ella in with him. I'm sure of that. They left here together in the morning. They've been talked to already. Some detective woman went looking for them, in Winnipeg. Doesn't she work for you? Don't you know all about that?"

"My boy's done nothing wrong," Armin said, his mood darkening. He had definitely taken offence. "You don't want to be sitting here asking us these kinds of questions. What do you think we are? Criminals? Leave us, and Nick, out of this. See us? We're good, hard-working people. Raised our kids right. Didn't hand them off to someone else to raise while we went back to work, like you're doing, when that one still's so little." He waved his buttery knife toward Dee.

"Why don't you go home and take care of your own?" He set the knife down, got to his feet, stomped to the back door, yanked it open, and walked out, letting it swing shut behind him.

"Sorry about that. Don't worry about him," said his wife. "He gets mixed up about things sometimes."

"Is he losing his memory?"

"Sometimes. He's tired. It's hard for him to keep up with everything that needs doing around here. He loves this place, but it's a lot of work."

"Isn't Nick going to take over here? Doesn't he help out already?"

"That's what we thought, but Armin's older brother had a heart attack not long ago." Vera put down her spoon, clearly worried. "He's Nick's uncle and never married, so he's got no kids. Now Nick's looking after his place and trying to finish his degree at the same time. Turns out he's going to inherit all that land. It's a real farm, much bigger. Not just a few acres of market garden, like this.

"Armin's turned seventy. It's not just the forgetfulness; he's got arthritis and is in a lot of pain. We should maybe sell, but where would we go? I can't move him into an apartment. A man like him needs to be outside, doing things. He'll never take well to town life. I don't know what we're going to do."

"I'm sorry." Roxanne wished she hadn't had to ask all those questions. Vera obviously had enough to worry about. She decided it was time for her to go. "Thanks for lunch. It's okay if Dee stays for the rest of the day? I still have work to do today." She went to the sink and wet a paper towel so she could clean up her baby before she went.

"No, leave her, she's no trouble. She makes me laugh, she's such a happy girl." Vera lifted Dee out of the high chair. "Say bye-bye to your mommy!" She brought the baby close to Roxanne's face. Dee gave her a sloppy red kiss. Vera took the wet paper towel from her and wiped the baby's face, then handed it to Roxanne, so she could clean her own.

"See you later," Roxanne said.

"Don't work too hard!" she heard Vera call to her as she disappeared out the back door and down the steps.

Roxanne set off back across the stubbly field. A brisk wind out of the south was blowing the clouds away. Above, there were patches of blue sky.

She would need to speak with Nick and Ella Klassen herself to confirm what Vera had said. Perhaps one of them knew who Meagan had been with when she left the bonfire that night—if she had been there at all. She also needed to track down the other two lifeguards again; they might have been at the bonfire, especially if it was the last one of the summer. She'd need to find time for another trip into Winnipeg, and call Vancouver to have someone in the RCMP check on Owen Bradshaw, the other beach patroller. Not that she suspected him, but he might know where Meagan Stephens had gone and who she'd been spending time with during her final days at Cullen Village.

Coop Jenkins, Rob Marsden, and Willa Stein had all died here, in the Interlake. Willa might have been at the bonfire in Klassens' backyard that holiday Monday. She could have known who Meagan had left Cullen Village with, too. That might be why she had died. But wouldn't Willa have said something as soon as Meagan went missing?

She noticed a flash of red among the trees. Andrea Carlson was just visible behind some poplars, looking her way. Andrea waved and pointed in Roxanne's direction. It looked like she was shouting, but the wind carried her voice away. Then Andrea ran toward a cleared patch of path that led directly into the field. Roxanne could see her face clearly now. Her mouth was moving as if she was screaming. But Andrea wasn't pointing at Roxanne; she was aiming at something behind her. Roxanne turned to look.

At the edge of his yard, just beyond the house, stood Armin Klassen. He faced Roxanne and held a shotgun in his hand. He was loading it.

Roxanne was completely exposed, standing in an open field as she watched Armin raise the shotgun to his shoulder. She reached for her own gun, turned and ran for the cover of the trees. A rut in the mown field caught her foot and she fell to the ground just as a blast rang out. He had fired. Roxanne lifted her head in time to see a blur of colour as Andrea ducked behind a tree.

She rolled over onto her stomach to face the house. Armin was still in the same spot, feet apart, reloading his shotgun, preparing to fire again.

Roxanne had no choice. She stood up, took aim and fired just as Vera rounded the corner of the house, running toward her husband, calling his name. He stepped back. The bullet missed him, but Vera crumpled to the ground.

"Drop your gun!" Roxanne shouted, but she doubted that Armin heard her. She watched him walk past his wife, barely looking at her, go to the side of his house and disappear inside, still carrying his shotgun.

Then she was running. Vera lay bleeding on the ground. Armin was inside the house, still armed, and so was Dee.

Roxanne had never run so fast. Her gun was in her hand, still drawn, when she reached Vera, who was conscious and moving, blood oozing from a wound in her thigh.

"What's he done now?" Vera gasped, struggling to sit up.

"Stay still. We'll get help," Roxanne said, gulping to catch her breath.

"Where is he?"

"Let me handle this." Roxanne left Vera and headed toward the back door of the house. Then she slowed, suddenly aware of how afraid she was. She pulled out her phone and dialled Ravi Anand's number.

"Armin Klassen tried to shoot me. I've wounded his wife. He's gone inside the house. My daughter's in there." She was still breathless from running, struggling to catch her words.

"Cars are on their way," he told her. "The Carlson woman just called in. Don't go inside, Roxanne. Wait for help."

She hung up. Sirens were already wailing nearby. A patrol car must be close, but right now, she needed to know that Dee was safe. She pocketed her phone but kept her gun in hand as she approached the door. The outside screen door, held by a spring, had swung shut again. She carefully opened it, then cautiously pushed the inner door open.

Inside, Armin Klassen sat in his usual chair at one end of the table. Dee was opposite him, still in her high chair, the bib around her neck stained crimson. The shotgun lay on the tabletop between them.

The siren blared again, closer this time.

"What's going on?" Armin said. "Been another accident out there on the highway?" He seemed oblivious to what had just happened, that he had shot at Roxanne and that his wife lay bleeding outside.

"I decided to come get Dee after all, Armin," she said, trying to keep her voice steady.

"DADADA!" yelled Dee, banging her hands on the tabletop.

Roxanne holstered her gun. Armin noticed.

"What's that? What are you doing with a gun here in my house?" He rose to his feet, slowly, his joints stiff. One weathered hand reached for the shotgun. "Where's Vera?" he asked. Then he appeared to remember something. His brows lowered. "She's still out there. You shot my Vera."

She grabbed her gun once more as he raised the shotgun. Suddenly, he door behind her slammed open and another shot rang out. The bullet struck Armin squarely in the forehead, and he toppled backwards.

Dee wailed as Armin fell towards her, blood splattering her face.

Lucas Bell stood in the doorway, his gun in his hand.

Roxanne ran to her daughter, moving around the table past Armin's sprawled, bloody body. She lifted Dee and held her close. Dee buried her face in her mother's shoulder, smearing her with blood and tears.

"Don't cry, baby," she whispered. "Everything's all right."

But it wasn't. Armin Klassen lay dead across the table. Lucas Bell stood white as a sheet, the gun still in his hand, shocked at what he had done. Vera Klassen limped in the door.

"What's this?" she cried, her voice raw with pain—from her wound, but even more from the sight before her. "You've gone and killed my Armin!"

28

RAVI ANAND WAS good at handling a crisis. Once he had secured Roxanne's and Lucas Bell's weapons, he quickly sent them on their way. They needed to go home right now, he told them. He'd come by later to take their statements. Maybe Roxanne could drop Lucas off. Right now, Ravi had other urgent matters to handle, including a wounded woman and her dead husband.

Dee clung to her mother. She looked like a child from a battle zone, eyes red from crying, still whimpering from the shock. Her face had been wiped clean but the onesie she was wearing was spattered with Armin Klassen's blood.

"Can you drive?" Roxanne handed Lucas her car keys. He was still pale, stunned by what he had done. He'd never had reason to use his weapon before, far less kill anyone. But he took the keys and waited for Roxanne to strap Dee into the car seat behind him. She climbed in beside her baby and reached for a squeaky toy, anything to distract Dee's little mind from the gory, violent scene she had just witnessed.

"We'll be suspended?" Lucas asked as they left the scene. More cars had arrived by then, bringing Todd Brewster and Sam Mendes with them, along with an ambulance. Vera was being prepared for transport to the hospital. Armin's body would remain where it lay until the medic and forensic teams arrived from Winnipeg.

Cars were stopping at the roadside. It was the afternoon when people came to pick up their weekly allotment of vegetables, and news of the recent disturbance at the Klassen farm was drawing them out. Brewster had been tasked with fetching the bags Vera had filled and placing them at the end of the driveway. He handed them over quickly, sending curious onlookers on their way. Taciturn and grim-faced, he told them nothing about what had happened.

"It's routine." Roxanne answered Lucas's question. She squeaked the stuffed toy, trying to get Dee to smile. "There will need to be an inquiry. It happens every time one of us fires a gun. Don't worry. You did the right thing. I'll vouch for you."

"But you were going to shoot, too." He glanced at her in the rearview mirror, not convinced. "You'd have brought him down. Maybe I acted too fast."

"I don't think so, Lucas. Armin might have beaten me to it. The shotgun was loaded and on the table, right by his hand. If you hadn't acted as quickly as you did, he'd have got me first. That was a pretty good shot, by the way."

She tried to ease his anxiety, but he was right. Questions would be asked. Lucas would be grilled for shooting to kill instead of using his taser. She would face scrutiny too, since she had wounded Vera. But Roxanne had been through inquiries before. She had fired in self-defence, and Andrea Carlson had witnessed it.

"I wasn't aiming for his head," Lucas was saying. "I wanted to hit his body, like you did with his wife. I thought I'd get his shoulder or his arm. I didn't mean to kill him."

"I didn't intend to hit Vera either," Roxanne admitted. "I aimed at Armin, but he moved. So did she, right into my line of fire." Dee was dozing off. Roxanne put down the toy and came to sit in the front seat. "You reached us really fast," she said, trying to focus on the positive. "That was lucky. Let's go, shall we?" Curious glances were coming their way from the highway.

Lucas had been nearby on patrol when the call came in. Andrea Carlson had reported that Armin was armed and shooting.

"Has that old guy killed all three of them, Sarge?"

Was it possible? Had Armin shot at Coop Jenkins and then attacked both Rob Marsden and Willa Stein? He might be forgetful, confused and arthritic, but he hunted and was handy with a gun. It was likely that he carried heavy metal tools in his truck, a tire iron, a hitch, ones that he could have used to hit Rob Marsden and Willa Stein. But why?

He had been annoyed with Roxanne and had tried to hunt her down. Was that how he now reacted whenever he thought someone was a danger to himself or his family? Had some old instinct taken over his addled brain, driving him to act this way? Had he killed Coop out in the back field because he believed Coop was a threat? But going after Rob and Willa would have required more planning. Rob's body had been found near where he was struck, but how could Armin have disposed of Coop's and Willa's bodies without help? Vera might know, if she was willing to say, but right now she was in shock, injured, and on her way to Winnipeg.

Both Klassen children had been in Winnipeg when Rob Marsden and Willa Stein died. Only Vera could have helped Armin. If that was true, she must have known all along. And kept quiet.

Roxanne looked back at her sleeping baby. She had trusted Vera to care for Dee, never imagining Vera could be involved in the murders or pretending to be friendly while hiding the truth. Perhaps Vera had agreed to take Dee into her care so she could find out what Roxanne was doing and what she knew. Roxanne realized she had allowed herself to be duped. She'd needed someone to watch Dee so she could focus on the case and had never considered Vera and Armin as suspects, perhaps because she didn't want to believe it. She must have got that wrong.

Lucas was pulling into the driveway of a winterized cottage owned by a city dweller who only used it in the summer and was happy to have a police constable as a tenant for the winter months.

"I suppose we'll have to wait," he said as he clambered out of the car. "We can't do anything else, can we?"

"That's right, Lucas."

She watched him unlock the door. Jude Andreychuk's Jack Russell bounded out to greet him. Lucas waved and went inside, the dog following close behind.

Roxanne drove to the end of the road and stopped. The lake stretched out before her, calm and placid, reaching all the way to the horizon. Dee murmured softly in her sleep but didn't wake. She cut the engine.

If Meagan's body was found in one of the Klassens' large freezers or buried outside, Armin would be considered guilty and the case would be closed. For Roxanne, it probably already was. She'd been too involved with the Klassens and had made a serious error in judgment.

The baby slept on. How was Roxanne going to explain all this to Matt? Dee had seen a man's brains blown out. Blood and gore had sprayed her as Armin fell. She'd screamed in terror. Lucas Bell could have missed and hit Dee instead. The thought made Roxanne shudder.

But Dee was safe. The worst hadn't happened.

She started the engine again. She needed to get her baby home, give her a bath, change her into clean clothes, and call Matt. He would hear the news soon enough and head straight home, she was sure. Roxanne needed to be ready with answers.

MARGO WISHART SUBSCRIBED to the Klassen farm's weekly vegetable sale program. She was one of the customers who drove by, later that afternoon, to pick up her allotted bag of vegetables and to see for herself what was going on. She drove straight to Sasha Rosenberg's house after, as she always did. The bag held far too much food for one person to eat in a week, so she shared it.

"The house is taped off, you can't get near. There are police everywhere. Someone else who was getting vegetables said that they're over at the Carlson house as well. The Provincial Medical Officer's van is sitting in the Klassens' driveway, so someone must be dead."

"I hope that's not Vera." Sasha stopped sorting a bunch of carrots into two equal piles.

"Me neither. An ambulance has been and gone. So someone's maybe injured, too."

"Wasn't Roxanne's kid there today? Isn't it Vera's day to babysit?" They both knew that Dee was not with Roberta. On Thursdays, she drove to Winnipeg to deliver eggs.

"I hope not." Margo pulled out her phone. Calling Roxanne was probably futile, but it was worth a try.

After a few rings, an automated voice cut in: "The person you are calling is not available." She wasn't surprised, but she did leave a message. "Just checking to see if you and Dee are okay. Please text me if you can."

She hadn't seen Roxanne or her car at the Klassens' and the constable who had handed her the grocery bag wasn't saying anything. He'd just told her to hurry along.

"I think they're looking for another body. There were police dogs sniffing around," she said to Sasha, "and someone in uniform was backing up Armin Klassen's tractor, the one with the front-end loader."

"They must be looking for that beach patrol girl. You know, the one that's still missing."

"How can Vera Klassen be mixed up in anything as awful as this?" Margo asked. "She's a lovely person, isn't she? Always friendly, when I see her."

"I dunno. That old man of hers can be a bit crabby sometimes." Sasha lifted a knife and cleaved a cabbage into two halves. "Maybe the kids know something. Have you ever met them?" Margo had not. "They're both smart. At university these days though, so they're not around much."

Margo's phone rang. She grabbed it. It was not Roxanne, but Roberta Axelsson, who had just got home.

"What's going on?" Roberta asked. She'd returned from Winnipeg via the fast highway farther west—the one that didn't pass the Klassen farm—but her route had taken her past the Carlson house, where a police car was parked outside.

"Tell her to come over," Sasha said. "And to swing by the Klassens' while she's at it. She can fill us in on what's happening there."

But Margo was busy talking: "Does Vera take care of Roxanne Calloway's baby on Thursdays?" she asked Roberta. After listening, she hung up.

"It is Vera's day to babysit," she said, worry creeping into her voice. "I just hope nothing has happened to that little girl."

A CLIENT HAD told Matt Stavros that there had been trouble at the Klassen house. He called Roxanne as soon as he was alone.

"There was a shooting. Armin Klassen was involved," she said.

"And?"

"I can tell you all about it when you get home." Roxanne didn't want to explain on the phone. Dee was in her bathtub, splashing the water, back to being her usual gleeful self. "Dee's here with me. We're both fine."

"No. Tell me now."

She gave him the condensed version. She'd been at the Carlsons' and learned that Meagan Stephens had attended a barbecue in the Klassen's backyard the night before she disappeared.

"There's a stretch of woods between the Carlsons' and the Klassens' houses. I went to check it out. There was just a field between them, so I walked over. I thought I'd have a casual chat with Vera and see what I could find out."

"You took this investigation into their home while Dee was there?" Matt's voice was level.

"It was just a friendly visit." She tried to make light of it.

"No, it wasn't, Roxanne," he said firmly. "You went there to ask questions about a murder."

"A missing person," she corrected him. "Anyway, I stayed for lunch and everything was fine until Armin took offence at something I said."

"About what?" Matt Stavros never expressed anger or alarm, he just grew quieter, as he was doing now.

"About being neighbourly. How things aren't like they used to be. It looks like he's got dementia. He couldn't remember who I was when I first got there. Vera keeps feeding him facts. It looks like she's been coping with this for a while. Anyway, he left the kitchen before me but when I was walking over the field, back to Carlsons' to get my car, he aimed a shotgun at me. Fired it, but he missed."

"Jesus, Roxanne." Matt went silent for a moment. "Where was Dee when all this was happening?"

"In the kitchen with Vera." Roxanne fell silent, unwilling to say more.

The pause stretched. Then he asked, "Is that it? Did you arrest Armin Klassen?"

"No. He reloaded. I fired at him, but Vera came running out of the house and he moved. I wounded her instead."

"So, let me understand this." She could hear him trying to stay calm and reasonable. "You were out in the field behind the Klassens'? Vera was wounded? She fell?"

"Yes. Beside the house."

"And where was Armin?"

"He'd gone back inside."

There was another moment's silence, then Matt said, so quietly she could hardly hear him. "And Dee was still in there."

"He didn't hurt her!"

"So what happened?"

She had to tell him. She made it quick: "I went in. Armin saw that I had my gun and reached for his shotgun. Lucas Bell came in the door and fired. Lucas killed him."

She didn't mention that Lucas's bullet had blown out Armin's brains. She certainly didn't tell him about the blood raining down on their baby. But Matt could guess.

"Dee was there? She saw all this?"

"She's right here, playing in her bath. She's perfectly okay, Matt."

"Why is she having a bath in the middle of the afternoon?"

Roxanne couldn't think how to answer. There was another silence, then he said, "Give me an hour or so. I need to make some calls, then I'll come home. Don't go anywhere for now, okay?" He ended the call.

She dried Dee off. A message came in from Inspector Schultz: CALL ME BACK, ASAP.

She didn't make the call. She already knew what Schultz would say—that her temporary secondment to the MCU was over, that she'd be the subject of an inquiry, and that she wouldn't be returning to work until it was complete.

More importantly, she needed to consider what she should say when Matt got home. Yes, she and Dee had been in danger, but what else could she have done? The important thing was that they were both safe now. The good news was that she'd be home for a while. She wouldn't be leaving Dee with the neighbours again.

When Matt's car rolled up the driveway, she took Dee out onto the veranda. The dogs bounded down the steps to greet him. Dee bounced in her arms, shouting "DADADA!"

Matt, however, was not convinced that all was well.

"I've closed the office for today and Monday," he told her. "Dee and I are going to go visit her grandma." Matt's father was dead. He had been of Greek origin but his mother came of English stock. She had moved to Victoria, B.C.

He took Dee from Roxanne. "Hey, you," he said. "We're going to go on an airplane."

Roxanne took a step back, surprised and shocked.

"When are you leaving?" she asked.

"Eight tonight," he said. "Just for the weekend. We'll be back Monday night." He looked her straight in the eye. "This can't go on, Roxanne. I asked if Dee was safe, and she wasn't. You kept insisting Vera Klassen was a great babysitter, but now it looks like her husband might be your killer. And Vera? She must've known something. Maybe she was using you. She could have been making sure you didn't suspect them. Guns were fired, Armin was killed, and Dee was in the room. She could've been hit.

"You put the job first. You knew it was dangerous, and you carried on regardless. Now our daughter's been exposed to a trauma that could stay with her for life."

"She's all right, Matt," Roxanne protested. "Just look at her." Dee was beaming up at her father, babbling happily. She certainly looked like her usual cheerful self.

"We'll see," Matt said. "I'm going to make sure she has a good time these next few days. Let my mom spoil her. But from now on, no one takes care of this baby unless they're qualified. I'll see to that.

"And we need some time to figure out what happens next. You need to decide where your priorities lie, Roxanne. We'll talk when I get back."

He turned and went upstairs to pack a bag for himself and his daughter.

29

LUCAS BELL HAD had enough. Life in the RCMP was not turning out as he'd hoped. Corporal Anand had just informed him that he was officially suspended pending an investigation. At least he was still being paid, but Ravi didn't know how long the process would take, which meant Lucas could be left in limbo for months. And when the inquiry finally happened, it sounded like it would be tough. They would want to know why he hadn't tried to de-escalate the situation first, or why he chose to use his gun instead of his taser.

He hadn't wanted to kill Armin Klassen but what else could he have done? He knew the old man had already fired his shotgun at Sergeant Calloway. Naturally, he'd gone in armed, gun at the ready. Wasn't it a good thing he had? He'd been able to fire immediately. Otherwise, Klassen could easily have shot the Sarge. Hadn't she said that herself? And what about the baby in the kitchen? Klassen had practically taken her hostage. What might have happened to her? Would they be blaming him—Lucas—for not acting quickly enough if things had gone the other way? For hesitating? For not being decisive?

"Just tell them how it happened and you'll probably be fine," Ravi Anand had said. Probably? How about, "Thank you, constable. You did the right thing."

No such luck. Lucas would probably keep his job, but he'd get a reprimand—just like last time, when he hadn't reported meeting that woman PI in the middle of the night at the Andreychuk place. He'd thought he was doing the right thing then, too. He'd waited to tell the Sarge because it was MCU business, wasn't it? Wasn't the

PI working for them? And wouldn't she have already known about the woman setting up surveillance cameras? But no—that wasn't how things were done in the force. Lucas had been led to believe the RCMP valued resourcefulness, encouraged its members to take initiative. But in reality, it was all about following procedures. That was what the job was all about.

Maybe he should quit. And then what would he do? He could become a PI, like that woman he had met, planting cameras out in the dark so she could keep an eye on the Andreychuks. She did what she thought was right. Didn't have to take orders from anyone. She had given him her card. Maybe he should talk to her. Ask her what that kind of work was like.

HAILEY JENKINS ANSWERED his call. Sure, she remembered him. What was going on out there in the Interlake? All she had heard was what was on the news. Someone had been killed by a cop?

"That cop was me," he told her.

He really shouldn't disclose information, but if he was in trouble and thinking of quitting the force anyway, what did it matter? He needed to talk to someone and Hailey Jenkins was willing to listen. She was appreciative when he told her what he had done.

"You went in alone? Even although he was armed? And you shot him? Saved Roxanne and her kid? That took guts," she said, adding, "I've been trying to get hold of Roxanne but she's not answering. I think her phone's turned off."

"It's been a big day."

"Have they found Meagan Stephens yet?"

"No, they haven't. They think she must be dead. They've searched the Andreychuks' farm and last I heard they were using a front-end loader to turn over their gardens, but it doesn't look like she's been buried there."

"Vera Klassen has been taken to the hospital? Here in Winnipeg?"

"I expect so."

"Have they talked to the kids? Nick and Ella?"

"I don't know."

"Okay. I still want to know why my dad got killed and that must have happened because he was looking for Meagan Stephens. I'll see if I can track them down. Call me if there's any more news out there? Talk to you later."

Vera Klassen had been wounded, so Nick and Ella were probably with her at the hospital. But which one? Hailey got lucky on her second call. Mrs. Klassen had already been discharged, she was told. But where would she have gone? The farm near Cullen Village would be off limits. She might have checked into a hotel, but Hailey suspected money was likely tight in the Klassen household. Why else would Vera have been working part-time as a babysitter?

Wasn't Nick Klassen looking after a big farm south of the city? Wasn't that the most likely place for him to take her? But where, exactly, was it? One of Nick's roommates might know.

Her neighbour agreed to look after Liam once more. She dropped her son off, went back to her townhouse, washed every trace of makeup from her face, fastened her hair back and donned the polyester pants once more. The heeled shoes were useless so she opted for her black sneakers. They looked okay when she put on the belted raincoat.

The man who answered the door at the house Nick Klassen shared kept her standing on the doorstep, just like Nick had, but he wasn't hostile. He looked like he'd just woken up, and was wearing a T-shirt and shorts, hair a mess, unshaven, yawning, his eyes bleary. It seemed he knew nothing about the attempted murder out in the Interlake. Hailey chose not to tell him.

"I'm a private investigator hired to help find a missing girl. Nick knew her and I need to talk to him."

"Well, he's not here," the young man said with a yawn. "I can't help you." He started to close the door.

"Whoa!" Hailey stuck out her foot to hold it open. "He might be staying at a farm, right? One that belongs to his uncle?"

"Yeah, maybe. Look, I really can't help you. I've got to get to work and I'm going to be late already," he said. "How about you move your foot?"

Just then, a bike rolled into the driveway. Another man, about the same age, in his early twenties, probably another grad student, got off and removed his helmet.

"Go ask Kel," said his buddy, impatient to see her gone. "He might know."

Kel opened the door to the attached garage, which was cluttered with discarded furniture and other junk. He wheeled his bike inside. Hailey followed him and watched as he locked his bike to a central post.

"I need to talk to Nick Klassen," she began, but he interrupted.

"What's this about a murder out in the Interlake?" He finished fastening the lock and stood up. "It happened at a market garden? Some old guy got shot? Is that Nick's dad?"

"Yes," Hailey replied. "That's why I need to talk to Nick."

"Did someone else get hurt?" The man was wearing bike shorts and a helmet. He was clean-shaven and fit, a stark contrast to his roommate. "It wasn't Nick?"

"No. His mother was wounded, but she's okay. And she's been discharged from the hospital. I'm wondering if she's with him. I need to find her, too."

He stood back and folded his arms, regarding her suspiciously. "You're not from the press, are you?"

"No!" She fished in her pocket for her PI licence and held it out for him to see. "I'm helping out with the investigation. I'm looking for a missing girl that's linked to the case. The Klassens knew her. It's important that I talk to them and I think it's most likely that they're at the farm that Nick's taking care of. The one that belongs to his uncle."

Kel studied the licence and nodded.

"We've hardly seen Nick since the old guy had that heart attack and he had to go out there and work the farm," he said. "I went out there to see when he first got it. It's a big dairy farm. He's got a herd of cows to take care of. He'll get the lot, he thinks, when the uncle dies."

"So you know where it is?"

"Yup. It's about ten klicks south of the Trans-Canada on the road to Steinbach. There's another farm at the road end where you turn off. It's got a big, hip-roofed barn painted red. Go east from there and it's the next farm, south side of the road. If you see Nick, tell him I'm asking for him. Get him to call me."

The man yanked the garage door shut and walked back toward the house. Hailey got into her dad's truck. It was still rush hour so it took more than half an hour to get out of the city, but soon she was driving along the Trans-Canada Highway. Then she followed the signs to Steinbach and turned south. The road was busy; people in this area commuted to Winnipeg and were eager to get home after a day's work. Before long, she spotted a red barn up ahead at an intersection. She turned east, just as she had been directed.

The next farm she reached was large. Hailey slowed as she approached. There were grain bins, a livestock barn, a hay shed, and some white cattle with nearly grown calves grazing in a field. Charolais? Weren't those dairy cows? Nick Klassen must have to milk them every day, on top of helping his dad at the market garden two hours away, plus trying to finish a postgrad degree at the university. That was quite the workload, and a lot of driving.

A single-storey house sat beside a paved front yard. A truck and two cars were parked outside, all covered in dust from gravel roads. It was nearly 6:00 p.m. Nick Klassen might be busy milking his herd. If so, Vera could be alone in the house. This might be Hailey's best chance to talk to her.

She drove up to the front of the house, acting as if it were a routine visit. There wasn't much of a garden. A strip of shrubs, a couple of dogwoods and a cotoneaster grew along the front. Three steps took her to the front door. She rang the doorbell.

The door opened a crack, and a young woman peered out. She wore jeans and an oversized men's shirt. Her dark hair was long enough to reach her collar. Hailey recognized her face from a time, not so long ago, when her hair had been shorter and she'd been smiling for a camera.

"You're Meagan Stephens!" Hailey blurted, then pushed the door so it swung wide open.

The girl shoved her away with both hands. Hailey staggered backward. Meagan pushed her again, and this time Hailey fell all the way down the steps, her head hitting the hard surface of the yard. Meagan took off toward the big barn, her shirt flapping behind her.

Dazed, Hailey struggled to her feet. Her head and hip ached. Meagan had already reached the barn door and gone inside. Hailey followed, knowing there was no need to hurry. Neither Meagan nor Nick Klassen would leave without Hailey seeing them.

Still feeling groggy from the fall, she took out her phone and texted Roxanne Calloway and Lucas Bell: *At Klassen farm on 52N off highway 12. Meagan S is here.*

Just then, the barn door opened.

Nick Klassen burst out. He wore grey, shiny overalls and heavy rubber boots, and was striding toward her with a stick in his hand. Meagan appeared behind him, standing in the doorway, watching with her hand pressed to her mouth.

Hailey turned and ran, ignoring the ache in her hip. But Nick was fit and had a longer stride. He caught up just as she reached her car. She spun around as the stick came down, missing her head but smashing into her shoulder. She cried out in pain. Nick raised the stick again, ready to strike a second time.

"Too late! I called the police already," she shouted at him. He dropped the stick and looked back to Meagan.

"Meg!" he called. "Come on. We've got to get out of here." He disappeared into the house. Hailey grasped her shoulder. Something was broken.

Meagan ran over and followed him, leaving the door wide open. Another young woman appeared in his place. She hurried to Hailey's side and helped her to her feet. She looked like Vera Klassen.

"I heard you! Is it true you called the police?" she asked.

Hailey clutched her arm and nodded. It wasn't exactly true yet, but she hoped Lucas or Roxanne would see her text and respond.

Nick Klassen emerged from the house, having shed his waterproof overalls and boots, now pulling on a jacket. Meagan ran past them to one of the cars—a newer SUV—and they both climbed inside.

"Let's get you into the house. You look like you're going to pass out, said the young woman.

"I need to go," Hailey was groggy. If she held her arm close to her body, it didn't hurt so much. She was fairly sure her collar bone had been hit. Maybe she could drive herself to a hospital. Call the RCMP from the car.

The SUV roared out of the driveway, disappearing down the gravel road in a cloud of dust.

"Wait here. We can call an ambulance. I'd drive you to the hospital, but my mom's inside and I can't leave her right now. I'm Ella, Nick's sister. Who are you?"

"Hailey Jenkins. A private investigator. We were hired to find Meagan. Has she been with your family this whole time?"

Ella had helped her to the doorstep but now she paused, looking perplexed.

"Jenkins? An investigator? Like that man who died?"

"Yeah. Cooper Jenkins," Hailey said. She gasped with pain again and she felt like she might throw up. "We worked together. He was my dad."

"You've gone white. You need to come inside." Ella reached out to help her up the steps. "This is all that stupid girl's fault—Meagan Stephens. She's the one who shot your father, and my brother's been making sure we cover up for her ever since."

30

"NICK THINKS HE can let Dad take the blame for all of this?" Ella said. "No way."

She had called 911, then found some Tylenol. Hailey swallowed a couple of the pills, but they weren't helping much. Vera was sound asleep, Ella told her, in a bedroom, exhausted and knocked out by more effective painkillers.

She and Ella sat at a worn wooden kitchen table, glasses of water in front of them. She still wore her raincoat. Trying to take it off was impossible.

"Nick's always been able to get his own way," Ella said. "He's the boy in the family, y'know. Mom's always given him everything he ever asked for. In her eyes he can do nothing wrong but this time he's really done it." She had her mother's round, cheerful face and warm brown eyes, and, like her, she bustled around the kitchen.

"Your dad tried to shoot Roxanne Calloway earlier today," Hailey reminded her, then her phone beeped. She had a reply from Lucas Bell. He had received her earlier text.

Sarge not answering. Location? U OK? Will get help.

She sent him the coordinates, hoping that the police would soon be on their way.

She held up the phone so Ella would see her hit the record button before she pocketed it but Ella didn't seem to notice. She was too busy talking.

"Dad's got Alzheimer's and Mom's been pretending he's okay. All this trouble's made him much worse," she explained. "He's always been protective of us and the farm and now he gets confused. He saw Meagan shoot a man out back of the house. Maybe that put the idea into his head. He imagined that Roxanne was dangerous and he thought he was defending his home."

"You're saying that Meagan shot my dad out in your back field?" Hailey interrupted.

Ella glanced away, embarrassed. "That happened a week after she disappeared," Hailey continued. Dad was looking for her. Is that why he was killed? Was Meagan hiding out at your house the whole time?"

"She wasn't there for long." Ella sat down. "Just since the end of the summer. We had a barbecue, the Monday of the September long weekend. She and Nick are a couple, you know. They took one look at each other and that was it. I've never seen anyone as much in love as my brother. He'll do anything for Meagan." Hailey opened her mouth to speak but Ella pushed one of the glasses of water closer to her. "Drink some of that," she said. "And just listen, will you?"

"Meagan was in a bit of a state that night. It was the end of the summer. She didn't want to go back to Winnipeg the next day. She'd have had to go home to her parents' house, she said. She wasn't sure she wanted to go back to university, but she also didn't know where else she could go. If she went home she was sure her parents would take over her life again and they would stop her from seeing Nick. Nick was beside himself with worry about that. He said he couldn't imagine living without her. The Stephenses are all believers, you know. Call themselves people of faith. We're not. Dad grew up Mennonite, but he gave up going to church years ago, and Mom only took Nick and me to Ukrainian Christmas and Easter. The Stephenses wouldn't have liked that. They wanted their girl to marry a good Christian boy.

"Nick told Meagan she could take a break from university to figure out what she really wanted. She could always go back later if she changed her mind. Her parents were paying for it, she said, but we told her that was okay—she could always get a student loan. Mom and Dad were out, but when they got home, Nick persuaded them to let Meagan stay with them for a while. He told Mom that Meagan probably just needed time to figure things out, and this way, she and Nick could see how serious they really were. I was heading back to Winnipeg in the morning, so Meagan could maybe have my room. Give herself a week or two to think things through.

"So Mom and Dad agreed." Ella rolled her eyes. "Nick drove Meagan over to Susan Rice's house the next morning—that was the Tuesday—and she picked up her things. He brought her back to Mom and Dad's house, then he and I went off to Winnipeg to start classes. He said he'd be back every weekend to see her.

"It turned out that Mom and Dad liked having Meagan around." Ella drank some of her water. "She wasn't afraid of hard work and she made herself useful. She helped them with the gardens. They're way behind the trees, so nobody needed to know that Meagan was there. She was scared that her parents would come looking for her, so they needed to keep it a secret that she was there, but they never showed up. After a while, Mom began to hope that Nick and Meagan would get married. She thought that Meagan would be a good wife and mother someday and it made her happy to think that Nick would marry someone that she could be friends with. Meagan was good with my father, too. Patient. Never tried to tell him what he should do."

"Then the Stephenses hired my dad and he came looking for her."

"Stop interrupting, will you?" said Ella. "It's hard enough to tell you all this. My mother is going to hate me for doing this. I was told to promise that I wouldn't tell."

"Sorry." Hailey grasped the glass with her one good hand, frustration simmering. She needed Ella to get to the main part of the story—how Meagan killed her father—before the police arrived. But she couldn't rush her.

"We never saw your dad when he came out to the Interlake. It was a Saturday; Nick was back for the weekend. He and Meagan were always so happy to be together.

"My dad and Nick go hunting every fall. They bag a deer and butcher it for the freezer. Some geese too, and ducks. Dad wanted to go shooting, as usual. He was really keen to go, kept talking about it. Nick wasn't sure about taking Dad out alone, but Meagan offered to go along and help. Dad listened to her, so it seemed like a good idea. Nick decided to show Meagan how to load and fire a shotgun, just so she'd know what Dad needed to do, so they took the guns out to the back field. Nick set up a target. He showed her how to aim and pull the trigger.

"I looked out the back window and saw it all happen. Meagan shot at the target and she missed. She was shooting in the direction of the trees. They didn't think anyone was there, but we know now that your dad was staying at the house that the Carlsons rent out, the one that's at the far end of the wood. He must have gone for a walk along that path through it and he must have seen them. He stepped out of the wood, waving his arms, like he was trying to tell them that he was there, but he appeared just when Meagan had reloaded and fired. The cartridge smacked right into him. He must have been dead before he hit the ground." She looked down at the table, then back up at Hailey, apologetic.

"So how did he end up hidden in a sunflower field?" Hailey demanded, unimpressed. Both Ella and Vera had known what happened to her father but had kept quiet about it. They'd told no one, even when others had been suspected of his murder.

"Well, everyone panicked," Ella said, spreading her hands in defense. "Meagan was hysterical. I ran outside, but by then Dad was already taking charge. He could still be clear-headed sometimes, and he was used to being the one in control. Nick was trying to calm Meagan down. Dad checked to make sure your father was really dead, then went to fetch the quad. He knew how to load a body onto it. He'd done it with deer plenty of times. He couldn't quite lift your dad, though. Mom and I helped with that," she admitted. "He told us he'd handle everything after that and that we weren't to worry. Once Dad sets his mind to something, there's no stopping him.

"He was only gone about half an hour. He wouldn't say where he'd taken your father. I think he'd already forgotten. He was confused again. It happens like that, you know. He can be okay for a little while, but it never lasts. We knew he couldn't have gone far, but we didn't find out how close the body was until those two men walked through the sunflower field that night and found him. We thought he'd made it farther, maybe into the bush somewhere."

"And left my father there, for the coyotes to get him?" Hailey felt sick again at the thought. Ella wrapped her hands around her glass and leaned toward her.

"What else was I supposed to do?" she hissed. "My whole family was involved. I told you, I was sworn to keep it all a secret. Nick took over, like he always does. He got rid of the target out back and put the gun away in the office, where Dad always keeps them. He told us all to act like nothing had happened. He'd make sure that everything would be okay. No one needed to know a thing. If the body was found, the police would think it was a hunting accident. He took your dad's phone and ID so it would take longer for anyone to identify him if his body was found. I don't know what happened to them. Maybe he got rid of them.

"There was no reason for anyone to suspect that Meagan was involved, but it was best that he should take her away from here. He'd go back to Winnipeg and find a place for the two of them to live.

"Meagan calmed down at that. I could tell that she trusted Nick and it meant they'd be moving in together. I went back to Winnipeg, and we all carried on as if nothing had happened. Dad didn't seem to remember a thing and Meagan was all excited about her and Nick becoming a real couple. She was almost as starry-eyed as he was. Mom told me she spent most days working hard out in the gardens or helping her in the kitchen. Every night, she talked to Nick on the computer.

"Then Jakob, Dad's brother, got sick and ended up in the hospital. Nick brought Meagan here right away, to live with him in this house. Meagan told me that her prayers had been answered—that being able to live here, together, was a miracle, meant to happen. She's still pretty religious, you know. They were already talking to a pastor about getting married.

"Jakob's never going to be able to work this farm again. Nick will get it. He and Meagan settled right in here. She behaves like a good little farm wife. Feeds the cattle, loves the calves. Our cousin, Conrad, lives nearby. He comes over sometimes to help. Between them they take care of things when Nick needs to get to class or go up to Cullen Village and check on Mom and Dad."

"The cousin's sworn to secrecy too?" asked Hailey.

"I don't think he knows anything. He just knows that Meagan is Nick's girlfriend. The one he's going to marry."

"It's not just my dad that got killed," Hailey reminded her, appalled at the whole story she'd just been told. "There's the RCMP sergeant who got hit on the head at Cullen Village and the girl that worked with Meagan all summer when they were both lifeguards. Nick was going whack me on the head. That's exactly how they both got killed."

There was a loud banging on the door. Two burly constables from the Steinbach RCMP detachment stood on the doorstep. They listened, took notes, and called for backup. There had been an assault. The missing girl the MCU was searching for had been there. She had taken off. The guy with her was connected to the family in the Interlake, the same one involved in the shooting earlier that day. He had assaulted this woman. The officers got the make and colour of the SUV that Nick and Meagan had driven away in. It was registered to Jakob Klassen, the owner of the farm.

One of them needed to get a statement from Ella. The other would drive Hailey to the hospital in Steinbach right away.

"No," she told them. "I can't get home from there. Take me to Winnipeg."

Vera Klassen appeared in the hallway, wearing a nightgown, her hair straggling around her shoulders, looking bewildered. She was leaning on a crutch.

"What's happening?" she asked. "Where's Nick? Where's my son?"

They told her the basics.

"You talked?" Vera accused her daughter. "You made a promise."

"It was time, Mom. He can't keep going like this. It wasn't Dad who killed those other people, was it? Was it Nick?"

Vera looked confused. She didn't answer. Her daughter wasn't finished, though.

"You think Nick's perfect," she snapped, "but he's not, is he? He's just like Dad. Everything has to go his way, and when it doesn't, he explodes. Dad's hit you sometimes. Me and Nick too, when we were younger. When he loses his temper he turns violent and you've always kept quiet about it. Nick was crazy about Meagan, but he gets just as angry when he's frustrated, you know that. I'll bet he would have done the same to Meagan, sooner or later, if she'd married him. You should have seen him come after Hailey here with a stick. He looked like he was ready to kill her.

"Was it him? Was it Nick who killed that police sergeant and Willa Stein, Mom? You need to tell the police everything."

But Vera's mouth clamped shut. Whether she knew or guessed the truth, she wasn't going to say. And Hailey had already sent the police a copy of the recording that she had made.

MEAGAN AND NICK had made it as far as a shopping mall on the western edge of Winnipeg. They needed cash, Nick said, and enough supplies to last them a while. He'd have to use his bank cards, but only this once. The cops could trace the transaction.

He'd withdraw as much cash as possible and charge everything else to his credit card, just this time. They needed food. Clothing.

"You stay here, Meg," he told her firmly. "Don't let anyone see you. I'll get hair dye, so you can go blonde. We can't risk anyone recognizing you."

Once it got darker, they'd need to find a car he could hotwire—somewhere quiet, not too noticeable. Maybe between here and Brandon. After that, they'd keep heading west. They'd need fake IDs.

"Think of a new name for yourself while I'm gone. Don't worry about a thing. I've got this all planned out."

He kissed her on the cheek and walked toward the mall. Meagan watched as the doors swallowed him up. She counted to five hundred. Once she was sure he was gone, she opened the car door. At the far end of the parking lot, there was a Burger King. She walked straight to it, opened the door, and headed to the counter.

"Order, please," the server said, barely looking at her

"My name is Meagan Stephens," she said loudly, her voice steady. "And I need your help."

An elderly man sitting nearby lifted his head, listening.

"I've been abducted. The police are looking for me. Please call them. Right now."

31

MEAGAN STEPHENS WAS eager to tell all. The problem was that her story didn't match what the RCMP had already heard on the recording PI Hailey Jenkins had made earlier that evening.

"It was Nick who killed Cooper Jenkins," she declared. According to Meagan, Nick had taken a shotgun out behind his parents' house to show Meagan how well he could shoot. But a man had been walking in the nearby woods, and Nick had hit him instead, killing him instantly.

"It was an accident," she insisted, facing Constable James, sent by the Major Crimes Unit to question her. She had his full attention.

"I'd never seen anyone die before, officer!" Meagan was just as cute and pretty in person as she appeared in the photographs circulated during the search for her. It was easy to see how a man could fall for that wide-eyed, innocent look and feel compelled to protect her, as Nick Klassen apparently had.

"Nick said we shouldn't tell anyone. His dad took the body and left it in a sunflower field, where it wouldn't be found until winter, but later, he didn't think that was right. He thought that the man should have been given a proper burial, and I kind of agreed. We could have laid him to rest, y'know? Had a bit of a ceremony? Said a prayer for him? There's a big old ash tree at the back of their garden. That would've been a good spot, but Nick said to leave him where he was. It would still look like a hunting accident. It was too bad his dad hadn't taken it further afield and dropped it out in the bush somewhere, but if the body was found in the sunflower field after the season was over, he figured everyone would still assume that was how he had died.

"Nick's clever," she told the nice-looking young police officer. "And he's very well organized. A bit too good at that, though. He can be very controlling. He always needs to have his own way."

"You thought that but you still stayed with him?" asked Nolan James.

"I didn't know it at first. I liked him and didn't want to go back to living with my family, and his parents offered to help me. They said I could stay with them until I knew what I wanted to do with my life. I enjoyed living there. They have a market garden. You know, I think I might take up horticulture, the organic kind."

"So it's not true that you fired the shot that killed Cooper Jenkins?" Constable James asked.

"Me? Never!" Meagan turned her wide eyes on him, full beam. "Who said that? It was Ella, wasn't it? Nick's sister? She's never liked me. Or their mother. She'd do anything to protect Nick. You know that, don't you?"

"It's going to be hard to prove," Nolan James replied, unmoved. "It's your word against theirs."

"You know he attacked that woman who came looking for me tonight," she reminded him. "And I know that he killed all those other people."

"You do?"

"He told me, today, after we drove away from the farm."

"Sergeant Marsden? And the other beach patroller who worked with you?"

Meagan slowly nodded. "He said he had to do it, to protect me, but I knew that wasn't true. He was making sure they didn't find out it was him. That's when I realized I needed to get away from him."

"What exactly did he say?"

She raised a finger to her mouth and nibbled a fingernail before she spoke, then she began.

"He said he'd made a mistake. The sergeant had come by the farm, asking about quads. He knew the make of the one that drove into the sunflower field. It was tucked away, out of sight, inside the garage, but Nick said it was away getting fixed, just in case the man demanded to see it. Later, he realized that had been stupid. The repair shop for quads like theirs was in Fiskar Bay and the police might go and ask if it was there, then they'd know that Nick had lied to him. That would make them suspicious.

"That Tuesday, Nick came by and we worked in the garden. He dug up potatoes, and I washed the dirt off. Later, he went to pick up Chinese food from the hotel in Cullen Village. He saw the sergeant leave his car and go jogging along the path near the beach, heading toward the wood. No one else was around so Nick took a tire iron from the truck and followed him. He wanted to shut him up. That's when he did it."

"And Willa Stein?"

"That was later. By then, we were living at Nick's uncle's farm. His dad's tractor needed a part, so Nick picked it up and then headed out to his parents' place later that afternoon. He'd told me he was planning to stay over. He got his cousin to come by and milk the cows, but otherwise I was completely alone on a Saturday night. That was scary." She chewed at another fingernail.

"Nick's parents go to bed early and he was on his own that night too, so he went to call on Willa. They've known each other most of their lives, you know. She usually has friends over but that night she was on her own so they had a couple of beers and that was when she told him that she'd seen his truck parked near the beach the night that the sergeant died. She hadn't seen him. Where had he been?

"Nick didn't know how to reply, right away. Then he laughed it off and said he'd been out walking himself, in the other direction, while he waited until it was time to pick up our order at the Chinese. He told her he hadn't seen a thing, but she'd noticed him hesitate. He could tell from the way she looked at him. She yawned and said she wanted to go to bed, right after. He was sure she was faking it. She wanted him to leave.

"By morning, he'd made up his mind to go find her. He was lucky she hadn't told anyone yet, but he figured she probably would, especially after a few beers, just like she'd said more than she should the night before. He knew she liked to swim off the pier at the end of her street, and all the cottagers down that way had already left for the summer. It was real early. He hit her over the head and threw her off the end."

The machine on the table recorded every word. They needed to find Nick, but he had disappeared. The car he'd been driving was still parked outside the shopping mall. A bag of clothes and another filled with groceries sat on the back seat. He must have returned to the car, found Meagan gone, realized she'd turned herself in and would probably tell all. There was regular bus service to the mall, and he'd withdrawn cash from an ATM: maybe he had friends who would hide and protect him. The fact that he had fled supported Meagan's story.

However, Constable Nolan preferred Ella's account of how Coop Jenkins had died. It explained Meagan's need to stay with the Klassen family where she was protected. If Ella was correct, Meagan Stephens had shot Coop. Vera Klassen had been there that day and must know what really happened.

He reported his findings to Inspector Schultz. The inspector agreed. They needed to get Vera to reveal what she'd seen. Sure, she'd been wounded, but the bullet had only nicked a bone; she'd be fine. Her husband had just died, too, but sometimes tough questions had to be asked.

Nolan James found himself in a police car, heading to the large dairy farm where Vera and her daughter were staying. He'd been thoroughly pissed off when called out that night, told he was the only one available to question a suspect. He liked working from his desk and knew that there was a future in the RCMP for members like him, who understood how computers worked and were thorough. But as he thought about it, interviewing people and getting them to open up wasn't so bad once you got the hang of it. It didn't hurt to sharpen that skill set, and he'd just earned points with his boss, which didn't hurt either.

HAILEY JENKINS WAS stuck in the emergency department of a Winnipeg hospital. She'd been triaged but hadn't yet been X-rayed. It would be a while before that happened. The room was crowded, filled with people in worse condition than her. Ambulance drivers wheeled in a couple of stretchers while she waited. This was going to take a long time.

She messaged the friend watching Liam to let her know she wouldn't be home for hours. Maybe Liam could sleep over? She was stuck in Emerg, probably with a broken collarbone.

Then she received a text from Lucas Bell, asking if anything interesting had happened. Using her one good hand, she typed back:

Sure has! Looks like you guys found out who killed my dad. Meagan S is still alive!

Where are you? he replied.

At the hospital, just my luck, she wrote back. *I'll be here all night. It's busy.*

Roxanne Calloway was still not answering her phone. She must have turned it off.

ALMOST TWO HOURS later, Lucas arrived at the emergency room entrance. At first, neither he nor Hailey recognized each other. They had only met that one night outside the Andreychuk farm, in the dark, but when he called her number, her ringtone sounded nearby. He waved and walked toward her.

"You don't look like I remember," he said.

"This is my disguise for when I need to get people to talk to me." She grinned, glad to have company.

A couple sitting nearby was called in to see a doctor. Lucas made sure they took the vacated chairs, side by side. He fetched Hailey a cold drink and badgered a nurse into giving her a couple of painkillers. Then he listened as she recounted what had happened at the farm.

"So it was Meagan who killed your father?" he said when she finished. "I never thought of that."

"Me neither. I wonder if anyone's told Roxanne?" She was thirsty and swallowed most of the juice he'd given her.

"Maybe not. She's suspended, like me."

He described what had happened that afternoon—how he had shot Armin, and how Roxanne had wounded Vera. He had barely finished when a nurse called Hailey in for treatment.

An hour later, they left, her left arm in a sling and taped to her side.

"Could you drive me out to the farm where Nick and Meagan were staying?" she asked Lucas. "I need to pick up my truck." She was pretty sure she could drive one-handed. The roads were quiet at this time of night.

A Jack Russell terrier was curled up on his driver's seat.

"This is Charlie," Lucas said. "He belongs to Jude Andreychuk, the woman who lived in that house where you put up those cameras. Her husband's been arrested for smuggling drugs. He was released on a promise to appear in court and the pair of them have taken off—out of province, maybe. She was supposed to pick up this little guy but she hasn't. I guess he's mine for now."

The Klassen farmyard was deserted, with only the yard lights on. As Hailey got out of the car to start her dad's old Silverado, a man emerged from the house. It was Conrad, the cousin of Armin and Jakob Klassen, who helped take care of the cattle.

"The police have been back, like we haven't had enough trouble today. They took Vera in for questioning, can you believe it? After everything she's been through. She just lost Armin. They'd been together since school, and they'd never do anything wrong. Well, I mean, Armin did shoot at that woman cop, but he's out of his mind these days. He doesn't even know what he's doing half the time."

Ella Klassen could be seen at the window but didn't invite them inside or come out to talk. She and Conrad watched as both Hailey and Lucas drove away.

Lucas followed Hailey home and waited until she was safely inside before heading back up the highway to Fiskar Bay, with Charlie sitting beside him for company. He had said he'd stay in touch with her. He wanted to know more about what it was like being a private investigator. He wasn't sure if the RCMP was for him. There were just too many rules and regulations, but no one could fire you if you worked for yourself. Maybe Hailey could use a partner, he thought, hopeful and curious. It was definitely worth checking out.

VERA KLASSEN SAT in the Steinbach police station and wept. None of this was her son's fault. He had always been a good boy, always done things the right way. Just look at how he had stepped up to help his father when Armin began to decline. He worked hard to keep his grades up, even while keeping Jakob's farm running.

He had only been trying to protect the girl he'd fallen in love with—Meagan Stephens. She was the one who had shot the man walking in the woods behind their back field one Saturday afternoon. Nick had convinced Vera and Armin to let Meagan stay with them until they could find a place of their own. He was head-over-heels in love. He told his mother he couldn't imagine life without Meagan, and everything had been falling into place so nicely. They'd moved onto the farm and were going to get married, just like they were meant to.

Her boy had always done what was right. He'd taken care of his parents, and then he'd done the same for Meagan. But now, look how everything had turned out.

Yes, he had been visiting around the time that the police sergeant had been killed at Cullen Village, but he came to help out at their market garden whenever he could. There was nothing unusual about that. And he had brought some parts from the city on a Saturday and stayed to help fix Armin's tractor. Was that when that other beach patrol girl had died? She couldn't be sure.

What she did know was that her son was blameless. Yes, he had struck out at that woman tonight, but what did you expect? Wasn't she snooping around his uncle's barn? She just wished he hadn't run off like that. It made him look guilty when he wasn't.

Was her husband ever violent? Not really. Sometimes he lost his temper and acted rashly but that was just the illness talking. They wondered if she was telling the truth about that.

Vera was sent back to the farm near Steinbach in a taxi.

Two witnesses had described how Meagan Stephens had caused the accidental death of Cooper Jenkins, and Nolan James formally charged her. Meagan broke down, sobbing.

"I want to go home," she wailed. "I want my family."

After she was led back to her cell, he called her parents. They deserved to know their missing daughter had been found. They also needed to be told about the criminal charge she was now facing.

John Stephens listened silently, then said, "Thank you for letting us know. We will be having nothing more to do with Meagan. She's no longer a daughter of ours."

Then he hung up.

32

ROXANNE CALLOWAY WAS keeping to herself. She had turned off her phone the night before. No one would be telling her anything about the case, and she didn't want to talk to Matt if he called, which he hadn't. He had only texted that he and Dee had arrived in Victoria. That was it.

It was a long time since she and her son, Finn, had been alone together. She had driven him to hockey practice the previous evening. The parents there had been welcoming, surprised to see her instead of Matt. Some of them knew that she'd been investigating the recent murders and asked questions. She told them nothing. They chatted about the usual topics—the weather, curling, pickleball; the new principal at the school—while their padded and helmeted children swooshed around the rink in pursuit of the puck.

Roxanne noticed Vassily Kovalenko on the other side of the rink, walking on crutches, accompanied by a woman who had to be his wife, Zlata. Their son, Andriy, must be part of the team. He looked to be about the same age as Finn. She walked over to greet them and express her sympathy for Vassily's injury. They smiled politely.

"Not to worry," they said. They would manage.

Vassily would walk with a limp for the rest of his life, and physical labour was no longer an option. But he and Mike McBain had an idea they hoped might work. Vassily could retrain, too, and try to qualify as an engineer in Canada. In the meantime, Zlata still had her job at the bakery, and since Vassily had been injured on the job, there would be compensation. They would get by.

Roxanne hadn't seen her son play for a while. Matt was a good stepfather and Finn liked him. If she and Matt broke up over this, she'd be compromising that relationship as well as her own. She found a quiet spot where she could watch and think.

She loved investigating and felt compelled to do it, but she couldn't transfer back into the Major Crimes Unit, she told herself. She'd quit it once before and moved to Fiskar Bay so she could raise her boy where the job was safer. Now she had another, younger child. The problem was compounded.

Matt was devoted to his daughter. If they split up, he'd never let Dee go and neither would she. They would share parenting and Matt's business tied him to this area, so she'd need to live close to the Interlake until Dee was grown.

She had managed the Fiskar Bay detachment long enough that the job held few surprises anymore but was that really such a bad thing? Did she truly need the challenge of a murder investigation? Was it worth giving up everything she had here just for the thrill of chasing down a killer? She told herself it was time to accept that she'd be back in her old position by December. Time to get back to reality and deal with the daycare issue. If she sorted that out, Matt would be happy again and everything would fall back into place.

It was now Saturday. She still avoided calling the detachment for updates, but she did turn her phone back on. The radio carried the news: a suspect had been located but had escaped from a farm near Steinbach.

She could guess who it was. Not her problem, she told herself.

The missing Meagan Stephens had finally been found. She must have been with Nick the whole time. Roxanne was curious to know more but she figured she'd find out soon enough.

She dropped Finn off at his friend's house in Fiskar Bay. He was spending the afternoon there, working on a science project. Another boy was already there.

"Hey, Andy!" Finn called out as he stepped inside. Andriy Kovalenko must be a new buddy.

Roxanne had brought the dogs with her and headed to the dog beach near Cullen Village, where Maisie and Joshua could run off leash. A sharp wind whipped across the lake, and the temperature was dropping. She pulled up her collar and tucked her hands into her pockets. No one else was around—just her, the dogs, a long stretch of empty beach, and grey waves rolling steadily toward the shore.

Her phone buzzed. She looked down at the screen.

"Hi, Izzy," she said.

Izzy McBain had just left her mother's house, west of Fiskar Bay. Her assignment in Churchill was over and she had expected to have a few days off, but she'd been asked to head up to the Interlake first. Inspector Schultz wanted her to wrap up these murder cases. She was checking things out up here, but her mother was also overdue a visit and had insisted she come for lunch.

"I am stuffed. Stay where you are and I'll join you. I can walk some of this off while we talk."

THEY STROLLED ALONG a wooded path, the ground littered with wet fall leaves of red and gold that clung to the soles of their shoes. The wind didn't reach them here. The path led them past the spot where Rob Marsden's body had been found. Scraps of yellow police tape still fluttered from a few tree branches.

Izzy had already been briefed by Inspector Schultz about most of what had happened the night before. She knew that Hailey Jenkins had tracked down Meagan and Nick, they had escaped by car, and how Meagan had later turned up alone and surrendered.

"That Hailey sounds like a smart one. I might want to keep in touch with her," said Izzy. "I could maybe put some work her way."

The police had not found Nick Klassen, but they were optimistic.

"He's got a limited amount of cash. He won't get far. We're not sure if he or his father murdered Rob and Willa Stein, but the fact that he's taken off makes it looks like he's our killer. We just need to prove it and it would be good to get a confession."

They emerged from the shelter of the trees and arrived at the boardwalk that edged Cullen Village's main beach. The wind was at their backs, blowing in from the southwest, stripping more leaves off the trees. Fall was coming to an end early this year. Roxanne called in the dogs and leashed them. It wouldn't do for Sergeant Calloway of the local RCMP to be seen breaking regulations.

"Nick's smart. He could take on a false ID. It sounds like he planned to go west and start a new life." Roxanne agreed with Izzy. "Look what he's left behind—a grad fellowship, his uncle's farm. Why would he walk away from all of that, unless he's guilty?

"Willa Stein's neighbour mentioned seeing a car outside her cottage around the time she died. Nick's father drives a truck, so it's more likely the car belonged to Nick. He must be strong enough from all that garden work to load a body into the car and heave it off the pier."

Roxanne had to raise her voice over the wind. Out on the water, a paraglider soared above the waves, his sail billowing overhead.

"His sister Ella said he's always had a short fuse. That he lashes out when things get tough." Izzy had read up on the case as soon as she knew it was hers. "Maybe Meagan Stephens is better off without him."

Out on the water, the paraglider fell close to the water, then swooped back up into the air.

"I'm sure she must be the one who killed Coop Jenkins. She stayed hidden all that time. Everyone who knew her at the beach here this summer says she's sociable. She liked to be out and about. Why would she vanish like that unless she had something serious to hide? Did you know that it looks like her family has disowned her? She's got no one to help her, poor kid. We've got Ella's witness statement and my guess is that Vera will back her up. There will be no love lost between the two of them now that Meagan has said that Nick confessed to her that he killed Rob Marsden and Willa Stein."

They reached the end of the boardwalk, where the beach patrol hut stood closed and shuttered. The kayaks and lifesaving equipment were safely stored inside for the season. Outside, a wooden picnic table sat beneath a round, roofed pavilion, the spot where Meagan, Willa, Joe Russo, and Owen Bradshaw had spent most of the summer. They had watched over the crowds of beachgoers and children as they splashed in the water and sunbathed, charged with making sure no one drowned.

"Where's Matt?" Izzy asked. "And the baby?"

Roxanne told her.

"He thinks you messed up?"

"Says I put our daughter in danger. And I did, Izzy."

"Yeah, but nothing happened to her. She's fine, isn't she? And look what you managed to do! We'd never have come so close to solving this case if you hadn't gone after it the way you did. Doesn't Matt get that? Do you want me to talk to him?" Izzy had been in a relationship with Matt Stavros years ago. She knew him almost as well as Roxanne did.

"Don't do that." Roxanne sat down at the picnic table. A cluster of trees sheltered it from the wind. "I'll sort this out. I'll go back to my old job. Find permanent daycare for Dee. Make sure we all stay safe."

"There's no such thing as safe." Izzy sat beside her. "We both know that." The dogs lay down beside them. "You know I've passed my tests for inspector?" she said. "I got the results last week."

"Good for you. Congratulations!" Roxanne had planned to go that route once. Now Izzy, younger than she, ambitious and unattached, had passed her on the road to promotion. Izzy was rising within the ranks, Roxanne was not.

"You know that Schultz is going to retire? I think I should go after his job."

Roxanne had once considered doing that herself. Now it was out of her reach.

"We could use your talent back in Major Crimes, Roxanne," said Izzy.

"Not a chance. I live here in the Interlake. I broke with the MCU so I could raise Finn out here, and now I've got Dee as well." Roxanne watched the paraglider out in the bay, soaring above the waves, his sail a bright blue and red curve against a cloudy sky. He wasn't scared to take a risk. Then she realized something:

"I think I know where Nick Klassen will have gone." She turned to Izzy, her gloomy mood evaporating as she spoke. "He'll have come back here, to his parents' house, to get clothes, maybe his passport. Armin's old truck is there and Vera had a car. He could change his appearance and try to get across the border. All he'd need is some help from one of his relatives to get himself here."

"Well then!" Izzy jumped to her feet. "We'd best go see."

33

ROXANNE'S GUESS WAS right. Nick had called his cousin as soon as he had realized that Meagan had run off. He could trust Conrad. They'd known each other all their lives. They'd been born within months of each other. They were family.

Conrad drove to the mall to pick Nick up and took him back to his own farm, the one next to Uncle Jakob's, which Nick had hoped to inherit. Nick's mother and sister were still staying there.

"Maybe you should sleep in the barn, in the tack room," Conrad suggested. If his wife or kids saw Nick, they might run next door and blab. So Nick spent the night listening to the heavy breathing of the herd, their snoring and belching.

Morning chores had to be done on a farm. His cousin went to milk Jakob's herd next door and make sure that Ella and Vera were not going back to the Interlake today. Nick mucked out and fed Conrad's beasts in return. Conrad's wife worked at the Steinbach Credit Union weekdays. On Saturday mornings she took the kids to their music classes. She stayed in Steinbach and shopped while she was there and visited her mother. She'd be gone for hours so that was when they could drive north to Nick's parents' house in the Interlake.

Out behind Jakob's place was a silver Ford F-150, not unlike the one Armin Klassen had owned. Conrad helped himself to the licence plates. Nick would need them.

"If the police find out, just tell them I stole them," Nick had said.

He was now hiding out in the empty farmhouse near Cullen Village. Conrad had dropped him off and offered a blessing before leaving. He still practised the Mennonite faith.

Nick would soon be gone. He had packed a bag with clothes from his closet in the room that had always been his. He had the hair dye that he'd bought for Meagan. He looked quite different with fair hair. He shaved and showered then changed into a suit and tie so he would look businesslike, then he polished a pair of black dress shoes.

His passport and birth certificate were in a briefcase, but he wasn't going to chance the border. They might be looking out for him. His parents kept an emergency stash of cash in a home safe, and he knew the combination. Inside was more than $7,000 in cash. Taking both the money and the truck seemed fair to him. It was probably all he'd ever get from them anyway, he reasoned, so it didn't feel like stealing. He took their computer too. He used it more than they did. He'd head for Alberta. All he needed was a false name and a fake identity. He'd see if he could get some work on the oil patch and make some real cash for now.

He was almost ready to leave when two cars rolled into the yard, blocking his way out. One of them was driven by Roxanne Calloway—he recognized the red hair. If she hadn't interfered, everything would have gone according to plan. His father would still be alive, he would have married Meagan, and they'd be living on Jakob's farm. Nick hated her.

But it wasn't Roxanne approaching the door. He remembered Izzy McBain from their days at Fiskar Bay High School. She was RCMP now, wasn't she? And wasn't that a gun in her hand?

His father's shotgun had been confiscated, but there was another one in the gun cabinet in his parents' office, just down the hall. He headed there.

The back door creaked open. Izzy was already inside. There was no time to load the gun. He gripped it like a club and took position behind the door.

She must be crossing the kitchen now. He held his breath and listened. A floorboard squeaked. She was coming down the hallway. The door creaked open, swinging slowly toward him. As Izzy stepped into the room, he lunged forward, raised the rifle butt, and brought it down hard on her head.

Izzy crumpled to the floor, her gun slipping from her hand. He bent to pick it up.

"Stop right there," said a voice.

Roxanne Calloway stood in the doorway, the kindling hatchet that usually lay outside by the Klassens' woodpile gripped tightly in her hand.

She raised it and threw.

IZZY WAS CONCUSSED. Her forehead was swollen. She was going to have two black eyes. She had been released from the hospital into the care of her mother and was propped up on a heap of pillows in her old bedroom.

"That was great. You nailed him." She grinned at Roxanne, who sat beside the bed.

It was almost an apt description. The hatchet had struck Nick Klassen in the arm that held the rifle. He had screamed in pain and stumbled backward, dropping it. Roxanne had kicked it out of reach. There had been a lot of blood. She arrested him on the spot and called for help.

"I won't be able to interrogate Meagan Stephens after all." Izzy had been ordered off work for ten days. "Too bad you can't do it either. But not to worry. Nick will blame her for killing Coop Jenkins, for sure, now that she's walked out on him. We'll get him for the others, though. Rob Marsden and Willa Stein. Has Schultz called you yet?"

Roxanne hadn't heard from him, but she'd been busy. She had stayed at the Klassen house until Ravi Anand and Aimee Vermette arrived, and Izzy was taken away in an ambulance. Another ambulance had transported Nick to Winnipeg under police supervision. Roxanne gave her statement and left. After all, she was still officially off duty.

"He'll definitely want you back. You saved me from getting my skull bashed in. I saw you throw that hatchet! That was brilliant." Izzy sucked a Slurpee through a straw. Her brother Mike had brought it for her. Mike was downstairs, being fed dinner by their mom.

"Thanks, Izzy. It was a lucky hit. I've never done that before."

It was also pure luck that the Klassens' woodpile was close enough to the house door for her to grab the hatchet before she went in.

"You've got to come back to work with us," Izzy said. "You know what you need? A live-in nanny. That way, you could come and go as you please. You two can afford it, and you've got the space. Give her the spare bedroom with the bathroom. Matt can keep an eye on things when you're away. Let him make sure his kid is raised the way he wants."

It was a good suggestion. Roxanne promised to think about it.

She headed downstairs. Dinner was pork roast, and Mary McBain insisted she stay. She and Mike wanted to know everything. Roxanne told them as much as she could.

"Nick Klassen was always smart. Got good grades," said Mike. He'd played hockey with Nick when they were teenagers, too. "He had a temper, though. And boy, could he get pissed off when we lost. Always liked to swing a stick around."

Mike was doing fine. Any blame he'd felt toward Roxanne seemed to have faded. Work at the new building would wrap up in a couple of months, but that was okay with him. He and Vassily Kovalenko were thinking about going into business together.

"Did you know Vassily's an engineer, back home?" he asked. "He's a smart guy, too."

They planned to start a renovation business. Vassily would handle the designs, estimates, supplies, and payroll, while Mike took care of the hands-on work. Out here, there was always demand for people with those skills and they'd make good money. But Roxanne had heard Mike talk like that before. His ventures never lasted long.

Zlata was still working at the bakery, though she worried her hours might get cut now that winter was coming and the summer visitors were gone. The Kovalenkos needed the income. The sooner Mike and Vassily got started, the better.

Mary McBain carved thick slices of pork and packed them into a container with mashed potatoes, cooked carrots, a tub of coleslaw, and half a pumpkin pie.

"I can drop it off, if you like," Roxanne offered. "I'm heading that way." She still had to pick up Finn from his friend's house.

BY THE TIME Matt arrived home late Monday with their baby girl, Roxanne had spoken with Inspector Schultz. She could rejoin the Major Crimes Unit as soon as the inquiries into why she had shot Vera Klassen and thrown a hatchet at Vera's son were concluded. He would be glad to have her back. She had a week to decide.

"I talked to Zlata Kovalenko," she told Matt over a glass of wine. They sat side by side on the sofa. Dee was in bed, sound asleep, and Finn was engrossed in a video game. "She's only making minimum wage at the bakery, and her hours will be cut back this winter. Business drops off when the summer tourists leave.

"I offered her forty hours a week as our full-time nanny and home help. She needs job security and she's willing to do it." Roxanne watched out of the corner of her eye to see how Matt would react. "She'll start as soon as I go back to work, one way or another. It means that we don't need to worry about daycare. I don't think we'll have her forever, but it will take care of the next year or two.

"They're having trouble getting workers compensation sorted out for Vassily's accident. Could you help them with that?"

"Possibly. Do you really want to go back to the MCU?"

"I could stay on managing the detachment, but investigating's what I do best, Matt. You know that."

Matt took a deep breath and puffed it out through his lips. He reached over and took her hand. "Do what's best for you, then. Just don't get yourself killed, Roxanne. Promise me that."

Roxanne remembered Izzy McBain saying: *There's no such thing as safe.*

But she didn't say it herself.

"I'll do what I can," she replied, and gave his hand a squeeze.

Acknowledgements

I'd like to thank Karen, Ashley and the marvellous team at Signature Editions for all their help and support in the making of this book, Doug Whiteway for continuing to be my patient and thoughtful editor, and Terry at Doowah Designs for creating a cover design that keeps on working.

Kirsty Macdonald and Ann Atkey are my trusted beta readers, Bill Martin actually did build a straw house (and knew how you might hide a body in it) and Susana Harder told me about quads and how they work. Peter Williams gave me advice on shotguns and Christine Hannah answered my questions about forensics.

My thanks to you all.

About the Author

Raye Anderson is a Scots Canadian who spent many years running theatre schools and presenting creative arts programmes for arts organizations, notably at the Prairie Theatre Exchange in Winnipeg. Her work has taken her across Canada, from the Pacific coast to the Atlantic coast, and as far north as Churchill and Yellowknife, as well as to the West Indies and her native Scotland. She now calls Manitoba's Interlake home, where she is part of a thriving arts community.

Had a Great Fall is the fifth book in the Roxanne Calloway Mystery series, which includes *And We Shall Have Snow* (shortlisted for the CWC Best Crime First Novel and the WILLA Literary Award for Fiction), *And Then Is Heard No More*, *Down Came the Rain*, and *Sing a Song of Summer*. She has also published *The Dead Shall Inherit*, the first book of her Elspeth Laird mystery series.

Eco-Audit
Printing this book using Rolland Enviro100 Book
instead of virgin fibres paper saved the following resources:

Trees	Energy	Water	Air Emissions
4	7 GJ	2,000 L	246kg